The Sculptor

DS McGregor Book 1

Alison Aitchison

The characters and events portrayed in this book are fictitious. Any similarity to real persons, living or dead, is coincidental and not intended by the author.

Printed in Great Britain.

Cover design by: Alison Aitchison

ISBN - Paperback: 9798332583346
First Edition: August 2024

For my Dad,

who always believed in me

x

Prologue

As he slipped the noose around her neck he watched her bright blue eyes widen in fear as she finally realised her fate. She kicked and punched wildly at him, whilst desperately trying to get her hands underneath the rope. Trying so hard to free herself and stop him from squeezing the last drop of life out of her. But he was too powerful for her. He had already slung the other end of the rope over the branch above her head and was slowly pulling on it, lifting her feet off the ground.

She was no match for this brute of a man and they both knew it. She was fighting a losing battle. They were miles from anywhere, and no one knew where she was or who she was with. Damn it, she thought to herself - why hadn't she insisted on meeting him in town? She had broken all of the first rules of dating. Only she hadn't been sure this was a date, and there was no one to tell. Her family didn't even know where she was. She wasn't ready to die. There was so much more she wanted to do with her life. But sadly, this was to be the end for her. Alone, in this dark wooded forest. His dark wooded forest.

Her lungs were burning from trying to catch a breath,

her fingernails raw from clawing at the rope, and her hamstrings aching from trying desperately to take her weight on her tiptoes. As he pulled her head closer and closer to the enormous branch above her, she knew she was running out of time. She looked pleadingly into his eyes, willing him to stop what he was doing and let her go. But she got nothing in return, his eyes had turned almost black and he seemed fixed in some kind of rage, calling her by another girl's name.

One more pull of the rope and it was over, just like that. The last sound she heard was the strange gurgling noise that came out of her lips as the last of the air in her lungs rushed to the surface, and then she was silent. Her body twitched for a second or two before her arms fell limply by her side. He released the tension on the rope a fraction, just enough that her arms came to rest as though she was reaching for him.

A single tear escaped from her left eye and trickled down her face before landing in the leaves that were swirling at her feet. Then her head slumped forward, towards her chest, with it her beautiful long dark curly hair. It swung forward covering her face, the ends blowing loosely in the wind.

Had it not been for the rope around her neck, tethering her to the branch above her she would have fallen to the ground. But it held her upright, perched on her tiptoes, but leaning slightly forwards due to the gentle downwards slope of the land. The ends of her white leather Converse were embedded in the moist dark earth of the forest. She was so still – as still as a statue. The only movement was the wind in her hair and the slight flapping of her open jacket.

He secured the ends of the rope on a nearby tree and stepped towards her. As he reached her lifeless body, he gently lifted her chin, using his other hand he tenderly tucked her hair back behind her ears. The rage in his eyes had gone. She was perfect, exactly as he remembered her. He wrapped his arms around her limp body, pulling her into an embrace. For a split second, he was back in the past, caught up in happy childhood memories with her, but then he remembered.

Images from that fateful day came flooding back to him. The way she had laughed at him when he tried to kiss her out on the loch, blaming the wine. The look of disgust on her face when he unveiled his sketches and paintings of her. The names she had called him when he told her he loved her. And worst of all, the final look she had given him as she took off into the forest as if the very thought of being with him repulsed her. He immediately let her go. She was just like the others. Sent back to torture him over and over again.

The light was starting to fade; he knew he would have to move quickly before her beautiful innocent features were gone. He would have all the time in the world to admire her when he was done.

She would be back; he was sure of it. They had a bond that couldn't be broken. A pact they had made as children, to stay together, forever. Perhaps next time would be different. Maybe she would finally admit she loved him. This concept excited him as he set to work.

1

Friday 14th October 2022

Katie sighed as she watched another raindrop travel down the window and land in the little puddle that was forming on the outside of the black rubber window sill. At the same time, a single tear escaped and ran down her cheek. Although no one was in the room with her, she quickly wiped it away, vowing not to start crying again.

She was on the Caledonian Sleeper on her way to start a new life five hundred and sixty miles away in Inverness. A journey that she hadn't planned on making, and if you'd asked her twelve months ago, certainly not on her own. Yet here she was.

This time last year, she had been the happiest girl alive, or so she had thought. If only she'd known the truth. Surrounded by family and friends, she had just completed her advanced diploma in Emergency Care. She landed her dream job as an emergency nurse practitioner in the minor injuries unit within the accident and emergency department at Kings Hospital in London. She had also been busy making plans to marry the man of her dreams - Matthew Watson.

Matthew (known as Matt to everyone) was a thirty-five-year-old orthopaedic staff associate specialist whom she had met one hot summer evening five years ago, over an elderly patient in accident and emergency. The lady had fallen and twisted her ankle whilst getting out of a taxi after a night out with her friends. As a result, she sustained a particularly nasty fracture of her foot, which would require surgery to realign the joints and return the broken bone fragments to a normal position, if she was ever going to walk again.

Katie had been an A & E nurse at that time, whilst Matt was the on-call orthopaedic registrar who had been called to assess her patient.

Matt was six feet tall, with an athletic build, sallow skin, medium brown cropped hair, hazel brown eyes and the most amazing sexy smile that could just melt her heart. He could have easily passed as Italian; in fact, he had blended in very well with the locals when they had spent a long weekend together in Rome for his thirtieth birthday. Which had only been two months after they met.

Her patient had been terrified at the prospect of surgery. Still, Matt had spent almost an hour with her explaining the procedure in great detail, answering all of her questions and never once losing his patience, despite the old lady asking him the same thing repeatedly. She had fallen for him instantly, and when he asked her to go for breakfast with him at the end of her night shift, she hadn't hesitated in accepting.

They had been dating for a little over two years when he asked her to move in with him. He lived in a beautiful two-bedroom period property in a tree-lined street in the Peckham Rye area of London. The location offered them the best of both worlds. It was close enough to the green spaces they enjoyed together like Warwick Gardens, Peckham Rye Park and the common so that they could keep up their beloved running and cycling, whilst its proximity to the popular shops and cafés on Bellenden Road, meant they were able to socialise with their friends without worrying about getting a taxi home afterwards. The train station was also only a short walk away, making it a perfect commute to work for her.

One of their favourite spots had been Frankie's bar in nearby Rye Place. In the summer months, it is considered by locals to be one of the places to visit, as it has some of the best views in London from its rooftop terrace. Katie could see why. She had fond memories of walking the short distance home from there, often carrying her shoes as her feet were sore from wearing shoes that were too high to walk in (although not that she would ever admit that to anyone).

Katie loved her shoes; at only five feet three inches tall - the higher, the better. Her parents loved Matt, her friends loved Matt; in fact, everyone loved Matt. He was so laid back and easy to get on with. She had been so happy then, and last year he had made her the happiest girl alive when he had proposed to her on a moonlit beach on the final night of their holiday to the Maldives.

She closed her eyes and thought of this holiday now, of the beautiful deluxe beach bungalow they had stayed in, with its own private jacuzzi and outdoor rainfall shower. Each detached bungalow was surrounded by lush palm trees and had its own private little stretch of beach, which genuinely made you feel like you were marooned on a desert island.

They had filled their days sunbathing and snorkelling in the warm Indian ocean alongside the amazing array of colourful tropical fish and baby sharks. She had learned to scuba dive while they were there, completing her three-day PADI course through the island's Aqua Centre.

Their evenings had been spent under the stars listening to the island's visiting band 'The Wood' or watching a romantic movie together on the big screen, which was set up twice a week on the beach. It was the best holiday she had ever been on, and not just because Matt had proposed.

To her, the Maldives truly was paradise on earth with its pure white sand surrounded by the bluest ocean. They had stayed on an Island located in the Rasdhoo Atoll, arriving at the island by speed boat from Male Airport, the main international airport for the Maldives, taking the seaplane on their way back.

Matt had organised the whole holiday, she didn't even know where they were going until they arrived at Heathrow Airport. He had proposed on their very last night.

Her thoughts drifted towards that night. They had enjoyed a final meal in the island's Indian restaurant, the Tandoor Mahal. As they were making their way back along the wooden decked path to their bungalow he had suggested one final walk along the moonlit beach. She remembered slipping off her silver Jimmy Choo sandals and feeling the warm sand running between her toes.

Matt had bent down behind her; she thought to remove his shoes, but when she turned around to see why he wasn't following her, she suddenly realised why - he was on a bent knee holding out a small black box. Inside the box was the most amazing pear-shaped diamond ring, set on a beautiful narrow diamond-encrusted platinum band. It was sparkling away in the moonlight.

She almost forgot to breathe as he told her how much she meant to him and how much he loved her, before finally asking her to marry him. She had cried as she said yes, and he had instantly lifted her off her feet and spun her around before slipping the ring onto the third finger of her left hand. It had fitted her perfectly.

When they returned to their bungalow, the bed had been covered in pink Maldivian rose petals. There was an ice bucket in the corner with a bottle of Moët champagne chilling in it, with two glasses sitting on the nearby dressing table. Thank goodness she had said yes, or this could have been rather awkward for him. Not to mention messy for Farid (their housekeeper) to clean up. She remembered Matt had left him a very generous tip.

Despite the four-hour time difference, they had rung her parents immediately in Nottingham to share their news. They had been delighted for them, as had Matt's parents in Newcastle. She had been so happy that night.

Katie opened her eyes and looked down now at her bare left hand. Looking closely, she could still see the indent along with a small white band where the sun hadn't reached the skin underneath her ring. It had broken her heart to give up that ring and all that it meant, but she could not keep it, not after everything. There was no going back now. She shivered a little, pulling her cardigan around her and stared out into the darkness before closing her eyes again and drifting back into her thoughts.

Less than a year on from this holiday, here she was, on her own aged twenty-nine, sitting on a train heading from London Euston to Inverness. She had no return ticket. Inverness was to become her new home.

A lot has changed this past year. Her parents, Bill (a

retired police officer) and Sheila (a retired primary school teacher) had finally moved permanently out to Florida. They had a holiday home there and had always planned on one day making the most of their retirement and relocating there. Her dad suffered greatly from arthritis, which seemed much better in the heat.

Once they knew that Katie was settled with Matt, it seemed the right time for them to make that permanent move. They had begun proceedings just after Katie moved in with Matt and left shortly after they had returned from their holiday to the Maldives last September. The pandemic delaying their plans.

As an only child, Katie was very close to her parents. Her dad was the first one she called whenever she had a problem. This time had been no different. They had both urged her to join them in Florida. There were plenty of jobs for nurses, and they could act as her sponsor. Whilst that was very tempting, Katie had decided she needed to face this alone. She was almost thirty years old, and it was time she learned to stand on her own two feet.

She had, of course, gone to visit them immediately afterwards, but a chance discovery on the S1 jobs website (an online website for jobs in Scotland), one afternoon whilst sitting down by the pool, had found her clicking on the link for an application form for a nurse practitioner post. Before she knew it, she had an interview for the position of nurse practitioner in the accident and emergency department at Raigmore Hospital in Inverness.

It was an exciting opportunity for someone to set up and develop the service, working alongside two other trainee nurse practitioners. With her experience in London, it sounded like the job description had almost been written with her in mind. And just like that, she was home, had been offered the job and, as a consequence, a mere four weeks later, was sitting onboard this train headed for a new start in Scotland.

Her colleagues and friends were shocked at her decision to leave and tried everything they could to make her stay. They thought she was an amazing nurse who always went above and beyond the call of duty. Her patients loved her. Her colleagues loved her. But she had made up her mind. She couldn't stay a minute longer. Not after the heartbreak and humiliation she had suffered, and as they both worked in the same hospital, she felt she had no choice but to leave as it was all just too painful for her.

Not only that, with her working as an emergency nurse practitioner in accident and emergency, and Matt working towards becoming an orthopaedic Consultant in the same hospital, it was inevitable she would still bump into him. She just wasn't sure her heart could take that. Plus, she had nowhere to live and couldn't afford London prices on her own. Her parents had offered to help, but she had turned them down. They had been amazing, but she couldn't accept. She had her pride.

It all started to go wrong six months ago. Katie had come home early from work with a migraine only to discover Matt in their bedroom wearing nothing more than his boxer shorts, sitting on their bed next to her best friend, April. She had stormed out of their home, tears streaming down her face. Matt had run down the street after her, still wearing nothing more than his black Calvin Klein boxers. He stood in the freezing rain in the middle of March in his bare feet, pleading and begging her to return to the apartment so they could talk. If any of their neighbours were watching, he must have looked ridiculous.

This was not what it looked like, he had said. April had simply come over to bring back a handbag she had borrowed from her for a wedding a couple of months back. She was upset as she had just broken up with her boyfriend, and he had been trying to comfort her. He explained he had been in bed after his night shift when she knocked at the door, and when he had gone into the bedroom to get some clothes, she had followed him in, crying. Before he knew it, she had sat down on the bed, and he had simply put his arm around her to comfort her, and that was when Katie had walked in on them. Nothing happened, he said.

He was crying and pleading with her to believe him. She was in complete shock and wasn't sure what to believe.

He was her fiancé, the man she was supposed to be spending the rest of her life with, and April was her best friend and had been for almost twenty-two years. They had been through everything together. She was so confused and didn't know what to think.

This did sound like a logical explanation, after all her shift had been changed at the last minute, so maybe April had thought she would have been home, and Matt seemed genuinely devastated. They had just been sitting on the bed, and apart from her jacket and her shoes April had been fully clothed, so maybe this was true. Maybe her migraine made her blow things out of proportion, or perhaps it was PMT. By the time April had caught up to them, she was crying too and saying nothing had happened, pleading with Katie to believe her. She was her best friend, and she kept saying she would never do anything to hurt her.

April and Katie met at primary school. They had both started halfway through the term in their fourth year at primary school and had become firm friends ever since. Their dads had both been in the police force and had transferred to the same division at around the same time. They did everything together. April even followed Katie to London when she moved there after university. They shared an apartment for a while. Physically, they were the complete opposite. April was stunning, five foot ten, with long blonde hair and big blue eyes. She had a perfect hourglass figure that seemed to captivate men wherever they went, completely the opposite of Katie, who was a petite five-foot-three brunette with shoulder-length naturally curly (sometimes frizzy) hair.

April was always immaculately turned out, whilst Katie lived mostly in sports clothes as she was a keen marathon runner and was always out training whenever she wasn't working. However, she did love to dress up for nights out. All the men loved April. She only had to bat her eyelids, and she could reduce grown men to shrivelling wrecks in seconds. April was a flirt; Katie had watched her in motion many times on nights out together. She had witnessed her break many hearts over the years, but to the best of her knowledge, she had never done anything like this before. Katie had never felt threatened by her beauty. Not until now. But they had known each other for so long.

She chose to believe Matt and April that afternoon. A decision that she would later come to bitterly regret.

2

Katie watched as the train passed through Crewe, knowing they would reach Preston an hour later. The next stop after that would be Stirling. She lay down on the tiny bunk bed and closed her eyes, trying desperately to get some sleep, but the sound of the train on the tracks kept her awake, that and the events of the last six months.

It wasn't long before her thoughts drifted back to Matt again. Kind, sweet Matt, who she had thought had been the love of her life before he betrayed her in the worst possible way. And April, her best friend. Only a true best friend is someone who would never, ever do anything to hurt you. She tossed and turned, trying to get comfortable on the tiny bed.

Things had been strange at first between her and Matt following the incident with April. She couldn't quite get the image of them sitting on their bed together out of her head. There were so many unanswered questions. Why had April been off in the middle of the day? That didn't quite make sense to her. She was a paralegal at a large law firm in the city and should have been at work. And why had she followed Matt into their bedroom, especially when he had no clothes on? That didn't seem right, either.

However, when she thought of the layout of his ground-floor apartment, their bedroom was at the front of the house, next to the sitting room, so perhaps it did seem plausible that she had simply followed him through without thinking. After all, everyone joked April was like the sister she never had; she had known Matt for as long as Katie had. They were comfortable being around one another, and it wasn't like April was a stranger in their home. Still, something about the situation didn't quite sit right with her. Why hadn't Matt put some clothes on before he answered the door? It could have been anyone at the door.

In the following weeks, though, Matt seemed as attentive as usual. April seemed just like her normal self, so Katie tried to push these thoughts to the back of her mind and carry on as usual. She didn't want to ruin her relationship or friendship over something that might have been nothing.

She should have trusted her instincts, however, less than six months later, her entire world would fall apart.

Katie looked at her watch again, it was 2:55 am. She had boarded the train in London Euston nearly six hours ago, which felt like an eternity ago. This journey seemed to be taking forever. She knew she really should try and get some sleep. In five and a half hours, she would be arriving in

Inverness and would need her energy to try and find her way to the apartment she had rented.

She had only been to Inverness once, four weeks ago, in fact, for her job interview. She hoped she could remember her way around. It had seemed logical to rent somewhere until she made some friends and found out what areas were best to live in and where she should avoid. And she needed time to save for a deposit, although with the amount of money she would be paying in rent that might take her a while.

Her parents had helped her choose the apartment; thank goodness for FaceTime. She had shown them each of the five apartments from the shortlist they had drawn up together, which she had viewed the day after her interview (just in case) before helping her settle on one of them. The winning one, situated on Culduthel Park Road had been the nicest by far. It was also the most expensive. Guess that was to be expected, though, as it had recently been renovated to a very high standard.

Although that had been a big factor in her decision, it was also within easy walking distance of the town centre, which, considering she didn't own a car, would be handy for shopping and any possible future nights out. It also seemed easy enough for her to get to work.

Katie didn't have a car; there had been no need when she lived in London. Public transport was so good, and it took almost twice as long to get anywhere if you went by road. She had passed her driving test nine years ago, just before she graduated as a nurse from university. Although she had driven around Nottingham anytime she went home (before her parents emigrated), she had never really driven anywhere she didn't know. That would have to change. But then a lot of things would have to change for her.

The apartment was bright and modern, with beautiful walnut wooden flooring and white walls. It had a sleek light grey gloss kitchen with dark grey granite countertops. The main bathroom was also very modern, with a large freestanding bath, waterfall taps, and a separate double shower unit.

A small en-suite off the main bedroom was decorated with white porcelain tiles and a walnut vanity unit. The apartment had two bedrooms, which, although she didn't really need an extra bedroom, it would come in handy if her parents or any of her friends from London came to stay with her. And having an additional wardrobe for all her shoes was definitely a bonus. Except for the kitchen appliances and a couple of bar stools at the small breakfast bar, the apartment came unfurnished.

She had ordered a bed which was due to be delivered later that day. Once she had her internet connected, she could easily order the rest of the essentials online. Most of the furniture in her last place had belonged to Matt, so besides the three suitcases she had brought with her on the train and a few boxes she had organised to be sent up the following day, she pretty much had nothing.

She had left Matt's place in such a hurry she hadn't even had time to think about taking any of their beautiful engagement gifts with her or anything they had bought together, like the walnut dining table with grey velvet chairs and matching sideboard. It would have been a perfect match with the style of this apartment. Still, every time she looked at it would just be a reminder of her past, and she'd already decided it was time to let go. But that was proving easier said than done.

***

She let out another sigh and glanced out the window into the darkness, catching a glimpse of her tired reflection as she did so. It really was time she got some sleep. These dark circles would never disappear if she didn't start caring for herself again.

Sleep remained elusive, though, no matter how hard she tried to block it out, she just couldn't stop thinking about that fateful night on the 1st of July. She had just finished a run of four night shifts. Matt still had one more to go. An extra one he said, helping a colleague out so they could get away on holiday. That was just like Matt, always thinking of others.

They had enjoyed a takeaway together before Matt left for his night shift.

Katie opened a bottle of wine and poured herself a glass. She was off for the whole weekend and decided to make the most of her time off. It had been a particularly stressful week at work as they were even more short-staffed than usual, meaning she had been left to run the minor injuries unit single-handedly. She had a lovely girly evening planned for herself after Matt left.

She would run herself a bath surrounded by candles, pop a face mask on and just relax while listening to a podcast. Afterwards, she planned to paint her nails and toenails in preparation for the BBQ they had been invited to on Saturday night while watching her favourite movie '*Twilight*' for the millionth time.

She never did get to enjoy that bath, though. As she looked for her nail kit, which she kept in one of the drawers under their bed, Katie thought she could hear a mobile phone vibrating. She smiled as she thought it was probably Matt's, left in one of the pockets of the crumpled pile of scrubs on the bedroom floor. She picked them up. Apart from a couple of pens and a tourniquet, they were empty. Puzzled, she popped them into the laundry basket and bent down to check under the bed in case the phone had fallen out, but nothing was there. Strange, she thought – maybe she had imagined it...

She was just about to walk away when she thought she could hear the vibrations again, only this time, she was pretty sure they were coming from the drawer on Matt's side of the bed. She opened the drawer to check and found wrapped in an old T-shirt at the back of the drawer a mobile phone she didn't recognise. This was a Samsung. Matt had an iPhone. She immediately felt a pang of unease. Suddenly the phone started ringing again. She recognised the number instantly - it belonged to April - her best friend!

It stopped ringing, and then a photo came up on the screen of April in her underwear blowing a kiss to the camera with a message – "*Hey sexy, what's keeping you??? Hope you're not going to bail on me – bought this, especially for you*" followed by six faces blowing a kiss emoji.

Shaking in disbelief, Katie dropped the phone on the bed and stood there staring at the message on the screen – willing it to go away. Maybe this wasn't for Matt; April had accidentally sent this to him. She waited with bated breath for the message to be deleted or another message to come through – the one where you apologise profusely, totally mortified as the message was intended for someone else. Only this message never came.

Seconds passed, followed by minutes. Her heart was pounding in her chest, nausea slowly working its way up the back of her throat. Deep down, she knew. This was not an accident. Katie slumped down on the bed, oblivious to the bath water which was now overflowing in the background.

She tried to unlock the phone, which turned out not to be too difficult as it wasn't password protected. She was trembling so hard it still took her a minute or so, but soon she was able to look back at the history. The only number stored on the phone was April's.

There were hundreds of calls and texts between the pair of them, spanning back years. Loads of photos of them together enjoying cosy nights in and out – although not anywhere she thought she recognised. There were even holiday photos of them together, laughing and joking by a pool.

Tears filled her eyes – they were probably laughing at her now and how gullible she'd been. She thought back to all the medical conferences Matt said he had attended in Milan, Paris, and Chicago. They were always last-minute places, meaning she could never get time off to join him. Then there was April and her business trips, always careful to leave a few days before Matt or stay on for a day or so afterwards. Never in the same place - allegedly.

Katie could feel the bile rise in the back of her throat. Although she now knew the truth, she continued to scroll through the messages in total disbelief. She scrolled back to that afternoon in March when she had caught them in their bedroom together. There were several messages between them that day, mostly arranging to meet up – and loads afterwards joking about how they needed to be more careful in future and how they had almost been caught. Seconds earlier, and she would have caught them at it, it seems.

Katie dropped the phone, went straight to the bathroom, and threw up. Their whole life together had been a lie. She hadn't known Matt at all. April was not the friend she thought she was. It was then that her perfect world came crashing down around her.

She turned off the taps, leaving the water sloshing all over the floor, packed a bag and left.

3

A few hundred miles away, another person was busy trying to settle into a new way of life. Detective Sergeant Tracy McGregor had relocated from the outskirts of Glasgow to sleepy Inverness a little over a week ago and was slowly beginning to find her feet in her new role investigating cold cases at Inverness Police headquarters.

Just like Katie, this was not the move Tracy had been expecting to make at this point in her life either. Had her life turned out the way she had planned it, she would have been busy settling into a completely different role right now. That of Detective Superintendent (deputy to the Detective Chief Superintendent in charge of the CID unit) back home in Glasgow. But, due to a bad judgment call on a very high-profile case she had been working on, she found herself here instead - forced to step down from her previous role as Detective Chief Inspector in CID in Glasgow East to that of a Detective Sergeant. Oh, how the mighty had fallen.

To save face, she had moved to another region entirely. One where no one knew her or her reputation. That place was Inverness.

Still, at least she hadn't been demoted to Constable. Her old Assistant Chief Constable (ACC) had written a letter of recommendation on her behalf to the Police board. Although she had still been demoted, they had allowed her to keep the rank of Sergeant with the possibility of promotion again. But at forty-eight, she knew this was probably unlikely.

DS McGregor loved her job. A job that, although challenging and often upsetting, had given her much pleasure over the years but, at the same time, had taken a considerable toll on her personal life, including her marriage.

The irregular hours and frequent calls in the middle of the night meant she was hardly ever there, leaving her husband, Rob, to bring up their two boys, Callum and Finn, more or less on his own. He had been the one who went to school sports day, prize giving and rugby practice every Saturday with them, rain, hail or shine. He was there in the middle of the night when they were sick and ferried them everywhere regardless of the time of day or night. When the boys left home to go to university, Rob decided to call time on their marriage. Things became quite messy towards the end. Their only communication now was concerning the boys. Even then, that had become less frequent as the boys were both settled at university.

Callum was in his second year at the University of

Salford, studying for a BSc in Architectural Design and Technology. Finn had just started a BSc (Hons) in sports coaching and physical education at the Birmingham City School of Education and Social Work, allowing him to continue with his beloved rugby.

With her share of the sale of the family home and the help of some inheritance from her parents, she had bought herself a run-down three-bedroom cottage with half an acre of land attached to it on the outskirts of Nairn, a pretty town seventeen miles outside Inverness, leaving behind the hustle and bustle of her former life in Glasgow.

For the first time since joining the police force, she had regular hours, which she was struggling to get used to. She hoped this would finally allow her to take up some hobbies and maybe reconnect with her friends again, but as she'd always struggled to switch off, this wasn't going to be an easy task.

Her marriage wasn't the only thing to suffer. Over the years, her friendships outside the force had taken quite a bashing. She could never quite manage to keep the plans she made with anyone, and although her true friends were understanding, she could tell deep down they were hurting. She knew she had sacrificed a lot over the years, but she was so passionate about her work and often found herself happiest when on the job - eating, living and breathing a case.

Just like Katie, she was also struggling to sleep. The events of the last year kept rattling around in her head. She wondered if she would ever be able to sleep soundly again – but then again, maybe she didn't deserve to. A child had died because of her. Tracy sat up and checked the time on her phone which was sitting on a box at the side of her bed – 02:57, twenty-two minutes since the last time she had checked it.

She got up and padded downstairs to the kitchen, where she poured herself a large glass of milk (as she was out of wine), to wash down a couple of Prozac. She wandered aimlessly around the unfamiliar house, staring out into the darkness from each room, before finally climbing back into bed. When the alarm went off at 7 am, she was exhausted.

4

Katie put her head down on the pillow and closed her eyes. She must have finally drifted off as the next thing she heard was the sound of the alarm on her phone; it was 07:45 already. Just enough time for her to quickly wash her face and brush her teeth in the tiny little sink before the train pulled into Inverness. She swept her hair into a messy bun, and applied her trusted Clarins beauty flash balm and some Charlotte Tilbury magic away liquid concealer, in an attempt to hide the ever-present dark circles. With a quick spritz of her favourite perfume - Victor and Rolph Flowerbomb, she was almost ready to face the world again.

Hopefully, there would be a café near the station she thought, so she could grab a quick coffee to wake herself up before meeting the estate agent at the apartment. She had planned to catch an early breakfast on the train, but there was no time now. Her stomach growled, and she was feeling sick. She wasn't sure if it was tiredness, hunger or nerves. Or perhaps a combination of all three.

Elaine, the estate agent who had shown her around the apartment, had kindly offered to meet her there with the keys to save her from travelling to the branch to collect them after her long journey. She had taken pity on Katie, who was about the same age as her daughter, and the apartment block was only a short drive from her house. Elaine had been so easy to talk to, Katie had ended up telling her the whole story about Matt and April and why she was moving to Inverness.

At £895 per calendar month, the rent for the apartment had been a bit higher than she was comfortable with. Still, this seemed very reasonable compared to the apartments she had rented in London. It was the nicest she had seen by far. Katie had paid the hefty deposit along with her first month's rent with some of the money she had taken from her share of their wedding fund.

As the train pulled into the station, Katie took one last look at herself in the tiny mirror and let out another sigh. This time a nervous sigh. This was it, time to move on and get her life back on track. She had changed into a fresh pair of skinny jeans (which now needed a belt to hold them up as she'd lost so much weight these past few weeks). She teamed them with a white cotton t-shirt, navy blazer and her beloved white leather Converse. One last nervous look in the mirror. The tiny bit of makeup she had put on did little to hide the dark circles that were becoming an almost permanent feature lately. Still, nothing she could do about that now. Another quick spritz of perfume and she was done – time to start a new chapter.

She picked up her navy leather Michael Kors handbag and slung it across her body before deciding how on earth she was going to manage three large suitcases on her own. Her colleagues and friends Heather, Michelle and Lynn had come to see her off and had taken one each for her, so she had only had to worry about her handbag whilst she was walking through Euston station. As the cases were on wheels, they were easy enough to manoeuvre, but three on her own – this would be a bit more of a challenge. Thank goodness she was wearing flat shoes.

As she opened the door to her cabin, a kind elderly gentleman came out of his cabin simultaneously with her and when he saw she was on her own, he immediately offered to help her. Once they were safely on the platform, he suggested she try pushing two along together in front of her with one hand, whilst pulling the third one behind her in the other hand. This sounded like it might just work. She thanked him and hoped, a kind taxi driver would help her when she got out of the station. She might have to forget that coffee, though. Not enough hands.

The fresh cool October air hit her as soon as she stepped into the station. She reached into her handbag and pulled out a scarf to cover her neck. It was only 8:45 am, and she wasn't due to meet Elaine until 10 am. There was no point in heading out to Culduthel Park Road too early as she would be stuck outside on her own in the cold.

Looking around the station, Katie decided she would try to grab a quick coffee after all from the little express café tucked away in the corner, and maybe a chocolate muffin - if they had any. Her tummy rumbled at the thought. As she was making her way over to the café, the elderly gentleman who had helped her off the train, saw her struggling again as he came out of the newsagents and kindly rushed over to help her. He sat with her cases at an empty table by the door while she went to the counter to place her order. She bought him a coffee as a thank you.

Katie was so exhausted she didn't take any notice of the man sitting quietly at the back of the café on his phone, a half-empty coffee cup and a set of car keys in front of him. No one really noticed him. But he noticed her. As soon as she walked in, he was captivated by her. Careful not to draw any unwanted attention, he watched her using the camera on his phone. Quietly snapping away, taking lots of photographs of her from multiple angles. To anyone watching, he looked like he was just another lone commuter passing the time, glued to his phone. Oblivious to the attention she was receiving, Katie hungrily ate her muffin whilst she waited for her coffee to cool.

Sensing she was getting ready to leave, he casually got up before her, grabbing the keys to his Range Rover, which was parked outside near the taxi rank. Brushing past her as he left, he ensured he was just close enough to catch a whiff of her sweet smell without being noticed. Once outside, he kept his distance, lingering on the concourse in the middle of the station, pretending to check train times on the information boards, but he was only interested in her. Now that she was back, there was no way he was letting her out of his sight.

By 9:45 am, Katie was feeling slightly nervous again but sitting in a taxi heading towards her new home and her new life. Unaware of the black Range Rover that was intently following along behind her, the occupant eager to find out where she was headed.

***

He couldn't quite believe his luck. Heart pounding in his chest, he'd had to stop himself from approaching her in the café, but it was too soon. He'd waited a long time for her to return and judging by how things ended last time, he didn't want to scare her. But now that he'd found her again, he wasn't about to lose her. She was his, and he would stop at nothing to get her back.

5

Her predecessor had been very untidy, so Tracy had spent the first few days in her new job with the help of Betty, her secretary of sorts, organising and then re-organising the filing system in her tiny office, which was really no more than the size of a cupboard.

Once she had done this, she set about organising her desk and finally installing the whiteboard she had found gathering dust behind one of the metal filing cabinets. Some coloured pens and neatly placed magnets on the right-hand side of the board finished the transformation. Now she was ready to start working on her first case. Looking around the room, she was secretly quite pleased with herself.

They had arranged the cold cases into categories - murder, missing person and theft. Each with its own drawer. These were then subdivided by year and alphabetically. As she had spent almost thirty years of her career dealing with murder, she decided to stay away from this drawer for now - although to be honest, there were only two cases in it. She guessed not so many murders took place up here. Certainly not anywhere near as many as the inner cities of Glasgow and Edinburgh, where she had previously worked. In

Glasgow, there had been at least one murder a night, most never making it into the press as they either involved members of rival gangs or were alcohol or drugs related.

Still, despite her experience, she didn't want a reminder of her recent failure, so she chose to start with a missing person case instead. She knew the statistics; thirty-seven thousand people are reported missing in Scotland every year. Around ninety-seven per cent either come home or are found dead within a week, another two per cent within the year, leaving only around 1% missing for more than a year. Occasionally these people are found alive and well, living a new life somewhere different. Now, this was something she thought she could cope with.

There were no other officers directly assigned to her. Still, her new ACC had told her when she had enquired about the position, if staffing and budget permitted, he would see if he could spare any police constables from time to time to help her as and when required.

Tracy poured herself a coffee and settled down at her desk. The first file she opened was that of a twenty-three-year-old American girl, Erin Doherty, who had gone missing in Inverness in August 2012. She had left home on the 4th of August 2011 with her two best friends on a gap year following university and was due to fly back home to New York on the 7th of August 2012 before starting work as an accountant in a large firm in Wall Street the following week.

Reading on, she discovered the girls had initially travelled through Europe together and were on the last leg of their trip, visiting England, Wales, Northern Ireland and Scotland, before they were due to fly home when Erin had gone missing. Erin had stayed on alone in Inverness for a week as her friends, who had met two guys whilst they were in Edinburgh, had cut their time short in Inverness to meet back up with the boys again before flying home to the US.

They had just missed the Fringe festival when they visited Edinburgh, and having heard so much about it from the boys, her friends had decided they wanted to go back and experience some of the festival magic for themselves. Kind of like one final blowout before heading home and starting work. Tracy was pretty positive that was not the only reason. Not wanting to cramp their style, Erin had agreed to stay on in Inverness and join them in a week for their flight back home to the States, only she had never shown up.

According to a witness, Erin was last seen on Sunday, the 5th of August 2012. From her picture, Tracy could see she was a beautiful girl, petite at five-foot-three, with bright blue eyes and dark brown curly hair. Tracy pinned her photograph on the whiteboard and wrote her name and age with 'last seen Sunday the 5th of August 2012' underneath. At some point, she would need to interview the witness herself to see if they remembered anything that might help. Often people see significant things which they don't think are relevant enough to mention when initially questioned, and it takes a skilled detective to tease this information out of them.

Turning back to the file, she discovered Erin's friends had reported her missing when she hadn't shown up to meet them on Tuesday afternoon down in Edinburgh. The girls had contacted Erin's parents in America, who subsequently contacted the American Embassy, which contacted Interpol. As Erin was an American national, Interpol had initially been involved, but as per protocol, they had passed the investigation onto the local police force. The central working hypothesis was that she had simply run away, but Tracy wanted to keep an open mind at this stage. There didn't seem much to go on, and with no crime scene as such, this was going to be a bit of a challenge, but DS McGregor certainly did enjoy a challenge.

Reading on, she discovered the girls had been staying at the Inverness Youth hostel. Still new to the area, a quick look at the map on her phone confirmed this wasn't far from here. It looked like it was just a five-minute drive from the police station. There was no mention of CCTV at the hostel, so sadly, no video footage was available on the day Erin had disappeared or in the days leading up to or after her disappearance. Although not essential to an investigation, this was one of the first things officers often look at. It can help with timelines and, depending on the quality of the recordings, can often help identify suspects.

After a local police appeal, the only witness who had come forward at the time was a girl named Heidi, who was originally from Sweden. She was another international student staying in the hostel at the same time as the girls, whilst she was working at a local restaurant for the summer.

Heidi claimed to have seen Erin leave the hostel on her own around 18:30 dressed in blue skinny jeans and a pretty pale pink floaty blouse, which showed off her lightly tanned skin. She wore white leather Converse on her feet and had a pale pink leather bag slung across her body. Her hair and make-up were done as if she were going somewhere, like maybe on a date. She spoke to her briefly, but Erin didn't say where she was headed.

As their room had been paid for until the following Tuesday, no one had realised at first that she was gone, leaving all her things behind her (including her passport), until the cleaner arrived the day she was due to check out, which was two days after anyone last saw her.

This made the timeline of her disappearance sometime between the Sunday evening, and the morning of Tuesday 7th of August 2012, at 12:30, when the cleaner had let herself into the girl's room using her key.

As she was used to travellers leaving things behind, the cleaner had simply thought this was just another case of someone who had too much luggage for their flight home.

She saw it all the time; rather than pay for excess baggage, they left behind what they couldn't take with them for her to deal with.

She had bundled everything into a large black refuse sack and carried on cleaning. When she had finished, she left the bag securely at the front desk with a tag on it stating which room she had found it in and when in case anyone came back looking for it. These items are kept for them to either be collected by the owners or the contents donated to charity if no one claims them within a year.

When Erin hadn't turned up at the train station in Edinburgh to meet her friends, they had phoned the hostel and, on hearing this story about her belongings, had immediately insisted something was wrong. Her friends had promptly called her parents in the States, who then reported her missing.

The police had visited the hostel at the time and collected all of her belongings, which they had taken back to the station with them. They had subsequently been sent back to her parents in America. An itemised list of her belongings and photographs of all the individual items had been included in her file, which the original investigating officers had put together.

Nothing initially jumped out as being out of place, when Tracy looked through the photographs. There were photographs of the inside and outside of the enormous red duffle bag. Inside the bag, officers had found underwear; a couple of t-shirts; some vest tops; shorts; two pairs of jeans - one blue, one black; cardigans; a couple of jumpers; three summer dresses; a pair of khaki combat trousers; an old grey Pennsylvania university hoodie and a rather well- worn pair of navy canvas Converse. All standard items you would expect a young person who had been travelling for a year to be carrying.

The other items which had been left behind in the room had also been placed inside the plastic bag by the cleaner. These included a make-up and cosmetic bag; a hairdryer; a bag of dirty laundry; a pair of pyjamas; a winter jacket, and a rather crumpled-looking rain jacket. Other personal items included costume jewelry; an iPad; an iPhone charger; a universal travel adaptor; and Erin's passport. Again, all standard things you would expect to find. Although Tracy couldn't help but think to herself, how on earth someone hadn't realised, this was a bit more than a few items left behind was beyond her.

Sadly, as the room had been cleaned, there was no way the original investigating officers could have known if there had been anything suspicious left behind in her room, or if anyone other than her friends had been there. There had been no suspicion of foul play in the room; thus, sadly, forensics had not been asked to attend. Photographs of the room after it had been cleaned had been taken.

The room was a triple room containing three beds (single bunk beds and a separate single bed) and a small wardrobe. There was one window with a radiator underneath and a sink in the room's far corner. It was functional and clean, exactly as you would expect for a hostel.

Isa, the cleaner, had worked there for years. She was sixty-two years old and had no prior police convictions. The officers in attendance had interviewed her at the time, but she had only been able to tell them she didn't notice anything out of the ordinary - it was just a typical young girls' room.

The only bed with linen on it had been neatly made, but she remembered clothes were left lying scattered on top. She had put this down to someone choosing which items to pack and which to leave behind.

But Tracy was already working on another hypothesis - could this be someone who had tried on several outfits before deciding what to wear when heading out for an evening? And if Heidi's assumptions had been correct and she was on her way to meet someone, that someone had never come forward or at least, there was no record of him or her doing so in her tiny police file.

Looking back over the cleaner’s statement, Isa said she didn't remember seeing anything to suggest a struggle had taken place in the room. Although it wasn't a single room, she didn't think anyone else had been there as the other beds had been stripped after her friends had left for Edinburgh, and their dirty sheets had already been taken away for washing. Only a pile of clean linen lay on top of their unmade beds. Bed linen was changed once a week.

The girls had paid for their room in advance for a two-week stay. This was before Mollie and Olivia had decided to cut their visit to the Highlands short and head back down to Edinburgh a week early, leaving Erin behind. The hostel was full, so the girls had cut their losses and Erin had stayed on in the same room alone.

Guests are asked to strip their beds and leave the laundry neatly piled on the bed weekly or before leaving. As Mollie and Olivia had already left the week before, their dirty laundry had already been removed and replaced with clean ones, which they hadn't touched. Tracy wondered at this point why Isa didn't think it strange that Erin's bed was still neatly made when the other girls had stuck to the rules. And, surely, if you were planning not to follow the rules, you certainly wouldn't have even bothered making the bed in the first place. This suggested to her that Erin had intended to return to her room, but something or someone had prevented her from doing so, and she was determined to find out why. As a former lead detective in the CID, Tracy found this strange no one had thought to question this at the time.

The bathroom had been shared between them and two other rooms on this floor, so there had been no way of telling if Erin had left anything behind in there. A small wash bag and make-up bag had been listed within her possessions, which suggested probably not.

Once she was satisfied she'd had a good read through the small file, Tracy decided to start her own investigation by visiting the hostel. Although it was a long shot, she thought she would see if anyone still worked there who might have remembered Erin and her friends or even remembered anything about the night in question. Plus, being a previous DCI in the CID, she wanted to see the room for herself and check entrance and exit points to see if anyone could have sneaked in and taken her without being seen, especially as there was no CCTV.

Tracy also wanted to speak to Heidi, Isa and Erin's friends and parents, so she scribbled names and numbers in her new notebook. Of course, she had no idea if these were still the correct contact details for everyone, as over a decade had passed since Erin had gone missing, but it was a starting point. As a parent herself, she could only imagine the anguish they must be going through. It must be terrible enough to lose a child, but even worse, not knowing what happened to them, never knowing if they were alive or dead or if there was anything you could have said or done to change the course of events. Call it a hunch, but she couldn't quite think there was more to this, and this wasn't an open-and-shut case of a girl who had simply run away.

6

As the taxi pulled up in front of the apartment block, Katie saw Elaine eagerly waiting outside for her. Elaine helped her up the four flights of stairs to the second floor with her three heavy suitcases. Sadly, there was no lift. Usually, Katie preferred the healthy option, but that was ok when you didn't have three heavy suitcases in tow. As soon as she walked in through the front door of the apartment and closed the door, she immediately felt safe.

The apartment was just as nice as she remembered it, and the view from the French doors in the living room over the woods was incredible. Looking around, she felt happy for the first time in a long while.

Elaine had kindly left her a box in the kitchen containing tea, coffee, milk, a kettle and a couple of mugs as a little housewarming gift, which thankfully she had brought up before Katie arrived. Her kindness almost made Katie burst into tears. She had been so preoccupied with other things she hadn't even thought about needing these simple things.

After she had gone over the basics and explained where everything was and how everything worked, Elaine stayed for a quick coffee with her before leaving her alone to settle in. Luckily enough, there were two chairs at the breakfast bar to sit at. Katie was exhausted, but she would have to wait for her bed to arrive before she could sleep. She hoped it wouldn't be too long.

While waiting, she decided to keep herself busy, unpack some of her things, and at least hang her clothes up in the wardrobe. However, she soon discovered there were no hangers, so this was another thing that would have to wait. She could unpack her toiletries though, as the bathroom had plenty of cupboards. As she looked around the rest of the apartment, she realised exactly how empty the place was, much like her life at the minute. It would take time and money to have it looking and feeling like home.

She was beginning to wish maybe she should have taken her time moving out of Matt's, but it was too painful and she didn’t want to run the risk of bumping into him or April. That very evening she had found out about them, she had grabbed a few things and temporarily moved in with her friend Lynn, but not wanting to impose on her and her girlfriend for longer than necessary, had flown out to Florida as soon as she could to stay with her parents.

She had only returned to Matt's place once to retrieve her things. Lynn had come with her in case Matt had turned up, but thankfully there had been no sign of him. She took her things, leaving her keys on the dining room table alongside her engagement ring. Looking around now, she had perhaps been too hasty, deciding to leave everything behind. After all, some of the furniture had belonged to her, and half of their engagement gifts technically belonged to her too. But after learning of their betrayal, she wasn't sure she could bear to look at any of it. She wasn't sure what she ought to do with the gifts, weren't you supposed to return them? She decided Matt could deal with that. It was the least he could do after humiliating her. Still, no point in going over the past. She would pick new things, her things, this time.

Her bed arrived a little after 2 pm, so thankfully, she didn't have too long to wait. Fortunately, it came with a free duvet and pillows, which meant she didn't have to bring these bulky things along with her. She had paid extra for the install service, which meant the delivery guys unpacked it for her and built it up before taking all the packaging away with them. The beautiful grey velvet upholstered bed looked so comfortable. It was tempting to jump in immediately and fall asleep. But, Katie wasn't sure what time the shops shut up here, and she didn't want to leave it too late to go grocery shopping as she had no food with her. Plus, she hadn't eaten since the muffin at the train station that morning, so sleep would have to wait again for now.

She made up the bed with the duvet set she had brought with her (un-ironed as that was yet another thing she would have to buy) and picked herself out a warmer jacket from one of her suitcases that was now lying open on the floor of the walk-in wardrobe in the master bedroom. She had sorted the clothes within them into neat piles to try and save them from getting too crushed until she managed to pick up enough coat hangers to put them away.

She was beginning to wish she had ordered a sofa beforehand too, but only having been to the apartment once, she wasn't sure of the exact size and layout of the room and thought it best to wait until she moved in. Plus, she wasn't sure about access and didn't want to order something too big in case it wouldn't fit up the stairwell. Next had a great online range, and depending on which one she picked, she noticed some didn't seem to take too long for delivery.

Her television and laptop were arriving tomorrow via courier, along with a few other home comforts and treasured possessions. These included her family photos, a vast collection of shoes, and all her beloved books and childhood memories that she had never bothered to unpack when she moved from her parent's house to London. For now, the only other things she needed were bedroom furniture and maybe a coffee table for the living room. The spare room could wait. She suddenly felt quite excited at the prospect of choosing her own things.

The walk into town was quite pleasant. It was a bit warmer than it had been first thing, and the sun had come out, but Katie still felt the temperature difference between Scotland and England. It was definitely several degrees cooler up here. She would have to get used to this. She picked up the essentials for now after finding out from the checkout staff she could do a large shop online and have it delivered.

By the time she returned to the apartment, her arms were aching from carrying the four large bags back from town, and then up the four flights of stairs to her apartment. She dumped the bags in the hall whilst she scrambled in her bag for her keys again. As she brought in the last bag, an elegant, immaculately dressed older lady stepped out of the apartment next door. Katie went over and introduced herself, excited as this was the first person she had met besides Elaine since she arrived.

She discovered the lady's name was Lily Davenport and she was on her way to meet some friends in town at an Italian restaurant for dinner. Lily was very easy to talk to. She invited Katie to drop by sometime for a coffee with her, which Katie vowed to herself she would do, it would be nice to make some new friends, and she seemed as if she genuinely meant it.

After she put her shopping away, Katie decided on a simple microwave pasta dish with salad and garlic bread for dinner that night. She would have to learn to cook, though, now that she was on her own. She'd never survive very long on cereal, toast and micro dinners. Matt had done all the cooking when they lived together, so she had become somewhat lazy in the kitchen.

After a quick chat online with her parents, Katie decided on a long hot bubble bath followed by an early night. This time she slept like a baby, completely unaware of the dark figure nestled into the trees overlooking her apartment.

7

Grabbing her coat and handbag, and the car keys for her pool car, Tracy shouted to Jenny, the desk Sergeant, that she was heading out for a bit. The hostel, which was situated on Victoria Avenue, was only a five-minute drive from the station. On the way there, she noticed although it was just a short walk to the town centre, giving it great proximity to all the local attractions, such as the museum and castle, along with all the restaurants and bars, it was also located in a very quiet part of town, making it quite secluded.

It was a three-storey building, and its style reminded her a little of a ranch with its white exterior and orange slate roof. She parked in the car park at the rear of the building and made her way around to the main entrance. Entering through the single glass door, she walked along a narrow corridor, past a large notice board full of posters and flyers, towards the bright reception. After showing her warrant card to the young girl on the desk, she asked to speak with the duty manager.

She was in luck; the manager, Mr Johnson, was still the same person who had been there ten years ago when Erin disappeared. Jack Johnson was a frail little man now, unlike his photograph on display in reception, which was easily twenty years old. He was dressed in grey trousers and a cream and grey stripy shirt with a beige jumper over the top, which she noticed had holes in the sleeves. She guessed he was somewhere around seventy years old and wondered why on earth he was still working.

After showing him her warrant card and briefly explaining why she was there, he invited her into his small apartment, which was situated on the ground floor, to the rear of the property. As they walked along the corridor he explained his apartment was attached to the hostel and went along with the job. When they arrived, she saw it was more of a bedsit than an apartment. It was very cluttered, filled with oversized furniture, some of which had seen better days. He apologised for the mess, explaining his wife had been the housekeeper but she had died the previous year, leaving him on his own.

Tracy managed to find herself a seat in the small living room while he shuffled off into the tiny kitchen in the corner to make himself a tea and a coffee for her. She opted for a black coffee which he handed her in a chipped black mug. He placed a plate of chocolate biscuits on the coffee table before her, which she politely declined.

He remembered the case of Erin's disappearance very well. It had been around the time his wife had taken a mini-stroke, so he wasn't around that day like he usually was.

They didn't have children themselves and, as a result, welcomed many of the youngsters as if they were their own.

His wife Joan took pity on some of the younger ones and often did some washing for them if they couldn't afford to do it themselves, or she made them the odd meal or two whilst they stayed there, which again wasn't part of the deal. She had been a fantastic baker, and he told her he would often come home to find one of their guests sitting at the table enjoying a cup of tea and a slice of cake with her. It was clear from the way he spoke about his wife, he really missed her.

Erin and her friends had stood out as they had been particularly kind to them, helping him bring in his shopping one night and another night when he was struggling with his wife's wheelchair on the paving stones at the front entrance. They had seemed like nice friendly girls, keeping their room relatively tidy. It was apparent that Mr Johnson was still very upset at her disappearance, and Tracy quickly conceived he couldn't have had anything to do with it.

Although ten years had passed, Tracy asked if he would mind showing her around and if she could see the room Erin had been staying in. He took great delight in this. Tracy thought he seemed pleased to have something to do. As they walked along the corridor, he proudly told her there were forty-two rooms in total, with the ability to accommodate a maximum of one hundred and fifty-five guests. There were several communal spaces throughout the building, including a large well-equipped kitchen, café, TV lounge and laundry room.

He told her the ground floor has only one guest suite situated on it which is now their wheelchair-accessible room. The rest of the ground floor comprised the reception; dining area; a self-catering kitchen; laundry room; a small shop selling soft drinks, toiletries, etc., and the biggest of the two lounges, which he proudly informed her could seat up to twenty-five people. Tracy noticed each was brightly decorated; and although some areas were quite tired, the place was immaculate.

The girls had been staying in a second-floor room with a shared bathroom. As there was no lift, they had to climb the stairs, which took slightly longer as Mr Johnson wasn't as mobile as he once was. Once Mr Johnson found the key from the relatively large set he was carrying on the belt around his waist, he stood back to let Tracy enter the room first. No one was staying in this room at the minute, and nothing was left in it now that belonged to Erin; her things were long gone.

Looking around, Tracy noticed it looked exactly like a room in any other hostel, with its wooden bunk beds and small wooden wardrobe. Apart from perhaps a fresh coat of paint, the room looked the same as it had in the photographs. It had the same blue carpet, mattress, bedding, and light green curtains. Tracy wondered if they might even be the same ones.

At the time, Isa's statement mentioned she found some clothes hung up in the wardrobe, with a plastic bag stuffed full of dirty laundry at the bottom. Erin's sizeable red duffle bag had been neatly stored underneath the bottom bunk bed. Although she knew it was empty, Tracy still walked over to the wardrobe and opened it. As she looked inside, she imagined how the place would have looked and sounded when the girls were staying there.

Satisfied, she closed the wardrobe doors and turned her attention to the rest of the room. The sink, where again, according to the statement Isa had given - a single toothbrush had sat in a glass alongside a half-empty tube of toothpaste. A hairdryer had also reportedly lain unplugged on the floor next to an open make-up bag. A wet towel hung on the peg behind the door. The bed was neatly made, with a pair of short pyjamas neatly folded underneath the pillow of the single bed.

Nothing had looked out of place, according to Isa. Again, this struck Tracy immediately as strange – why leave the room like this if you were planning on running off? If she had been planning to disappear, surely, she would have cleared the room of every last trace of her and then just vanished. In her mind, this was more like a room left by someone who had headed out for the evening but was planning to return.

It also didn't sound as though it looked like she had left in a hurry either, and there was no evidence of a struggle in any of the photographs taken afterwards or according to Isa's statement. Nothing had been broken in the room, and there were no stains on the floor or marks on the walls. Although she would have loved it if forensics could have confirmed this - it was too late for this now.

Tracy walked over to the window. As she had already noticed from the photographs in the file, no one could have climbed in or out this way, as the only opening part of the window was a small hopper-style section at the top. This would not have been big enough for anyone other than possibly a very small child to climb through. But given that they were on the second floor, this too would have been difficult without a ladder and probably impossible without someone seeing or hearing anything in the rooms below. Photographs taken at the time of the inside and outside of the door indicated no damage, meaning the only way in or out of this room was if you had a key or were with someone who did. Given the door locked on closing, it would have been difficult for anyone to have entered the room without a key.

She thanked Mr Johnson very much for his time and said she would see herself out if he didn't mind her having another quick look around. He shuffled away and left her to it. She looked at the entrance and exits (including the fire exit) and had a wander around the perimeter of the property. She wasn't sure exactly what she was looking for but was working on a hunch that something sinister had happened to Erin. Seeing the window from outside further, emphasised that climbing in or out this way would have been impossible, and why would you when you had a key? Although reception was only open until 10 pm, she noticed on her way in, there was an emergency number you could call if you'd lost your key. There was no ledge or drainpipe near the window either. Everything she had seen and heard so far pointed towards Erin leaving of her own free will, but what had kept her from returning was a mystery. A mystery she was itching to solve.

Climbing back into her car, she looked at her surroundings, trying to imagine where you would go on your own on a Sunday evening as a young woman. The town wasn't completely strange to her, the girls had been here for a week already when Erin had decided to stay on for a bit longer, so it was possible she could have met someone. It might also have been why she was so keen to stay on here alone. She made a mental note to ask her friends about this possibility.

The only witness was Heidi, who had met Erin as she was heading back to the hostel after she had finished her shift. Tracy felt the next logical step in her investigation was to speak to Heidi to try and find out what direction Erin had been headed. She turned the engine on, popped the car into gear and drove back to the station.

As she was driving back, she started thinking about the girls. Was it possible they had had an argument and something could have happened to Erin? Was this just an elaborate story they had concocted between them to cover up a murder? Or was she just being cynical having worked in CID all these years? Given that her friends were in Edinburgh at the time of her disappearance, and they were also the ones who raised the alarm, she felt it was unlikely they were involved in her disappearance. However, this was not impossible. She would have to do some digging into their backgrounds before speaking to them.

Then there were Erin’s belongings - were there any clues hidden in her duffle bag? Erin's bag had been taken back to the US by her parents, who had flown over the moment they discovered their daughter was missing. It had been fingerprinted on the insistence of her parents, but only Erin's and those of her friends were found on the zipper and padlock. If she had run off – why leave everything behind? Or had she left everything behind? Was it possible she could have taken some of her clothes with her? There had to be a clue as to where she had been going on her own that Sunday evening. And maybe that duffle bag might hold the answers she was looking for. Tracy knew she would have to talk to Erin’s parents soon anyway, as it was only courteous of her to inform them she was taking another look at the case, and she fully intended on asking if they still had that bag.

Once she was back in the office, Tracy decided to try and track down Heidi next, since she was the only person they knew at this stage, who had been the last person to see her before she disappeared. Although she had a copy of her statement, she wanted to hear it for herself. See if there was anything extra that hadn't been recorded. Tracy knew only too well that people often do see things which they fail to mention at the time as they think they are insignificant. Sometimes these memories are buried deep within until someone says something that jogs this memory, and she was good at teasing this information out of people.

A quick search in the police database revealed Heidi was now married and settled in Auchterarder, which is a small town just outside of Perth. She looked at her watch. It was two-thirty in the afternoon - too late now to make that round trip in a day, so she opted to call her instead to see if she could set up a meeting for the next day or so. Although she could have spoken to her on the phone, Tracy wanted to see her face when she talked to her, and make sure she was telling the truth. She got her voicemail and left a message on her mobile asking her to call back.

In the meantime, she switched on her computer and logged on to Facebook. Erin's Facebook account was still active. As is the case with missing persons, it had been left active in case she posted on it. However, there seemed to be no further posts since the night she had disappeared. Her last update was posted on Friday, the 3rd of August 2012, when she checked into Duff House, a beautiful Georgian estate house in Banff, Aberdeenshire.

She posted twenty photographs of the interior and exterior of the building, which is currently owned by Historic Scotland and is part of the National Galleries of Scotland. It was designed by the famous Scottish architect William Adam. Tracy looked back through the content of her posts over the last few months, trying to see if she could build up a profile of Erin. She found various posts and check-ins from lots of locations all over Europe.

It looked like the girls had started their trip in Milan before heading to Venice; Bologna; Tuscany; Florence; Rome; Naples, and Sicily. They had regularly posted updates, including photographs of them together doing various things like visiting some of the high-end fashion shops in Milan (and trying on a few things in the boutiques) to visiting some of the historical monuments such as the Colosseum, Trevi fountain; Pompeii; the Herculaneum; Mount Vesuvius and the Spanish steps to name but a few. From Italy, they had worked their way through France, Spain, Germany and Prague before finally flying to the UK.

There were lots of photographs of the girls having fun, larking around, drinking limoncello cocktails and eating pizza and gelato in Italy; wearing sombreros and drinking sangria in Spain; climbing the Eiffel Tower in Paris, and visiting the Brandenburg gate in Berlin. Some posts included photos of them with various handsome waiters, and there were a few with other travellers they must have met along the way. Tracy made a note to ask her friends who these people were in case she had kept in touch with any of them. Could one of them have followed her, or had she decided to meet back up with one of them, and they had run off together?

All of these were possibilities. Often missing people don't want to be found. But her gut and experience were telling her something about this case didn't quite add up. Erin had her whole life ahead of her and had landed her dream job with an apartment waiting for her in America when she got back. According to statements from her friends and family in the States, she was really looking forward to going home. Her disappearance didn't make sense to any of them.

Looking back further, Tracy could see Erin had joined Facebook in 2007 whilst she was in her second year at university. She had attended Pennsylvania University, which was around a four-and-a-half-hour commute from her parents' house. As an only child, she was very close to her parents. They appeared regularly in her posts and photographs. It was amazing how much you could find out about someone from their social media accounts. Young people seem to live their lives online. Being a very private person, Tracy found this behaviour strange.

There were various posts, as you would expect from someone this age, of nights out at parties with what looked like other students, and she seemed to have had a boyfriend for a while from what appeared to be early 2008 to sometime in 2010. A sporty-looking guy named Josh Sadowski, who judging from his photographs seemed to play ice hockey for his university or college team. There were loads of posts of her at matches supporting him.

Tracy wasn't familiar with American university crests or colours, so she wasn't sure if they attended the same university or not, but concluded this was possibly how they met. Although she wasn't entirely sure this was relevant, as he seemed to disappear from her posts towards the end of 2010, and her status on Facebook (although it hadn't been updated since 2012) was currently listed as single, so she wasn't sure yet if there was much point involving him.

She clicked on his name anyway but found his profile was private. Still, she wrote his name in her notebook anyway. It wouldn't do any harm to find out where he was when Erin disappeared, as if her calculations were correct it had only been six months since they split up before she left on her gap year. At least if he was still in the States when she went missing, she could eliminate him as having anything to do with her disappearance.

Scrolling through her photographs and old profile pictures, she found family photos of Erin at birthdays, weddings, christenings and eventually her graduation. Every one of them portrayed a happy, content girl enjoying life. But Tracy knew only too well a picture can tell a thousand lies. There were many family photos of her and Rob smiling and happy, looking like the perfect family unit when the truth was she had just arrived moments before the photograph was taken or left immediately afterwards as her job always seemed to need her more.

She sighed as she thought about Rob and her boys and how badly she had treated them. She missed them all terribly, but sadly she couldn't turn back time. Rob was happy now; he had moved on and met someone else. Somebody with regular hours. Somebody who worked to live instead of living to work. She was happy for him, but it still didn't stop her longing for what they had had in the beginning, when they were just a couple of teenagers madly in love with their whole life ahead of them.

They had known each other since school but didn't start dating until they were in their final year. Rob had taken an apprenticeship as a joiner with his dad, while she went to university to study criminology before joining the police force. They had been happy at first, moving into their first home together, getting married then having each of their boys. But as her career began to take off, her work took up more and more of her time. It became an obsession, and she didn't know when to stop.

Tracy let her mind wander back to the case. Looking back over her notes, Erin was last seen on Sunday evening, but that didn't necessarily mean she had gone missing that day. Her flight wasn't due to leave Edinburgh until Tuesday, so technically, there were at least two days her movements were unaccounted for. The girls had been staying self-catering at the hostel, but with no key card entry or CCTV, there was no way to figure out exactly when the last time was she had been in her room at the hostel.

Isa said the towel behind the door had been wet, but how wet - same day wet or damp from several days of use and left drying behind the door? Was the window open? Tracy had so many questions, she wished had been asked at the time. It was summer, so presumably, there would not have been any heating on in the room and without any proper ventilation, the towel could easily have been there for days. However, this was impossible to comment on without any officers seeing the actual towel at the time.

But maybe if she knew how often the towels were changed, it might just be possible to work this out – if they were changed daily for example, a wet towel meant Erin had to have been there Monday evening or even Tuesday morning. Meaning Erin could have returned to the hostel after Heidi had met her after all. She made a note to ask Isa or Mr Johnson that, as this may help establish a more accurate timeline of her disappearance.

It was also possible she could also have brought someone back with her, although she doubted that from Isa's description of how the room had been left. There was no mention either in the report if the hairdryer had been warm. Warm to touch would have indicated recent use.

Looking back at Facebook, she scrolled further to see if there were any clues hidden online. Tracy noticed Erin's last post (before the one on the Friday before she had gone missing), had been Saturday the 28th of July 2012.

The girls had been to Loch Ness for the day and posted photographs of them using binoculars, looking out over the loch, searching for the famous Loch Ness Monster. They returned to the hostel to get ready before hitting the town for their last Saturday night out together. They had gone to a few bars before partying in the local nightclub 'The Electric Room'.

Erin again looked happy in all of the photos. She had then commented on one of her friends' posts from some of the shows they had visited back down in Edinburgh at the festival on both Friday and Saturday evenings and left comments on a few posts her friends back home in the States had posted. Saying she couldn't wait to catch up with them. Then nothing. Drawing a blank, Tracy logged out of Facebook and rubbed her eyes which were sore from staring at the screen all afternoon. She was craving another coffee.

Spreading the contents of the file out on her desk, she sipped her coffee as she looked over Erin's mobile phone records, which had been pulled at the time. The last call Erin had made had been when she had spoken to her parents for forty-five minutes on the Saturday afternoon (which had been morning in the States), then nothing. Without the actual phone itself, she couldn't see what messages had been sent or received though. The same went for other communications apps, such as *What's App*.

Her mobile phone had never been found. It wasn't amongst the things she had left behind in her room, and it appeared to have been switched off sometime after she left the hostel on the Sunday evening and didn't appear to have ever been switched back on again. Her phone records had only confirmed the hostel as the last general area in which her phone had last been used. The *'find my iPhone app'* was also useless as the phone had been turned off. Officers had searched the undergrowth along Crown Avenue, the road she had last been seen near, but had found nothing. It was beginning to look as if she had vanished into thin air.

Just as she was lost in thought, her phone rang - it was Heidi returning her call. She was free on Sunday afternoon, so after writing down her address, Tracy agreed to visit her at 2 pm.

8

Saturday 15th October

Katie woke to the sound of the birds singing from the trees just outside her bedroom window. It was a lovely sound. Today was Saturday. Usually, she would have had loads of plans for a rare Saturday off, but with all of her friends more than five hundred miles away – this Saturday, she had no plans at all. She didn't know whether to feel happy or sad. Tempting as it was to pull the duvet back up over her head and feel sorry for herself, she forced herself to get up. She pulled on her running kit and trainers and decided to go for a run to check out her new surroundings. Running always made her feel better.

She ran out past the golf course and headed towards the hospital before turning left and heading back towards the town centre via the Moray Firth. She wasn't due to start work for another three weeks, but she just wanted to get her bearings. It turned out to be a lovely route, full of greenery, and the air was so fresh, unlike running through the streets of London. She felt happy, sure she was going to like it here. She thought she might sign up for the Loch Ness Marathon next September.

Absorbed in her new surroundings, she was totally unaware of the black Range Rover with the blackened-out windows that was following along slowly behind her, or of the man inside who was growing more obsessed with her as the hours went by.

After breakfast and a long hot shower, Katie headed into the town centre to check out the local shops. She needed to pick up some more towels, and curtains and make a start on the vast number of coat hangers she was going to need for all her clothes. She had a feeling TK Maxx, and Next were going to be her home from home for the next few weeks. Her boxes from London had arrived, too, so by late afternoon, the place was slowly beginning to look and feel a bit more like home.

That evening she ordered a television unit, coffee table, and some bedroom furniture to be delivered from IKEA and a plush grey fabric corner sofa from Next. Her parents had very kindly offered to buy her a sofa as a housewarming gift.

She temporarily set the TV up on top of the empty boxes in her bedroom. Having nowhere to sit, she settled into bed to watch some of the regular Saturday night television shows. If she was lucky she thought, there might even be a decent movie on. She hadn't sorted out her Netflix account yet, but that was definitely on her to-do list. It wasn't long before she drifted off again into a deep, restful sleep, still blissfully unaware of the attention she was attracting from a tall, dark stranger.

Sunday 16th October

The next morning, she went for another long run. She had hoped she might have bumped into Lily again, it would have been nice to have somebody other than herself to talk to, but there seemed to just be silence coming from her apartment. In fact, despite there being around thirty apartments in the three-storey building, it seemed relatively quiet. Still, it was the weekend she reasoned. Maybe most people were out or sleeping in.

She had noticed a few people coming and going the day she arrived when she had looked out of her kitchen window. But, other than her next-door neighbour Lily, she hadn't bumped into anyone else to talk to yet. Still, it had only been two days; she kept telling herself she had to be patient, and she was sure to make friends at work – wasn't she? Perhaps running away to Scotland had been the wrong decision after all.

Katie pushed her doubts away and decided after lunch

to check the notice board she had spied earlier at the front door, near the mailboxes, to see if there were any adverts for any local groups she could join.

There were loads of adverts, all pinned neatly on top of one another. Not knowing how old they were, Katie decided to concentrate on the ones on the top. She found notices for guitar lessons, maths tuition, yoga classes, and a running group. Along with the usual ones reminding residents of refuse collection days, parking rules and regulations, and fire escape plans. Katie noted the numbers for the yoga classes and the running group and added them to her phone.

Just as she was about to climb the stairs to head back up to her apartment, a sudden gust of wind came in through the open window in the hallway. It lifted one of the flyers straight off the noticeboard. It sailed high into the air above her before gently floating back down and landing face down at her feet.

Feeling obliged to pick it up and return it, she lifted it and walked back down the hallway. As she approached the notice board, she saw one she had missed. There, hidden underneath the monthly timetable for refuse collection (until the wind decided to dislodge it), was what looked like a very grand invitation to something.

Its design looked so out of place with the others. It was A5 sized, printed on glossy cream expensive-looking paper and had what looked like a coat of arms embossed in gold print along the top, with a gold decorative border. Intrigued to find out what it was, Katie walked back over to the notice board and removed the pin that until a few minutes ago had been holding them both together. When she got closer, she saw it was indeed an invitation. Underneath the picture of the coat of arms were the only words on the front of it - '*You are cordially invited to join us on a tour with a difference*'.

Turning it over she saw underneath the writing, was a watermark of a colour picture of a beautiful baroque-style mansion home with elaborately carved details featuring colonnades and corner towers. Two large arc-shaped wings flanked either side of the main building, which had a ram's head staircase in the middle leading up to its first floor, neo-classical entrance. It had a vast sweeping gravel driveway with a fountain in the middle.

There were well-kept lawns on either side of the driveway, and although you couldn't see much in this shot, it looked like it had vast gardens surrounding the house, which sat elevated at the top of a small hill surrounded by trees. The beautiful stone staircase leading up to the front door had a pair of regal-looking lions positioned on either side at the bottom. It looked like something out of a romantic novel. Katie could immediately imagine ladies arriving in horse-drawn carriages wearing beautiful silk dresses and carrying matching parasols to shade them from the sun.

She carefully placed the refuse collection notice back

in its place but decided to take the invitation back to her apartment with her as she was intrigued by it, and wanted to see if she could find out any more online. Judging by how full the notice board was, she was sure no one would notice it was missing. And she would put it back.

Had Katie looked a bit closer, at some of the older notices - the ones tucked away at the bottom of the board, hidden beneath the layers. The ones that had been there so long the paper had turned yellow and was curling at the edges. Had she looked at any of these, then she would have discovered these were posters for a missing person – four of them, to be exact. Four missing girls. Their disappearances spanned six years, the first of which happened a little over a decade ago.

The first was for a twenty-three-year-old American girl, Erin Doherty. Last seen Sunday, the 5th of August 2012. She had bright blue eyes and beautiful dark brown curly hair. The second is Natalia Robertson, a twenty-four-year-old Italian girl. Last seen Sunday, the 20th of July 2014. Again, very pretty with blue eyes and dark curly hair. The third one Klara Eriksson, the youngest of them all, was a twenty-one-year-old student on a gap year from Sweden. Also, with long dark curly hair and big blue eyes, last seen Sunday, the 25th of June 2016, and finally, twenty-three-year-old au pair Jessica Fletcher from Canada, similar physical appearance, last seen Saturday, the 28th of July 2018.

These girls had all recently arrived in Inverness and looked eerily similar. If Katie had looked at any of their photographs, she would have noticed that she also bore a close resemblance to them. So close - it was almost as if they could have been related.

9

The drive to Perth via Aviemore took Tracy two hours and fifteen minutes. She had stopped briefly in Aviemore for a coffee and a quick bite to eat. Heidi and her husband Paul lived in a new housing estate in Auchterarder, a small town on the outskirts of Perth. Pulling up in front of the large detached house, she noticed the sleek new black electric ix3 BMW sitting in the driveway in front of a large double garage.

She parked her drab police-issue Ford Focus next to the shiny new car and followed the pretty flagstone path up to the dark grey front door. It was one of these ultra-modern aluminium doors with a long matt silver handle and a really low letter box, which she thought must be a nightmare for the postman or lady. On either side of the door was a frosted glass panel. A *ring* doorbell was positioned on the right-hand side of the door underneath a sleek grey wall light. Tracy leaned over and pressed it. Heidi immediately answered the door and invited her inside.

Heidi was tall, almost six feet, with long blonde hair, which she wore in a ponytail. She wore a long black and white flowery dress that skimmed her calf. Her feet were bare, and her toenails painted a dark coral, which matched her fingernails.

The inside of the house was just as modern as the outside. The walls were painted an off-white shade and were stylishly adorned with contemporary, strategically placed artwork finished in floating black box frames. Tracy hadn't the faintest idea about art, but she wouldn't have been surprised if they were originals. A warm grey wooden floor in a herringbone design flowed throughout the entire downstairs.

Heidi led her through the hallway, past an equally beautiful sitting room with double oak glazed doors. As she walked past, Tracy quickly looked in and saw it was styled in the same off-white shade of paint with two large dark grey leather chesterfields set facing one another, a stylish coffee table in between them. Facing the doors was a large white marble fireplace positioned in the centre of the sofas, with a large mirror above. Beautiful matching abstract canvases sat on either side of the chimney breast wall, which was painted in a dark grey. Grey velvet Roman blinds, with grey and cream curtains, framed the bay window. They passed another two solid oak doors, which were both closed, before reaching a door at the end of the hallway which led directly into the kitchen.

The open-plan kitchen, which ran the entire length of the back of the house, was no different. Tall matt black wooden handleless cabinets reaching all the way up to the ceiling lined the left-hand side of the room, whilst a large island finished in a waterfall edge of white Calcutta marble was positioned lengthwise in front of them. Five grey velvet bar stools were neatly tucked underneath the island's overhang.

Facing her was a massive set of dark grey aluminium bifold doors which led out into the garden. The opposite side of the room had a large grey fabric corner sofa facing a wall-mounted TV with another impressive fireplace underneath. This one was built into the wall with a log storage unit on either side of the gigantic television.

Looking through the bi-fold doors, she could see out into the garden, which had been professionally landscaped with a pergola and hot tub in one corner and a patio and BBQ area in the other. No one overlooked them. There were just fields as far as the eye could see behind their home. Heidi invited her to sit on one of the velvet chairs at the island whilst she set about making coffee for them in an elaborate-looking coffee machine, which seemed to be hidden away on a shelf inside one of the cupboards. She set down some homemade chocolate and banana muffins. Although she should be watching her waistline, Tracy helped herself to one - they looked too good to resist.

Setting her empty coffee cup down, Tracy pulled out her notebook and began asking Heidi some questions. Heidi had been working at a local café in Inverness during her summer vacation from Robert Gordon University, where she had been studying for a BSc in Biomedical Science.

She had been about to go into her final year when she had decided to travel up to Inverness so that she could be closer to her boyfriend during the holidays. This also allowed her to see a bit of the highlands at the same time. Working enabled her to support herself so that she could stay up there for the whole summer. Her husband (who had been her boyfriend at that time) was originally from Inverness, so this meant they could continue seeing one another as he always went home for the holidays.

DS McGregor took her back to Sunday, the 5th of August 2012. Heidi set down her empty cup and began. She could still remember that day like it was yesterday. The coffee shop where she worked had closed as usual at 5 pm. By the time she and another girl had washed the last of the dishes, cleaned the tables, mopped the floor and set up for the breakfast rush the following day, it had been around 6 pm.

They had locked up as usual, and Carly (the girl she had been working with) had walked to the bus station, whilst she had made her way back to the hostel. It was only a fifteen-minute walk back. As usual, despite having been together all day, she had stopped and chatted with Carly for another fifteen minutes outside the café before finally returning to where she was staying. She had met Erin on the street just around the corner from the hostel and had stopped and chatted with her for a few minutes. Erin had seemed her usual bubbly self and didn't seem anxious to get away.

Erin and her friends had been staying on the same floor as Heidi, and they had gotten to know one another as they had met in the shared kitchen the night the girls arrived at the hostel. The girls had been looking for a bottle opener so they could enjoy a glass of wine whilst they got ready to go out. She knew Erin's friends, Mollie and Olivia, had headed back to Edinburgh earlier than planned, but remembered Erin seemed quite relaxed about being there on her own. It had been her idea to stay on by herself.

She had loads more places she wanted to explore before heading home and wasn't afraid to go alone. Plus, she didn't really want to play gooseberry to her friends, who had both met guys they were keen to hook back up with down in Edinburgh. And she didn't want to spoil their fun either, by making them stay in Inverness with her. It was their trip of a lifetime too.

Erin had stopped and chatted with her for a few minutes before heading toward the town centre. Heidi remembers she had gone off with a spring in her step, almost as if she was excited about something. At the time, Heidi thought maybe it was because she was due to go home in a few days, but the more she thought about it, Erin had been glowing.

It hadn't been a particularly hot day, and rain had been forecast for later that evening, but Erin was dressed for summer, wearing a pair of ankle-skimming dark blue skinny jeans with a pale pink floaty blouse and a vest top underneath. She had a pink leather bag worn across her body and white leather Converse on her feet. Heidi didn't remember seeing her carrying a jacket, but she may have had one in her bag. A small foldaway pack-a-mac could easily have fitted inside her small bag. She was wearing a lot more make-up than Heidi had seen her wearing before, and her hair had been styled, too, making Heidi think that she might have been on her way to meet someone. Heidi never saw her again after that.

It was only when she saw the flyers her family had been distributing around town, along with a local police appeal a few days later, that she realised Erin was missing and that she was possibly one of the last people to see or speak to her before she had disappeared. She had immediately come forward and given her statement to the police. No one had followed it up again until now. Heidi asked Tracy if they had finally discovered what happened to Erin. All Tracy could tell her at this stage was that she was looking into the case again.

Tracy pulled out her phone and, using *Google Maps,* asked Heidi to show her exactly where she had been when she met Erin and which direction she had headed off in.

Heidi was able to point out exactly where they had met. Using street view, Tracy was able to see the exact location for herself. It was a leafy road with a single pavement on one side of the road. The other side of the road had a tall metal fence with trees and shrubbery beyond. She asked Heidi if she remembered seeing anyone else on the street, anyone who could have been following Erin, perhaps even someone walking on the other side of the road or any suspicious vehicles?

Heidi took a deep breath and closed her eyes as if trying to imagine that evening again. She eventually opened her eyes and calmly said she remembered walking past a large black Range Rover with blackened-out windows parked on the corner of Crown Avenue, which is the street before you turn down towards the hostel. It had been parked just before the bend, on double yellow lines meaning she had to move out onto the road to get past it. As it was parked on the corner, she had been cautious about passing it in case another vehicle had been travelling in the opposite direction, and the driver didn't see her in time to stop.

She couldn't see if there was anyone in the car or not due to the privacy glass, but it struck her as strange now as if it had been parked, it would have been a bit of an odd place to park. All the houses on this stretch of road had long driveways, so if you were visiting someone, there was usually plenty of space to park in their driveway. She hadn't mentioned it at the time as no one had asked, and as she had passed it before she spoke to Erin, she hadn't thought it relevant until now. It had been so long ago she had no idea if she had noticed any of the number plate. Then she suddenly remembered the tail lights were on, so there must have been somebody in the vehicle or somebody nearby, maybe a delivery driver or something.

Heidi got quite upset at this point and started blaming herself - asking if this was relevant and if someone could have snatched Erin. Not wanting to upset Heidi any more than she already was or wishing to start any false rumours; Tracy placed her hand over hers and spoke gently to her, telling her this might be absolutely nothing. Although she was pretty confident this was just the lead she needed - even if it was ten years too late!

Realising that Heidi had told her all she could remember, she closed her notebook and left her card with her mobile number on it in case Heidi remembered anything else. Before she left, she asked to use the bathroom before her long drive back. The downstairs bathroom (which was located back off the hallway through one of the closed doors she had passed on the way in) was decorated in the same theme.

The walls were half-tiled the whole way around the room in a light grey porcelain ripple effect tile. The wall above it was painted the palest grey. A black pendant light hung from the ceiling. A large black mirror hung above the pale grey wood vanity unit, which ran the entire length of the wall. The unit was finished off with a sparkly white quartz countertop complete with a white undermount sink, a black tap, and a matching waste plug. A large *Jo Malone* candle and reed diffuser sat in one corner on a black tray, whilst a white lily in a black pot sat at the opposite end. Matching *Jo Malone* hand wash and hand cream in their famous lime, basil and mandarin fragrance, sat side by side next to the tap. Heidi's house was stunning. It was all a bit too modern for her country cottage, but it was nice to gather some ideas, like colour schemes and flooring, that she could take away for her own renovations.

10

On her way back up to her apartment, Katie tried Lily's door again, but there was still no answer. It would have been nice to ask her if she knew more about Loch Wood House she thought; maybe she would catch her later in the day.

Sitting herself at the breakfast bar, she had a good look at the invitation. The border on the front of it reminded her of an ornate antique Baroque Rococo style, featuring floral garlands, birds, cherubs and two flaming hearts bound with a floral wreath all embossed in gold. At the centre, at the top of the garland, was an outline drawing of a coat of arms with the name Loch Wood House printed underneath. Gold embossed lettering in the centre invited the reader to join them for a tour with a difference.

Turning the invitation over, the writing said tours were held on either the first or last Saturday of the month from June through to October (wedding dependent as this was also wedding season for them). There was an email address and telephone number for further information along with social media links to their Facebook and Instagram accounts. There was no more information than that.

Intrigued, Katie decided to *Google* the house first to see

if she could find out any more about it. The first website she found said the house dated back to the early 18th century and had been home to the Campbell family since it was built. It had originally been designed by the Scottish architect William Adam. Sadly, he died before it was completed, so his son Robert Adam, also a famous architect, took over and finished his dad's creation. Although still very typical of Adam's style, several family members had remodelled the house, adding various parts to the building over the years. Some of the oldest features still stood, and the stunning facade was instantly recognisable as an Adam's creation.

It had an impressive eighteen bedrooms and was set in over 40 acres of private gardens and woodland. The current Laird of the estate was Fraser Campbell-McNair, who in 2003, at just twenty-five years old, had become the sole heir to the estate and family fortune after his parents and twin sister were killed in a tragic accident. There was a picture of him standing outside the house. He was a very handsome man, and no mention of a Mrs Campbell-McNair anywhere.

Katie felt herself blush. She couldn't believe she was actually thinking like this. Her heart was still too crushed to think of anyone in that way. Moving on, there were a few smaller photos of the gardens and some of the rooms inside the house. It looked absolutely stunning. The Laird obviously had good taste (or he paid someone who had good taste).

Katie was really interested in art and loved visiting places of historical interest. Her parents had been members of the National Trust, so she had many happy memories of visiting castles and stately homes across England and Wales while growing up. Maybe this was just what she needed to cheer herself up.

There was a link on this website that took you straight to Loch Wood House's own website. Katie clicked on it, and it wasn't long before she found precisely the information she was looking for.

The private estate, known as Loch Wood House, was located around fifteen miles outside Inverness and was only accessible via a private road. It had been used for several period dramas and magazine shoots over the years, and access was strictly limited to guests attending any of its many private functions. The Laird still stayed in the house from time to time. Interesting, she thought to herself. Katie felt her cheeks flush again.

There were many more photographs of the house's interior and exterior on the website, along with several more of the beautiful gardens. It had a private loch, complete with a small jetty and a couple of rowing boats. Private dinner parties could be held in the impressive dining room, which had a beautiful hand-crafted oak table that was able to comfortably seat around fifty people. There was a photograph of it set up to host an event, possibly a wedding which suddenly made her feel quite sad. She would have loved to get married in a place like this - if she could have afforded it. The sprawling grounds had their own private forest with an impressive walled garden that Katie thought wouldn't look out of place in a Jane Austin novel.

It had several outbuildings, including a stable block; ice house; fishing temple; small church; family mausoleum and a large orangery. There were links to several events held throughout the year at the house, including murder mystery evenings, a Christmas market, vintage motor shows and an enchanted forest Halloween tour.

Being a massive fan of Halloween, Katie clicked on the link for the enchanted forest, which contained images of families wrapped up warm, but clearly having fun with children carving pumpkin lanterns and bobbing for apples. Coloured stalls lined what looked like a field decorated for the event selling local crafts, gin, candy apples, hot chocolate and candy floss for the kids. There was a bouncy castle and various other Halloween-themed fairground attractions.

There was also a short video that led the viewer off into a dense forest trail lit by tiny little black carriage lanterns. As the person filming the video meandered through this dimly lit forest, small clearings would appear as if from nowhere, each decorated with a different scary theme. There were giant spiders; webs; witches; ghosts, and some really eerie-looking statues of girls hidden deep amongst the forest, almost as if they were playing hide and seek but were lost and had turned into zombies. Smoke was swirling like a mist in front of them. As she looked closer at them, she realised she couldn't see any of their faces as they were almost entirely hidden by their hair.

Katie shuddered when she hovered over these images. Had she not been able to see they were made of stone, these dimly lit creepy statues seemed almost lifelike. She felt you could half expect them to be actors who would suddenly jump out at you - designed to frighten you. Maybe they were. She counted four of them in total. They were almost identical in stature and built like carbon copies of the same person, but they were fixed in different poses. Each one was equally as creepy as the next one. She couldn't help but think there was something sad about them, too. Shivering, she hit the pause button on the video link and scrolled further down the page until she found the link for more information about the 'Tour with a Difference', opening up a new window.

As it said on the invitation, these tours ran from June to October, operating only on either the first or the last Saturday of the month. Katie quickly glanced at the calendar on her iPhone, she had either just missed one, or there might be one scheduled for a week on Saturday (the 29th), just before Halloween. Tours commenced at 8 pm.

Excited, Katie realised this must be a ghost tour; Katie

loved ghosts, and the thought of a tour of a haunted house in the dark excited her. Places were limited to thirty people, and a shuttle bus was included in the price to ferry tour guests from Inverness city centre to the estate and back again. The tour cost fifty-five pounds, but this included canapés, prosecco, and transportation, which she thought seemed reasonable given what was included. Tour guests were invited to dress formally. This all sounded very sophisticated.

Katie was hooked, but as she read on, she soon discovered there was another twist to the evening. It was indeed a ghost tour of this fantastic property, but it was also a singles evening. She immediately closed her laptop and walked into the empty living room.

She stood there for a few minutes, just staring out of the French doors, watching the birds sitting on the branches of the large trees. Going out and socialising with people again was one thing, but she wasn't sure if she was ready to start dating again. She was still too raw after everything that had happened with Matt and April.

***

He was lurking in the shadows again watching her, nestled into the trees that backed onto her living room. Dressed all in black, he was standing far enough back so no one could see him. He was good at blending in and being invisible. Using his army-grade binoculars, he stared at her, zooming in on her face. She looked sad, he noticed as if she might burst into tears. He wondered what or who had upset her. Resisting the urge to run to comfort her, he suddenly noticed she was on the move, and quickly got ready to follow her, anxious to know where she was headed.

11

Katie grabbed her bag, jacket, and keys and headed out the door. She had decided to go for a walk and clear her head a little. It was a pleasant warm autumnal afternoon, the leaves on the trees were turning brown, and those that had fallen off were gathering into little piles at the side of the pavement. She scuffed through them like a child, heading down towards the town centre. It wasn't long before she found herself wandering towards Inverness castle, which sits in a commanding position overlooking the river Ness.

Sadly, the castle itself was temporarily closed for major renovations but would hopefully be re-opening in 2025. She walked along the river, speaking to various people as they passed her. It was so friendly here, unlike London, where everyone had their heads down, never looking at where they were going. He followed along behind her, staying just far enough back that she wouldn't see him.

Before she realised it, the sun started to set, bringing with it a cold icy wind. Turning back, she noticed several quaint little restaurants by the riverside. Suddenly hungry, she picked one, popped in, and treated herself to some home-cooked food. After settling on steak pie with all the trimmings, she treated herself to a large glass of wine followed by a rather generous slice of sticky toffee pudding with ice cream. Feeling totally stuffed, she headed home, unaware of the dark figure skulking along in the shadows behind her.

It was pitch dark by the time she arrived back at her apartment block, allowing him to blend perfectly into the shadows. Her phone rang suddenly, startling her as she walked up the path towards the front door. Pulling it out of her pocket, she smiled as she saw it was her friend Lynn. Distracted by the phone call, she took no notice of the man who slipped in behind her, carefully grabbing the door just before it closed, but staying outside long enough that she wouldn't see him sneak in behind her.

Making his way along the hallway towards the notice board, he had a quick check. It was gone. He hoped it was her who had taken it. Time will tell. Hopeful, he slipped back out unnoticed into the darkness and slinked back over to his position in the woods to watch her.

Once Katie returned to her apartment, she settled on her bed to chat with her friend. They talked for a while before Lynn gently told her she had some upsetting news for her – Matt and April had moved in together, and April was pregnant. They talked for a little longer before Katie excused herself. Heartbroken all over again, she curled up on the bed and sobbed until she had no more tears left.

Deciding to pull herself together, she wandered into the kitchen to make herself a coffee and noticed the invitation with her laptop sitting next to it in the middle of the countertop where she had left it. Instinctively she opened it up and saw it was still open on the last page she'd been looking at. Blowing her nose, she decided it wouldn't hurt to take another look. The exterior and interior of the house looked absolutely stunning. It would be pretty spectacular to see it, and this seemed to be the only way you could visit it unless she was attending another function which she very much doubted she would be likely to do. She came out of this website and searched Loch Wood House separately. There were many rave reviews on Trip Advisor, with an average rating of 4.5/5.

Scrolling further, she found several articles about the family and some about the Laird himself. Lady Campbell, Fraser's mum, inherited the family title and estate from her father when he died aged ninety-four in 2001. She had taken a double-barreled surname when she married in a bid to keep the family name. She and her husband, Harris, lived mainly in Loch Wood House but had another house just outside London. Apart from boarding school, they had brought their children up in Scotland and spent most of their summers here too.

She discovered Fraser was a Cambridge graduate, gaining a 1st class honour's degree in architecture. He had never married, although he had come close to it in 2003. The engagement had been called off after the tragic death of his parents and twin sister Emilia.

Emilia had a degree in Fine Art from Robert Gordon University in Aberdeen. After graduation, she moved to Paris, where she had a small show in a gallery there. There was a hyperlink to her work (all sold now), which was not really to Katie's taste – it was very colourful and reminiscent of Pablo Picasso's cubism style.

There was another link to a news article about the accident in the local paper, the *Inverness Courier*. Clicking on it, Katie learned that Fraser and his fiancée Isabella had been on holiday in the South of France at the time, but had flown back immediately. It was late Summer, and Emilia had been home for the weekend visiting her parents. She had been out riding alone when something had spooked her horse, causing her to come charging out of the estate at a terrifying speed. Her parents, who were returning home from lunch at a friend's house, had been driving back when Emilia's horse, White Spirit, had suddenly come charging out right in front of their Range Rover.

Witnesses say her poor dad had swerved to try and avoid hitting his daughter; but, the horse had panicked, simultaneously changing direction and causing them both to collide with an articulated lorry travelling in the opposite direction. His parents and the horse had been killed instantly, whilst his sister had clung on for three days in intensive care on life support before finally being declared brain dead. There were photographs of Mr and Mrs Campbell-McNair, who looked warm and friendly, not at all stuffy, and a photo of Emilia on her beloved Lipizzan white horse.

At the bottom of the article was a photograph of the crash. Thankfully you couldn't see any of the victims as the emergency services were in attendance and had cordoned the area off. Katie stared at this sad photograph, wondering how on earth her poor parents must have felt in their final moments. As she gazed a bit closer, she noticed another horse tethered only a few feet from the entrance to the estate. She thought this seemed a bit strange as the article said Emilia had been out riding alone. Still, it was a grainy photograph, and maybe the person this horse belonged to had nothing to do with the accident. Perhaps this was the person who had called for help.

There was a sad photograph of Fraser standing alone at the church whilst the three coffins were carried out to the waiting hearses. Katie felt absolutely heartbroken seeing this. Although she didn't know him, she couldn't imagine the grief he must be suffering from.

She thought again about the singles evening and how you never really know what is just around the corner. After all, she would be turning thirty soon and had always dreamed of getting married and, hopefully, at some point, becoming a mum. Laughing at herself, she thought – right – time to get a grip here - this was only a singles evening; it wasn't even a date. All she had to do was talk to people, and she was good at that; she might not even meet anyone she liked or anyone who liked her back. It was to be her third Saturday night in a new town; what was the worst that could happen?

Before she could change her mind, she turned to her laptop, and whether it was hearing Matt and April's news, reading this tragic story or some Dutch courage from the large glass of wine she had enjoyed earlier with dinner, Katie decided what the hell – life's too short. Sometimes you have to make change come to you; moving to Inverness had been all about change. It was time for her to live outside her comfort zone and try something new.

So, before she could change her mind again, she clicked on the link to apply for a place and immediately started filling out the online application form. Apart from the basic name and address question at the beginning, it seemed to ask loads of personal questions - like how long she had lived in Inverness, where she worked and for how long, whether she had family in Inverness, her weight and height (which she thought seemed rather strange). As she had never done anything like this before she carried on – thinking perhaps this was normal. It was late and she didn't really have anyone she could ask. All of her friends were in London and she was too embarrassed to tell her parents what she was doing.

It seemed to take much longer than the suggested fifteen minutes to complete. But then again, research marketing companies always lie about how long it takes to complete their surveys. Guessing this was no different, Katie carried on. It seemed a strange profile of herself though, certainly not what she was expecting, but then again, she had never done anything like this before, so she wasn't sure what to expect. Thankfully there were no questions such as *'What is the first thing people notice about you?* 'She hated questions like this. This format was more suited to someone confident, someone like April, who never had a problem promoting herself. She wondered what April would think of all this. This would be right up her street, having all eyes on her. She tried to push all thoughts of April aside. April didn't deserve her thoughts after what she had done to her.

Strangely, though, this type of form was easier to complete since there were no questions like that. It seemed to ask more about her lifestyle and friend network in Inverness. She had to upload a photograph of herself, and after great deliberation, she settled on her Facebook profile picture. She hadn't gotten around to changing it. In fact, she hadn't logged onto Facebook in a while.

It was an old photograph Matt had taken on their last holiday together in the Maldives. She was sitting on a wooden jetty, dangling her legs over the edge with her back to the ocean, not a care in the world. She wore a pretty red cotton sundress, an oversized hat to protect her from the sun and rose-gold Michael Kors sunglasses. She had a cocktail in one hand and flip-flops in the other, beaming back at the camera, her face filled with happiness. Where had this vibrant girl staring back at her gone? Time to get her back, she decided.

Once Katie had finished and submitted her application and payment details, she received an email informing her she would have to wait for confirmation from the organisers to find out if she had successfully gained a place. Strange, she couldn't imagine many people in Inverness signing up for this, but then again, you never know. Maybe it was more popular than she thought, or perhaps it was a numbers thing, and they had to ensure they met minimum numbers to make it a viable event for them.

By the time she had finished, it was well after midnight. Katie got up and wandered around the apartment closing the curtains as she went.

***

He stood outside again, watching, waiting patiently in the shadows, when suddenly he felt his phone vibrate in his pocket. Glancing at the screen, he was delighted to see he had received an email alerting him of her application. Smiling to himself, he left. Satisfied she would soon be his again.

12

Tracy went straight home after her drive back up from Perth. She decided she would take the pool car back on Monday morning. Home for her now was an old Victorian detached cottage on a rural road on the outskirts of the highland town (and Royal Burgh) of Nairn. It would take a lot of work and money to get the house the way she wanted it, but this was the only way she could afford to buy it in the first place.

The previous owner had been an old lady who she very much doubted had done any renovations in the last fifty or so years she had lived there. It didn't even have a fitted kitchen. The windows were draughty, and the flat roof in the kitchen extension leaked in the heavy rain - so she had found out the week before. Betty had recommended a local roofer to her, Bruce Baxter, who had come around right away and fixed it for her.

Her house was far from the beautiful one she had just come from. Still, it was hers; one day, she would get it how she wanted it. She shoved a ready meal in the microwave and poured herself a large glass of wine. After dinner, she ran herself a bubble bath in the enormous wrought iron claw foot tub (which had been the main draw to buying this house in the first place). She sank into the warm waters letting herself immerse in the bubbles.

It had been a tough few months, between the divorce and the disciplinary hearing to her relocation, and she wasn't sure she could take much more. Although not that she would let anyone see this. On the outside, she was still this steely emotionless woman who craved success at all costs. Only deep down she did care. She missed her husband and sons terribly and wished she could turn back the clock and have been there more for them.

And she bitterly regretted how she handled her last case. Blindsided by her own personal hatred of the man involved, she had allowed herself to miss out on vital evidence and temporarily taken her eye off the game whilst she focused on a big promotion that was coming her way. This was so out of character for her. She usually prided herself on her due diligence, leaving no stone unturned, and not stopping until the perpetrator was behind bars. She constantly drummed this into new recruits or colleagues at conferences. This would never have happened if she hadn't been so preoccupied with her divorce. A child had died because of the consequences of her actions. She would never forgive herself for this.

Tracy sunk down under the bubbles holding her breath for a moment longer than she intended before suddenly jumping up and splashing water all over the floor. She had to stop punishing herself like this. The past needed to stay in the past. She couldn't change anything. Her therapist taught her that. But a child had died, and she hadn't done everything she could to prevent it from happening. She knew she had to find a way to live with the consequences of her actions. Perhaps putting everything she has into her new role could help to put things right. Deep down she doubted it. But she had to at least try.

13

Wednesday 19th October

As DS McGregor headed into the office that morning, she couldn't help but think if the officers had just pressed Heidi further at the time, she would probably have remembered these details. Maybe the driver of this vehicle could have been traced or may have even come forward themselves if they had known the police were looking for them. Still, she couldn't blame the officers, one was only a probationer, and the other had less than four years' experience on the force.

Neither had worked in CID, and this was possibly the first missing person they had ever investigated. Plus, there appeared to have been a bit of an assumption by all that there had been no foul play, and this was simply the case of someone either choosing to wander off; or someone nearing the end of their visa who had wanted to stay on, and was willing to do it any way they could - even if this meant illegally. She guessed no one could really blame them. Having lived and worked in a city where bad things happened all the time, she was more inclined to think the worst and be proven otherwise.

What didn't make any sense to her was why, if this were the working hypothesis, officers wouldn't have wondered why Erin had chosen to leave everything behind. She hadn't touched her bank account, and unless she had access to a secret stash of cash or someone was helping her, then Tracy was pretty sure she would have been found before now.

An American girl in the Scottish Highlands could only stay hidden for so long. The money (if she had any) would have to run out sometime, so unless she had fled to maybe Ireland or England, she still had to be here in Scotland - somewhere.

Her passport had been found amongst her things at the hostel, so they knew she couldn't have left via any of the airports or ports. Plus, there had been an alert out for her in case she had tried to leave the country by any of these routes, meaning she still had to be here in the UK. Unless she had obtained illegal paperwork, but that seemed quite elaborate given the circumstances. There had been no bodies found either that matched her description. It was all very bizarre.

Logging into her PC, she set about trying to get in contact with Mr and Mrs Doherty. Her contact at Interpol was able to get this information for her. Although she would have preferred to make this visit in person, she would have to make do with a Zoom call as she didn't think her budget would quite stretch to a return trip to New York. She agreed that although they knew their daughter's investigation was still ongoing, due to the length of time that had passed and the fact there was no real news yet, officers from their local police department should visit them first so as not to alarm them. Once they had done this, she set up a Zoom call for 5 pm our time (noon in NYC). Just as she thought, they were anxious to hear any news about their daughter.

Mr Doherty was a tall thin man dressed in a blue and white striped shirt with navy trousers. He had short white hair and wore silver-rimmed glasses. Mrs Doherty was an elegant lady who bore a striking resemblance to her daughter. She had the same blue eyes, although the sparkle was long gone, and her hair, although dyed, was the same colour as Erin's. She wore it in a chic bob and had minimal makeup on. She wore a pink cashmere jumper, a black skirt, large diamond earrings, and a matching solitaire necklace. They both had an air of sadness about them. Tracy wondered how on earth they were coping.

She introduced herself to them and spoke of her extensive experience (leaving out the part about her recent demotion for gross negligence, of course), and informed them she was committed to finally solving the mystery of what had happened to their daughter. She explained what she had learned so far and described how she planned to progress. They sat quietly, listening to everything she had to say.

DS McGregor then started asking them lots of personal questions about their daughter. What kind of relationship they had with her, how she had seemed when they last spoke with her? She asked if Erin had any medical issues or if she had ever had any psychological problems or breakdowns?

She wanted to know how well she had known the friends she had gone travelling with. Could anyone they know have hurt their daughter? Did she feel safe on her own at the hostel? Was anyone bothering her? Did they have any idea why she would have disappeared? Could she have run off? These were all the same questions that had been going around in her parent's head this entire time, but every one of them had drawn a blank. If Erin had been suffering from any psychological problems, she had been masking it from everyone, including her parents.

Tracy learned Erin's parents had fully supported her trip and even funded part of it for her. As far as they knew, she had no access to funds other than her current account and a credit card that again, they had supported. Neither had been touched since her disappearance.

The girls had meticulously planned their trip before leaving, pre-booking most of their accommodation from the US. The only extras they needed were money for their food, transport and any excursions they planned on taking along the way. They had set out a daily budget for themselves, and as her parents had access to her account could see she more or less stuck to this. On the days where she spent more, she would spend less the following days.

As an accountant, it was one of the things Erin had been particularly proud of. She was always making spreadsheets and lists whenever she wanted to save for anything. Tracy asked if this account was still active and if they would mind sharing the statements with her. They both readily agreed but confirmed meantime, to the best of their knowledge, it had last been accessed three days before she went missing.

Once she was satisfied they did not know anything other than what they had disclosed already to the original investigating officers, she asked if they, by any chance, still had their daughters' belongings. Mrs Doherty revealed she had never been able to part with them and had left them on Erin's bed in her old bedroom, hoping that one day she would return to put them away herself.

Nothing had been touched inside the duffle bag, and only the dirty clothes in the separate plastic bag found inside the wardrobe had been washed. Now this was a stroke of luck, as Tracy knew if there was a clue somewhere in that bag, she was sure to find it. After promising to take good care of it, she asked if they would mind sending it to her for analysis. She would, of course, pay for this and return it to them again as soon as she finished with it.

They both agreed. Before ending the call, she promised

to keep in regular contact with them to update them on her progress. In the meantime, they agreed to send the bank statements from the year before Erin's trip, right up to her disappearance.

Closing her PC down, she thought she would like to speak to the friends she had been travelling with next. Before leaving for the evening, though, she walked over to her whiteboard and added the additional facts she had learned about Erin. These included a description of what Erin had been wearing and a photograph of the street where Heidi had stopped to speak with her.

She added ‘duffle bag on its way back for inspection’, then wrote 'black Range Rover with blackened out windows parked or waiting on Crown Avenue the night of Erin's disappearance' and circled this information twice. This driver had suddenly become a person of interest to her. Otherwise, why had they never come forward at the time?

It might have been nothing, perhaps a tourist who took a wrong turn and had stopped to look at a map or adjust their satnav. Or maybe someone from out of town who didn't know Erin had gone missing, or even someone who hadn't even realised they had seen her. But something niggling inside her told her this information was relevant and may just be the breakthrough she needed. Although it was a long shot, she was determined to track them down and was willing to do anything to do so. This was a case she was not prepared to lose.

Putting the lid back on her marker pen, she placed it back in the holder and called it a night. She had to keep reminding herself this job had regular hours, and she should have finished at 5 pm. It was just after 7 pm. She switched the light off, grabbed her coat and handbag and headed home.

She settled for another microwave meal for dinner and a walk before bed. A lovely trail ran past her home and led down into the town. While walking, she started thinking about her life and what she planned to do next. She was planning lots of renovations to the cottage starting next week. But she had also been thinking about getting herself a dog now that she had more regular hours, and it would be nice to have someone to come home to in the evenings. Perhaps she would consider visiting the local dog's trust and getting a rescue dog. Then she wouldn't have to worry so much about training a puppy.

It was pitch dark by the time she got home. Thankfully she had left some lights on this time. Despite her walk, she didn't sleep any easier that night either. She was dreaming about Erin this time and the black Range Rover, before the dreams evolved to include a dead child in the back of the Range Rover – little Robbie Denver. Waking up drenched in sweat, she padded downstairs and, pouring herself a glass of water this time, took another antidepressant from the kitchen cabinet.

14

Katie had spent the last few days going for a long run in the mornings and organising the rest of her apartment in the afternoons. Desperately trying to take her mind off Matt and April – and their baby! Her bedroom and living room furniture had arrived from IKEA, so she had built this up and finished off her bedroom by placing family photos and ornaments on them. She still needed some pictures for the walls, cushions and maybe a throw for these cold nights, unless she met someone at the singles evening. She blushed at the thought. It wasn't quite home yet, but it was getting there.

She had moved the television into the living room and bought a beanbag from the local charity shop to sit on until her sofas arrived. A few scented candles and a mirror above the marble fireplace helped give the living room a homelier feel. She hadn't had to do much to the kitchen, thankfully. It only needed a clock, toaster, storage jars and knife block. She had picked these things up relatively cheaply in the local supermarket, opting for a grey and chrome look to match the sleek grey gloss kitchen.

The small hall she felt could benefit from a console

table and maybe some coat hooks, but that would have to wait until she had a bit more money. It would also depend on how long she decided to stay here. She had signed a six-month lease but knew from Elaine that the owner was looking for a long-term let as he lived in Australia. She wondered if he would even be willing to sell it to her if things worked out for her, and she decided to stay. It was in such a beautiful setting. She had fallen in love with the place as soon as she stepped inside.

Katie received an email on Wednesday morning confirming her application for the following Saturday had been accepted. The email informed her she would be picked up along with everyone else outside Inverness train station at 19:00 prompt. She was advised to expect a black executive travel minibus with a placard marked 'Ghost Tour - Loch Wood House' in the window. Transport home for her would be in a private car. Perfect, she just assumed she would be dropped back at the train station afterwards. This meant she wouldn't have to wait for a taxi by herself. Seems they had thought of everything. She was reminded to dress formally and informed that photographs were strictly prohibited.

She walked into town that afternoon and booked firstly an appointment at a hairdresser for a long overdue cut and colour, and then an appointment at a nail bar for a manicure and polish. She knew she would have to remove the nail polish for work, so she opted for regular nail polish rather than the longer-lasting gel option.

When she got home, she decided to go through her wardrobe to look for a suitable outfit to wear. She wasn't sure how formal she should be, but she had plenty of wedding outfits, so hopefully, one of these would do. After a full hour and a half of trying things on, she had narrowed it down to just two - a beautiful black knee-length dress she had bought from Coast a few years ago, teamed with a black fur bolero jacket, or a stunning royal blue high neck calf-length dress with cover up she had purchased from Karen Millen for a wedding a few years back.

She had matching shoes and a handbag for each outfit, along with matching fascinators, although she knew she wouldn't need one of those. She didn't want to draw attention to herself, plus although they had said to dress formally, she was pretty sure it wasn't that kind of evening.

The black dress was her favourite. It was sleeveless, had a high neckline, fitted bodice, and a full skirt complete with a tulle underskirt. The whole dress was made of satin, but the skirt had a lace overlay with tiny black flowers embroidered on it. It had a v-shaped back which showed off a flattering hint of skin, without being trashy, and a silver zip complete with a diamanté clasp.

The blue dress was very floaty and rather summery in comparison. Like the black one, it was also high neck but had a halter neck fastening with two tiny little concealed silk buttons. It had an asymmetric ruffle that started at the neckline and crossed down the dress. It also had a fitted waist cinched in with a miniature ruffle flower.

Both were very elegant, and she had happy memories of wearing each one. She hadn't realised it, but she had lost so much weight recently these two options seemed to fit her the best. She would have to do something about that; she couldn't afford to become any lighter at only seven and a half stone to begin with. By the time she finished trying on outfits and putting everything away again, she was feeling quite excited and was glad her application had been accepted.

***

Whilst she was doing this he stood outside, in his usual spot, watching her from the shadows. He was excited to see she was making so much of an effort for him. Perhaps he had been wrong about her, maybe she did love him after all.

15

Thursday 20th October

Tracy spent most of the following morning arranging to have Erin's duffle bag sent over to her. Her connection in Interpol had been very helpful and organised for it to be sent via DHL; it would hopefully be here sometime the following week. In the interim, she decided she would try to speak to Mollie and Olivia (Erin's friends whom she had been travelling with) before she got to work on trying to identify the driver of her mystery Range Rover.

She also drove back to the hostel to check out the area properly, now that she knew precisely where Erin and Heidi had stopped to talk and where this Range Rover had been parked. Although there were houses around, the area itself was pretty secluded, meaning it would have been possible for Erin to have gotten into this car without anyone seeing her or for someone to grab her without being seen.

Heidi had mentioned rain had been forecast that evening. She had checked the weather from that day in 2012 and could see there had been light rain during the day, and at 18:30, it was around 12 degrees Celsius. So not exactly the type of evening when people were likely to have been sitting or working out in their garden. The doors had been canvassed at the time, but no one remembered hearing or seeing anything unusual.

She walked back down to her car, which she had left in the car park at the hostel and popped back in to see Mr Johnson to ask him how often the towels were changed and if he knew if Isa, the cleaning lady, still lived nearby. Mr Johnson confirmed guests staying for a week or more, had their towels changed twice a week - usually on the 2nd and 4th night of their stay, and bed linen once a week, but guests were always welcome to use the onsite laundry facilities at their own expense, should they wish fresh towels or bed linen every day. Most guests chose not to, as they were mostly students or families travelling on a tight budget.

This meant Erin's towel would have been changed for the last time on the Saturday, thus it could have been wet for either a day or so or almost three days of use, depending on how many showers she had taken and when she actually disappeared. Given the fact there would have been no heating on in July and the weather had been quite chilly, it was impossible to tell when it was last used. Sensing this was a dead end, she decided to enquire about Isa Ballantyne and was delighted to learn she was alive and well and living close by.

At seventy-two years old, Isa was retired and lived with her husband, Bobby, in one of the bungalows just along the road from the hostel. Mr Johnson didn't think she would mind if Tracy stopped by to see her. She decided to take a chance and swing by her home on the way back to the station. Driving along the road peering at the numbers, she eventually found it.

It was a quaint little dormer-style bungalow with beautiful pink rose bushes growing up either side of the pale blue front door. She found the doorbell hidden amongst the foliage. Thinking no one was home, she was just about to turn around and go when a spritely white-haired lady answered the door wearing a flowery apron, her hands covered in flour.

Her husband was out playing a round of golf, and she had been busy baking scones before she went to pick up her grandchildren from school. Millie and Mason were seven and nine years old and were pupils at the local primary school. She quickly ushered Tracy through into the small kitchen at the back of the house, which overlooked a beautiful walled country garden and set about making her a cup of tea in a pretty china teapot, which Tracy gladly accepted.

As the scones were still baking in the oven, she offered her some homemade tablet and a slice of banana bread and wouldn't take no for an answer. The smell coming from the oven was delicious, it reminded Tracy of her grandmother's home growing up. She had been an amazing baker, and always had something in the oven. Tracy found her tummy rumbling and remembered she had skipped breakfast. Two pieces of tablet and a large slice of cake later, she had satisfied her gurgling stomach, and probably increased her expanding waistline with it. She really needed to start eating a bit healthier.

Isa told Tracy all she could remember from that day, which wasn't much. She had met the girls briefly earlier in the week in the hallway. They were leaving their room on a day trip to Loch Ness and had held the door open in the hallway for her to bring her laundry cart through.

They had been relatively tidy guests, always making their beds every day, so it had seemed a bit odd when she came in to clean and found the bed still neatly made instead of being stripped and ready for her to turn over, with a few things still left lying around the room. So much so, that it had initially made her come back out of the room to get her chart to double-check whether the room was due to be vacated or not. When she saw she was correct - the girls should have checked out that day, and as it was after noon, she had been a little disappointed at the mess they had left, as this was extra work for her to do and she was already running behind schedule.

At first, she thought it was just a few things lying on top of the bed and the hairdryer in the corner. This was not unusual for foreign guests, though. They often brought too many clothes with them or bought cheap hairdryers that would only work in the UK, which they would then leave behind, as there was no point wasting space in their luggage for something that they might never use again.

It was only when she was vacuuming the floor that she noticed the duffle bag under the bed. It had been shoved so far back that if the strap hadn't caught on her vacuum cleaner, she wouldn't have even noticed it was there. That possibly explained now why Isa hadn't realised at first Erin had left behind her entire belongings. Isa said she always had a quick look inside the wardrobe and, on finding a few things in there too, had bundled everything into a black refuse sack and carried on cleaning. It was only when the police arrived and searched through her things that they discovered Erin's passport was still there.

Isa had felt terrible for not realising something was wrong, and Tracy could see she was genuinely upset; tears were welling in each eye. She apologised profusely for cleaning the room and removing any possible evidence. Placing a hand over hers, Tracy reassured her she wasn't to know—no point in upsetting an old lady even further than she already was. Tracy had just one more question for her though - did Isa remember what items of clothing were left on the bed? Isa thought for a moment before saying she was quite convinced it had been a couple of dresses and a blouse. This was just the answer Tracy had been hoping for, meaning her theory might just be right, and Erin could have been on her way to meet someone after all. She just had to figure out who and find them.

A timer buzzed next to the oven - the scones were ready! Isa insisted she took some back to the station for her and her colleagues to enjoy and promptly packed half a dozen into a freezer bag, along with a jar of homemade raspberry jam. She was instructed to let them cool before eating them. Tracy thanked Isa very much and told her she had been really helpful. She left her card with her, reminding her as she left that if she remembered anything else to give her a call.

16

Back at the station, Tracy made a cup of coffee and knowing she shouldn't, decided to treat herself to one of Isa's scones. They were huge. Just like the tablet and the banana bread, they were delicious. She left one on Betty's desk and handed the rest of them over to the duty desk sergeant, and asked him to share them with his colleagues.

Sitting comfortably in her office, she realised she still had a couple of hours before she would hear back from her contact in Boston PD about when she could speak to Erin's friends who had been on the trip with her, Mollie and Olivia. Just like Erin's parents, local police officers were going to speak with them first so as not to cause any panic. Officer Flannigan from Boston PD called just after 3 pm to say both girls were happy to chat over Zoom with her the following day. He provided email addresses for both girls to enable Tracy to set this up. They exchanged a few pleasantries although they had never met. Tracy filled him in on what she had learned so far. He wished her the best of luck and said if she was ever in Boston any time to look him up.

She quickly emailed each girl, asking what time would

suit them both. It wasn't long before each had replied, and she set up a Zoom call with each before heading home for the evening.

The weather was starting to turn, there was a definite chill in the air in the evenings now, and the leaves were beginning to change colour. Tracy loved this time of year. It reminded her of those happy times as a child when she would go and look for chestnuts with her dad. Tracy had lived in Hamilton as a child and would often go over to Chaterhault, a local country park or Dalziel estate in Motherwell (another Lanarkshire town), where she would run through the piles of leaves that had gathered in the grass, kicking them up into the air before trying to catch them again. They would find a large stick and, taking turns, would knock the chestnuts off the trees, competing to find the biggest one.

Her dad had also been a police officer and had been so passionate about the job it had been one of the reasons why she had followed him into the force. He was sadly no longer with us having died a few years back from lung cancer, but he had been so proud of her the day she became Detective Chief Inspector. She held back a tear and hoped he wouldn't be disappointed in her now.

When she got home, she changed into some old black leggings and a grey hoodie. Grabbing her wellies, she lifted the shed key from the hook behind the back door and headed out into her garden. The grass needed cutting, and there was no time like the present to start getting this place into some kind of order. Seeing Heidi's neat garden and Isa's pretty country garden had inspired her. Plus, the solitude gave her time to think about the case.

It wasn't long before she had the grass at the front of the house cut and edged and made a start on the weeds growing in the flower beds under the windows. She made a mixture of thin bleach and water and poured it onto the pretty flagstone path leading from the gate to the front door, using an old watering can she had found in the shed. A quick scrub and it wasn't long before the pretty colours began to shine through the years of dirt and grime. She had thought they were grey, but as they were drying, she could see they were emerging as shades of pink and beige. Looking around, she was pretty proud of what she had achieved. She still had a long way to go, but it was a start.

By the time she was done, she had worked out a strategy for talking to the girls tomorrow.

Friday 21st October

Tracy headed to work early again the following day, she wanted to get a head start on a mini-profile of each of the girls before she spoke with them. It was only three am in the USA, and she had organised to speak to Mollie and Olivia at ten am and eleven am, respectively. With plenty of time to kill, she logged back into their Facebook pages via Erin's account.

She quickly discovered Mollie was a thirty-five-year-old married mother of two - twins, a boy and a girl. She was currently on maternity leave, having only recently had the twins. Her profile states she is a pharmacist, working at her local hospital. Her husband Neil is a drugs rep for one of the large pharmaceutical companies; Tracy wondered if this was how they met.

They had been married for five years, it seemed and were currently living in the suburbs of Boston. Their house looked stunning, but it had been a big project by the looks of her multiple posts, and it got Tracy thinking about her house again and all the renovations she was planning. She hoped it hadn't been a mistake buying such a run-down, old property. Too late now.

Olivia was pictured holding the twins when they were only a few days old, so it looked like they were still close friends, even after all this time. Tracy longed for this. She had lost touch with most of her friends many years ago. Not that her friends hadn't tried, but they all had regular jobs with regular hours and couldn't understand why she was constantly checking her phone, answering emails when she was with them, or cancelling on them altogether at the last minute. But a police officer's job is never done. As a detective, you are constantly on call.

She turned to Olivia's profile now, also thirty-five; she was not married but was living with someone in a smart loft-style apartment in downtown Boston. She was a university lecturer teaching economics at Boston University. Her partner, Ryan, worked in finance but wasn't on Facebook, so she could only learn what Olivia had included on her page about him. It seemed he was a little older than her, having just celebrated his 40th birthday - skydiving, of all things. Doing something like this terrified the life out of Tracy. They seemed to be a very sporty pair who did a lot of travelling. There were photos of them climbing up to the base camp of Everest in Nepal, walking the Inca trail, cycling in Vietnam and snorkelling in the Great Barrier Reef.

Olivia, who wasn't teaching until noon, had opted to speak to Tracy first. She was wearing a bright blue blouse with navy chino trousers and wore her long blonde hair in loose waves framing her face. Although nervous, she had an air of confidence about her and sat with her arms folded loosely in her lap. She was anxious to know if Erin had finally been found after all this time, whether the news was good or bad. She just wanted to know what had happened to their friend.

Although she was expecting her call, Tracy showed her warrant card, explained a little about her role, and explained that she had only just taken up this role and was now looking into cold cases. She discussed her background in the CID unit in Glasgow and gave a brief synopsis of what she had learned so far. Olivia seemed satisfied with her explanation for contacting her and relaxed a little. She had been expecting to hear sad news when Tracy suddenly got in touch after all this time.

She chatted animatedly about her best friend, smiling as she remembered the good times they had shared. They had met at kindergarten (our equivalent of primary 1) and had been best friends ever since. Their trip around Europe had always been a dream of theirs, and they had planned it out together during their final year at university, having saved for it for years. It had been a trip of a lifetime, and they had loved every minute of it, that is until they learned of Erin's disappearance.

There hadn't been a day that had gone by since Olivia hadn't regretted leaving Erin behind in Inverness. When they had been staying in Edinburgh, they had met a group of Scottish lads who had invited them back down to celebrate the Fringe with them before heading home. They had looked it up online and, after reading about all the hype around the town and reviews for some of the shows, had decided it was something they had both wanted to do, plus Andy (one of the guys they had met) had been quite cute. Olivia blushed, ashamed to admit she had slept with him.

Not wanting to return to Edinburgh alone, she discussed it with her friends and discovered Mollie was up for it, too, as she fancied one of Andy's friends. Not wanting to cramp their style, Erin had opted to stay in Inverness alone. She had been to the tourist information office and had a bundle of leaflets for places she wanted to visit. The hostel seemed safe, and the staff were friendly. Although she couldn't remember the manager's name now, she remembered his wife Joan, who had become a bit like a surrogate mum to them while they were there.

Once Erin made up her mind about something, there was no changing it. As she was settled in their room and they had paid until the following week, there had been no need to switch rooms. Plus, the hostel had been pretty full. The girls ensured Erin had her return train ticket to Edinburgh before they left, and headed back down to Edinburgh on Tuesday afternoon. Erin had come to wave them off at the station. She had seemed happy and excited as she had made plans to keep herself busy for the rest of her week.

The girls had Face Timed on Friday night from Deacon Brodie's (one of the pubs in the Royal Mile in Edinburgh). Erin had seemed her usual happy self. Erin had a big day planned for Saturday, which she had seemed excited about. And they had messaged each other on Sunday afternoon, both with hangovers. They didn't hear anything else from her after that, which they found odd. Still, Olivia was ashamed to admit she was having so much fun with Andy that she hadn't noticed at first, and was even more embarrassed to admit she didn't pay much attention when her friend had been talking to her about her plans for the Saturday. The pub had been noisy, and Andy was trying to get her attention too.

It was only when Erin didn't get off the train to meet them in Edinburgh when she was supposed to, that they realised something was wrong. They both tried calling her, but their calls went straight to voice mail. After checking with railway staff in Edinburgh to see if the train had left Inverness as planned, they asked the staff to call the train station in Inverness to see if she had maybe missed the train and was perhaps on another train. The lady at the train station confirmed the train to Edinburgh from Inverness had left on time.

There were no other direct trains to Edinburgh that day. She had put a tannoy message out across the station in case Erin was perhaps waiting somewhere or in the toilet, but no one replied. The girls then rang the bus station, who contacted one of their drivers who was currently heading down to Edinburgh, to check if Erin was a passenger on his bus. On hearing she wasn't, they too, put out a tannoy call throughout the bus station, but had no luck locating their friend.

Panicking, the girls called the hostel, and on discovering Erin's belongings had been left behind, but there was no sign of Erin, they instinctively called Erin's parents and then the police. Olivia was visibly shaken after telling her side of the story. It was apparent she had shouldered much of the guilt for leaving Erin alone, even after all these years. All for a holiday fling. Sensing how upset she was, and conscious of the fact she was dredging it all up for her again; Tracy told her not to beat herself up. It had been Erin's choice to stay behind.

Olivia didn't remember anyone following them when they were on their travels. Although some of the other people they met might have been headed in the same direction, they never met up with anyone again. She confirmed Erin had broken up with her boyfriend, Josh, just after Christmas. It had been an amicable break-up. He was returning home to Chicago after university, whilst Erin planned to move to New York. They had just grown apart and the relationship had run its' course. Erin had been the one to finish it, but Josh had seemed to take it well.

She finished by asking Olivia if there was anything at all, even something she thought insignificant, to get back in touch with her ASAP. Olivia thanked her and said she just wanted to know what happened to her friend.

Ending the call, Tracy just had time to make another quick coffee before it was time to speak to Mollie. Mollie was dressed casually in jeans and a white t-shirt. She had minimal make-up on and wore her dark hair tied up in a loose wavy bun. Despite having two young children, she looked relaxed and a lot less frazzled than Tracy remembered she had been, and her boys were two years apart. Mollie explained that her mum had taken the twins out for a walk in their pram to give her time to talk to Tracy in peace.

Mollie gave a similar account of their friendship over the years, having also met the other two girls in kindergarten. In her teenage years, she had lived in the house next door to Erin. Growing up, they were always together. Her dad used to call them the three amigos. They used to get into trouble with their parents for running up huge telephone bills, despite having been together all day at school and then spent most of the evenings together. And still, they never ran out of things to talk about.

Erin and Olivia had been there for her when she lost her dad, who was a firefighter. He had tragically died when she was just fifteen years old. The floor had collapsed inside the building in which he was fighting a large blaze, killing him instantly. This tragedy brought them even closer as a group.

Mollie's parents had set up a savings account for her as a baby, and when her dad died, he left her and her brother quite a substantial sum of money. She had used some of this money to plan her trip with the girls. It had been their final adventure together before they started their adult jobs.

Mollie went on to talk about their trip before leading up

to the final leg in Inverness. Her version of events was identical to Olivia's except for one tiny detail. She mentioned a final trip Erin had planned for herself on her last Saturday in Scotland, to some nearby haunted house. Mollie didn't know the exact details, such as where it was or the name of the place and as Erin had never posted any photos of it on Facebook, she couldn't be entirely sure she had gone on the trip, but she remembered Erin had seemed excited about it when she was talking to them about it in the pub on that Friday night. Just at that, Tracy could hear a baby crying in the background. She presumed Mollie's mum had come back from her walk.

Tracy made a note of this in her notebook and ended the call by thanking Mollie for her time and promising to keep in touch if she had any new leads. She also asked Mollie to be in touch if she remembered anything else that might help. She closed her laptop and looked down at her notebook.

So far, she had written down - black Range Rover, possible date/night out and a tour of a haunted house, with question marks after all three. She was used to following leads when the trail was hot - not ten years old, but she wasn't about to let that put her off. Finishing up for the evening, she locked her office and headed home.

***

It was dark when she got home. She had forgotten to leave a light on. The house was cold too. Lighting the log burner in the snug, it wasn't long before she had the cottage lovely and cosy. She changed into sweatpants and a jumper with fluffy socks and settled down on her dad's old leather wing-backed chair in front of the fire with a nice glass of Rosé, thinking about what she had learned so far.

No bodies had ever been found matching Erin's description, but she knew this didn't mean she wasn't dead. It just meant her body hadn't been found yet. The area around the hostel had been combed at the time but had come back clear. As had the streets and wastelands surrounding the hostel. Without any more to go on, the police had no starting point to search anywhere else.

She guessed a combination of a cold trail and a tight budget had probably led to the investigation being concluded relatively quickly. Erin hadn't been classed as a vulnerable missing person, so it hadn't been thought initially that she had done something to harm herself. The initial thought had been that she'd met someone and gone off with them, and she would turn up alive and well in a few days. But, as the days went by and there was still no sign of her, the fact that all of her belongings had been left behind pointed towards suicide being the more likely scenario. But Tracy didn't buy it. There was no sign of depression.

She also didn't buy the theory that Erin had run off. If

she had run off, she would have disappeared without money, food, clothes etc., which didn't make sense. And if this had been her plan, surely, she would have just packed up and left as soon as her friends had returned to Edinburgh. This would have given her much more of a head start. The fact she had left her passport behind also bothered her about this theory.

To put this theory to rest, she thought she'd double-check with her friends when the backpack arrived - if this were all of Erin's clothes or if it was possible she could have taken some of her things with her after all. Meanwhile, she decided she could at least look into the haunted house tour. Surely that wouldn't be too hard to investigate?

The Range Rover would be harder to look into without a license plate, but she could at least check the DVLA records for the people who lived nearby at that time or perhaps check local rental agencies. Before she knew it, she had drained her glass; deciding against another, she stoked the fire and headed up the rickety stairs to bed.

She had a busy weekend in the house ahead of her. Her new windows and doors were scheduled to go in next week, so she had to take down all the old blinds in preparation for this, and she had planned to make a start on the living room by stripping the walls ready to plaster and paint. When she moved in she had lifted back the carpet and found the original floorboards, which were still in excellent condition despite their age, so she planned to strip them back and re-varnish them too. That had been a bit of a bonus.

She had another restless night, her dreams switching between Robbie and Erin again.

17

Saturday 22nd October

Despite her restless night, Tracy was still up bright and early as she had a local builder coming to look around her property and give her an estimate to start some of the rest of her renovations. The whole house needed gutting, which would cost her a small fortune.

It was built in the 1870s and still had some lovely Victorian features, such as a high-pitched roof, ornate gable trim and original fireplaces (that she planned to keep if she could), but the kitchen and its odd layout had to go. Rather than tackle a complete house renovation at once though, her budget had dictated she would have to live in the house and do the work in stages.

Doing part of it herself would also help to keep costs down. This was fine, as she was pretty handy, having learned a lot from Rob and her dad, so she was actually looking forward to doing some of it herself. It might be somewhat therapeutic. She finally had the time on her hands to do so.

The house had been re-wired and had a new central heating system installed before she purchased it, so thankfully that was two less jobs for her to tackle. She had kept back some money from her share of the sale of the family home to pay for the new windows and doors, which were being installed next week, just in time for winter. She had chosen dark grey sash windows with a matching grey cottage-style front door with a small square window in the upper middle section of the door and a black round old-fashioned door knocker underneath. It was finished with a black door handle and a black letterbox in the middle of the door. She was planning to have the gable trim of the house painted in a matching dark grey.

Allan (the builder) was due at 830 am, and sure enough, the bell rang at precisely 830 am. Allan was a jolly big man in his mid-fifties with a ruddy face, short white hair, and a closely trimmed beard. He wore navy combat trousers, a matching fleece with his company's name embroidered on the back, and heavy orange work boots, which he politely removed when Tracy invited him in.

The first big job on her long to-do list was to knock down the wall between the kitchen, pantry and dining room to make a large open-plan kitchen diner. Allan took lots of measurements and went upstairs, where he lifted back the carpet in one of the bedrooms to check the floor joists. It was just as he thought, it was a load-bearing wall, so, unfortunately, he would need his structural engineer to look at it to see if she would require a steel beam to support the upstairs. This was not the news she wanted to hear, but it wasn't altogether a surprise, it was an old house after all.

He couldn't give her an exact cost until his engineer had been out, but he was able to give her a ball park figure which seemed reasonable, so she asked him to get started on the paper work for her building warrant. Hoping to get back to her soon, he left her a brochure for Howdens, as she still had to choose her kitchen. She fancied something modern but with more of a country feel, maybe with a Belfast sink, but until she had the final figure to go on for the building works, she couldn't figure out exactly how much she would have left to spend on the kitchen.

After Allan had gone, she started on her tasks for the weekend. She dragged her old sofa, armchair and TV into the small snug with the log burner in it and lifted back the carpet in the living room. Once she had repaired any loose boards, she set about using the industrial sander she had hired. This turned out to be easier than she had expected and slightly less messy than she had anticipated, too, as most of the dust truly was caught in the vacuum attachment. Impressed she carried on.

Despite the early start, it still took her all day Saturday and well into the evening. However, she was secretly quite pleased with herself when it was finished. She covered the floor in heavy-duty plastic sheeting to protect it for now, securing it to the skirting boards with masking tape. She planned to stain the floor in a lovely dark brown after the walls and windows were done. Visiting Heidi's house had inspired her to paint this room in an off-white colour when it was finished. This would go perfectly with the original black fireplace she had lovingly restored the previous weekend. She would eventually treat herself to a new sofa and furniture for this room, but for now, the old mismatched furniture would have to suffice.

She was so grateful to be able to soak her aching limbs in the bath that evening. It also gave her a chance to think over the case and what her next step would be. Perhaps it was time to try and track down the driver of her mystery Range Rover.

Sunday 23rd October

Sunday's job was to strip the many layers of paper off the walls in the living room. She had hired a steamer to help her with this job. It was clear this was going to take much longer than a day. There had to be at least three if not more, layers of paper on the walls. Once she had finished this, she planned on using a heat gun to carefully strip away the many layers of paint from the original wooden doors in the house, as it would be nice to keep as many of the original features as possible. But one job at a time. Keeping busy helped her to stop thinking about the past, but it didn't make it go away. Little Robbie Denver was never far from her mind.

18

Monday 24th October

Katie still had two more weeks before she was due to start work. Determined to use this time wisely and keep herself busy, she had spent her weekend making up a tourist to-do list for herself. Armed with a bunch of information she had picked up from the local tourist office, and recommendations she found online in blogs and reviews, she had set about planning her week.

The man in the tourist office suggested starting with a trip on the hop-on, hop-off bus. There were two routes available (a red and a blue route), the red route covered the town centre whilst the blue route took her further afield. She settled on a ticket for both, as this would allow her to see most of what the inner city had to offer, without missing out on nearby popular attractions, such as the battlefield at Culloden, which once she knew where it was, she could always go back and visit at a later date.

It was a dry, crisp morning when Katie boarded the bus.

The sun was just starting to peak through the clouds. She had wrapped up warm and settled into her seat. It wasn't long before the bus filled up and they were on their way. She found the narrated audio tour interesting, as it provided her with an insight into the history of the city, whilst allowing her to decide when she wanted to stop off and visit some of the many exciting places along the way, such as St Andrews Cathedral, Flora MacDonald's statue, Inverness castle and the highland archive centre. She jumped off and visited each one (except the castle), stopping for a quick bite to eat at a local café with an elderly Canadian couple she had been talking to on the bus.

Choosing to sit on the upper deck of the bus as she headed out of town, she was also able to enjoy the magnificent scenery along the way, the breathtaking views of Tomnahurich Hill and the Caledonian Canal coupled with panoramic views of Kessock Bridge, the Black Isle and, of course, a view of the Inverness Firth all the way out to Fort George. She was thankful; it was a dry day.

Before today, Katie had no idea just how beautiful it was up here. She also felt happy being alone for the first time in a long while. Life in London was always so fast-paced, with everyone racing around at a hundred miles an hour. No one had much time to talk to you if they even bothered acknowledging you in the first place. From what she had witnessed, people up here weren't like that. They appeared friendlier and laid back, portraying a more relaxed way of life. People seemed happier somehow too.

All of this really appealed to Katie. Being on her own today had also helped her to take notice of her surroundings. If she'd taken this tour with a friend or a partner, she wasn't sure she would have been so attuned to it. Katie met lots of lovely people on the bus tour, and in the local shops she popped into along the way. Must be all that fresh air, she decided, keeping everyone's spirits up.

That evening she Face Timed her parents, filling them in on her adventures so far and eagerly discussed her plans for the rest of the week, leaving out the part about the singles evening for now. She was still slightly embarrassed about it and knew they would probably try and talk her out of it.

***

But still, Katie was oblivious to the stranger who had been following her again today, keeping his distance from her. No one noticed the quiet man sitting at the back of the bus, with the flat cap pulled down over his ears, collar turned up, glued to his phone. Only he wasn't glued to his phone, he was glued to her – she just didn't know it yet.

He knew he had taken a chance today, but the bus was almost full. While everyone was busy snapping photographs of their surroundings, he was busily snapping photographs of her. Looking back through them, he was secretly quite pleased with himself. He had quite a collection of her already in the short time she had been back, and it felt nice being so close to her today, soon they would be together again.

19

Despite her busy weekend, Tracy was at her desk bright and early again. A DVLA search revealed as many as a hundred and fifty-four residents owned a black Range Rover in 2012. This wasn't surprising as there was a local Land Rover dealership in Inverness, and the rugged terrain meant lots of people needed them to get around in the bad weather. But as a Range Rover is considered a pretty prestigious car, she hadn't anticipated there being quite so many, especially black ones, for her to check out.

She decided to discount the ones registered to people who lived on farms and large private estates for now and started looking at those addresses in and around a five-mile radius of the area where Erin had last been seen. This produced a much more manageable short list of just five people.

This list included a Mr William McVey, who stayed literally around the corner from the hostel. A background search into Mr McVey, revealed Billy who was seventy-two, was the retired owner of The Last Drop, one of the local pubs. His wife Wilma had run the catering side of the business. They had two girls, Melissa and Kristen, who were grown up and had children of their own.

Neither had ever been in trouble with the police, and neither had even had as much as a parking ticket. Looking up their address on *Google Maps,* she could see their house was located down the street from the hostel and had a large driveway, so she could see no reason for them to have been parked on the corner that evening. Still, it was a coincidence; and was worth a closer look. Plus, running a pub meant you often heard things you might not otherwise have heard. She decided to visit them later in the day.

Next on her list was Miss Marie Katz, a forty-eight-year-old business lady who ran an online beauty store. Around the time Katie disappeared she was living in a large Edwardian house in Union Street, one of the most sought-after areas to live in Inverness. She lived with her partner Mackenzie (or Mac as he was known locally). Mac Rennie worked as a steel fabricator. They too, had no police cautions or convictions. She ruled them out for the moment, as she could see no connection to either the hostel or to Erin but kept a note of their details in case they had perhaps been visiting anyone nearby that night.

Next on her short list was Johnny Baird, a fifty-four-year-old self-employed builder. He lived with his wife Sarah and their four kids in a large sandstone detached house on Crown Avenue, also situated around the corner from the hostel. Other than a police caution aged nineteen for being drunk and disorderly in the town centre after a local rugby match, Johnny was not known to the police for anything else. His wife Sarah, a music teacher, had nothing on record either. Tracy decided their proximity to the hostel was enough to warrant a visit.

Alix Sanderson, a thirty-three-year-old accountant, was next on her list. At only twenty-three at the time, she was the youngest person on her list. Alix was living at home with her parents at that time, who owned a massive sandstone property on Crown Avenue. Was it possible Erin had somehow met and became friendly with her? She decided this was worth following up on, given their closeness in age and the fact they were both accountants.

Last but not least on her shortlist was a seventy-nine-year-old retired GP, Dr Andrew Wilson. Dr Wilson was a widower now and he still lived in the same house he had shared with his wife Helen on Victoria Avenue, the road the hostel is situated on. Although unlikely, due to his age, she thought it was still worth a visit, even if just to rule out if he had parked his car on the corner that evening.

Just as she was about to get her bag and go and check on these leads, Betty popped her head around the door to thank her for the scone she had left on her desk a few days earlier. Betty was the station office manager, which is a civilian role within the police force. She was responsible for the clerical team, ensuring the smooth running of the department. Her duties involved, amongst other things, coordinating meetings for the Assistant Chief Constable and organising resources for everyone when needed.

Betty was a tall, elegant lady with short blonde hair and green eyes. She had been in the force for over thirty years. Although she was almost sixty years old, she didn't look a day over fifty, which, when asked, she put down to good genes and healthy living. She immediately recognised the name on the whiteboard and asked Tracy if she would be looking into all the missing girls?

Before Tracy could interject, Betty started off on a tangent, talking about four girls around the same age who had mysteriously gone missing in Inverness over the last ten years. They had all disappeared without a trace, never to be seen again. She was convinced their cases were linked, especially given the similarities in their appearance, but no one in the station had shared her opinion. There had been no evidence to suggest any connections, and they had laughed it off as she had become a bit of an armchair detective over the years.

Betty was still talking, but Tracy had stopped listening. She had already walked over to the filing cabinet and went straight to the section she had set aside for missing persons. Sure, enough, there were only three other files in this drawer. All girls. Natalia Robertson, a twenty-four-year-old Italian girl. Last seen Sunday, the 20th of July 2014. Klara Eriksson a twenty-one-year-old medical student on a gap year from Sweden. Last seen Sunday, the 25th of June 2016, and finally, twenty-three-year-old au pair Jessica Fletcher from Canada, last seen Saturday, the 28th of July 2018.

She carefully opened each file and took out a photograph of each missing girl. Placing them together on her desk, she took a sharp intake of breath as she put them next to the photograph of Erin, which she had temporarily removed from her whiteboard. There staring back at her, were four almost identical-looking girls. Their features were so close; that she could almost have been staring at images of the same person.

Perhaps it was her years of experience working in CID, but even in her almost twenty-seven years in the police force, this did not seem like a coincidence to her. She walked over to her whiteboard, rubbed off what she had written so far and pinned a photograph of each girl along the top. Dividing the board into four columns, she began writing what she knew about each one. Underneath each picture, she wrote their names, dates of birth, nationality and date last seen. She would need to read the other files to find out more about each of the other girls. Underneath Erin, she wrote student, Inverness hostel, black Range Rover, possible date/night out and haunted house tour.

Looking at the board, apart from their appearance, she

could see a pattern beginning to emerge. They were all foreign, were last seen on a weekend and had disappeared roughly two years apart. She didn't know how or why, but like Betty, she too had a sinking feeling these disappearances were somehow linked, and she was determined to find out why.

She also had a further sinking feeling this might not be over. 2020 was the middle of a worldwide pandemic. This was 2022. If Betty was right and their disappearances were linked, this could have happened again or may be about to happen again very soon. She turned to Betty and asked her if she knew if anyone fitting this profile had gone missing this year? Betty didn't think so, but as a civilian, she wouldn't necessarily have access to this information.

She logged into her PC and pulled up the current list of missing persons. Looking back over the last six months' cases: there was a seventy-five-year-old lady with Alzheimer's who had been found sitting on the doorstep of her old home; a sixty-three-year-old man who had turned up two weeks later living in Bolton with a man he had met online, and finally a twenty-six-year-old man who had disappeared after a night out in the city centre two weeks ago, who was presumed dead as he had been last seen walking along by the river. Police were expecting a body to be found any day now. There were no young foreign girls. Not yet, anyway. Closing her PC for now, she paused for a minute, then asked Betty if she knew of any haunted houses in Inverness.

Betty had a real fascination with ghosts and history and excitedly told her that Inverness is known historically as the key to the North. It has been long associated with a history of bloody battles and gruesome conflicts over the years, thus making it steeped in haunted histories. She knew of several places that were said to be haunted. The first of which was nearby Inverness Castle. While the current red sandstone fortress is relatively modern, she explained that several ancient castles have stood on the site before it. The first of which was built in the mid-eleventh century for King Macbeth. According to Shakespeare's Macbeth, this is said to be where Macbeth murdered King Duncan. The ghost of King Duncan is said to haunt the riverside beneath Inverness Castle.

There was also Eden Court Theatre which, although a modern building stands there now, the site is said to be haunted, and the most commonly seen ghost is that of the green lady who is thought to be the ghost of the wife of a Bishop who hung herself on that very spot.

Then there was the nearby Culloden battlefield, famous for the 1746 Battle of Culloden, one of Inverness's best-known haunted places. In a battle that changed the course of Scottish history, echoes of cries of the thousands of Highlanders that were cut down in a gruesome end to the

Jacobite rebellion, along with the sounds of swords being swung and guns being fired, are often reported as being heard today on the bleak moor.

Betty told her that a trip to the Ness Islands on an eerie autumn night is also very popular amongst those interested in the paranormal, and it is also home to the annual Ness Island Halloween show which was just over a week away. The area has been thoroughly investigated by various paranormal groups who have made many chilling and mysterious finds over the years, including a vision of a frightful woman accompanied by the smell of decay around an area located to the West of General Well's Bridge on the Bught Parkside.

Cawdor castle is another place also associated with the works of William Shakespeare as Macbeth became the fictional Thane of Cawdor and lived in Cawdor castle, which has a sinister past. Legend has it that Muriel Cawdor, daughter of the earl of Cawdor, fell in love with a rival chieftain's son. When her father learned of their love affair, he chased her up the highest tower. Trying to escape, she lowered herself out of the window where her merciless father cut off her hands, sending her to her death. To this day, the figure of a young handless woman in a pretty blue dress is said to haunt the tower.

Betty went on to talk about Black Friars' graveyard, which is all that is left of a Dominican priory founded in

1233 by the Black Friars. It is said to be haunted by the ghost of a medieval friar who walks the grounds at night.

And finally, there was Loch Wood House, a private estate outside Inverness designed and built by the famous Scottish architect William Adam in the mid-eighteenth century and owned by the Campbell family. Although she wasn't sure if they ran tours, Betty remembered attending a wedding there a few years back, and one of the guests at their table had been a close family friend. She knew of many ghostly stories that had been passed down through the generations. And she knew they ran a pretty unique Halloween enchanted forest experience for the kids. She had taken her grandchildren to it once and had been pretty freaked out by some of the scary statues hidden along the route.

Betty said the family had also been plagued by tragedy as the current Laird of the estate had lost both his parents and twin sister in a tragic accident on the bend of the country road, just outside their estate. She added she wouldn't be surprised if the ghosts of the family haunted this stretch of the road or even the house itself.

Tracy noted all of these places, intending to check each one out, as any one of them could quite easily have been where Erin was heading that Saturday. In the meantime, though, she wanted to look into Betty's theory and at least read through the other case files to see if they were dealing with serial abductions or a possibly even a serial killer (although she thoroughly planned to keep this thought to herself for now).

Determined not to make the same mistake twice, she knew she would need hard physical evidence before going to the ACC with something potentially as big as this. As she sat down to examine each case, determined to find a solid link, she had a feeling this would be a long night. She was going to need lots of caffeine. As she poured herself the first of many coffees, she opened the case file for Natalia Robertson.

20

Natalia

Natalia was a twenty-four-year-old Italian girl who had been touring Scotland after completing her master's degree in engineering at Strathclyde University. Unlike Erin, she had been travelling alone. She graduated at the end of June 2014 and decided to travel around Scotland for a month before finally heading back home to Tuscany.

Born to an Italian mother and Scottish father, she had chosen to study in Glasgow, where she had lived for the past six years. She completed her undergraduate degree before going straight on to study for her master's degree on a full-time basis. Her parents had funded her course, but she had supported her travels herself, having worked in various bars and restaurants in Glasgow whilst at university.

She had hired a car and was planning on doing what is known today as the North Coast 500 - a scenic 516-mile route around the north coast of Scotland, starting and ending at Inverness Castle. At the end of her road trip, she planned on spending her last few days in Inverness before flying home to Italy via London from Inverness. Only she never made the flight to London. Her parents had reported her missing when she didn't return home to Tuscany on the 26th of July 2014.

Reading on, there wasn't much to go on. Natalia had completed her planned trip and returned her hire car as planned when she arrived back in Inverness three days before she was last seen. Little was known about her whereabouts after this. Her parents hadn't been sure exactly where she had been staying, but a credit card search had revealed she, too, had been staying in the same hostel as Erin.

Tracy wasn't sure if this was significant at this stage but made a note to check it out. She made a note to speak with the manager again to find out about the staff working there when both girls went missing. See if there were any connections. Reading on, she could see the investigating officers had visited the hostel at the time. Staff could confirm Natalia had checked in with them. She had been staying in a single room on the top floor but, unlike Erin, appeared to have left nothing behind. As you are asked to leave your keys in a box at checkout in reception, no one actually saw her go, so it was impossible to say if she had personally checked herself out or not, but her keys were found in the box amongst the other guests' keys at the end of her stay.

Investigating officers had checked with local taxi companies and found no hires on that morning for anyone matching Natalia's description headed for the airport, or anywhere else for that matter. It was possible to catch the bus to the airport as it was only a short walk into town, and, if you weren't carrying much or you maybe had a case on wheels, this would have been easy enough. It seems the officers had thought about this already and checked with her parents, who confirmed they had taken most of her belongings home with them after her graduation. Anything she didn't need or want anymore had been either donated to charity or binned. As she was travelling light, it was considered possible she could have chosen to take the bus.

However, CCTV at the bus and rail stations had been reviewed, but no sightings of Natalia were ever found on any of them. Officers had trawled through footage days on either side and found nothing. It was as if she had just vanished, just like Erin had. There was CCTV of her handing the keys back to the hire car depo. Loading the file, she was able to view this footage for herself. Although there was no audio, Natalia appeared relaxed and chatted animatedly with the lady behind the desk. They had talked for twenty-two minutes before Natalia left. As the CCTV was limited to the yard and cars outside, she was only seen leaving and turning left down the street.

Just as she was about to switch off the footage - she

spied a black Range Rover parked at the very edge of the right-hand side of the screen. Only the vehicle's side profile was visible, but she knew her cars, and this one had blackened-out windows, just like the one Heidi had described. She zoomed in, but it was impossible to tell if anyone was in the car. The recording was just too grainy. She watched on, and the car sat for ten minutes before slowly driving off in the same direction Natalia had headed. As this was a fixed camera, she couldn't see where it went next or who was driving. Sadly, it wasn't at the right angle to catch any of the number plate. But surely this was no coincidence?

A search for Natalia's mobile phone had also drawn up a blank as it had been switched off whilst in the vicinity of the hostel where she was staying, sometime in the Sunday evening when she had last been heard of. Same as Erin’s.

Officers then turned to her social media accounts. Natalia regularly posted updates of her travels on Facebook and via her holiday blog. To try and see as much of the highlands as she could, Natalia had decided to follow the West coast route up to Inverness, which had taken her through Loch Lomond, Tarbet, Oban, and Glencoe, before taking the A87 across the Skye bridge into Skye. She had spent a few days on Skye visiting Broadford, the Uillins in central Skye, the beautiful but imposing Dunvegan castle, the Old Man of Storr on North Skye, Portree and the Talisker distillery, where she had pictures of her stopping for a wee dram. Next on her list was Eileen Donna castle and the picturesque Glenfinnan viaduct, where she had stopped overnight before heading North to Inverness to start the North Coast (NC) 500.

She had spent a couple of nights in Inverness before starting the NC500. Tracy made a note to try and find out where, as the hostel was mentioned at the end of this trip but not at the beginning - was it possible she had met someone there? Or could someone have followed her, knowing she was travelling alone? Well aware that people could use false names, she thought she should at least check to see if there were any repeat bookings from the same person on or around the times both girls went missing. After all, if these cases were linked, they had been getting away with this for over a decade now. Were there more missing girls that no one knew anything about?

There were transcripts of interviews with her lecturers and friends trying to find out what frame of mind Natalia had been in before she went missing. All said the same thing - she was happy, excited for her future and looking forward to finding out where the next chapter in her life would take her. She wasn't afraid of travelling alone. She'd lived away from home since she was eighteen years old. She had several job interviews lined up when she went home and had received a few offers in Scotland, which she was still mulling over. She didn't have a regular boyfriend but had dated a fellow student on and off over the last few years. Officers had interviewed him, but he was on holiday in Ibiza with his friends when Natalia went missing, so he had been dismissed as having anything to do with her disappearance. Plus, he seemed genuinely devastated to hear she was missing and had joined in with the search as soon as he arrived home.

Officers in Glasgow had joined in the search, too, in case she had simply headed back down to Glasgow, not wanting to return home to Italy. That search had also come up blank. Her lease for her flat had ended, so she had no base there now, and none of her friends had heard anything from her. Officers had visited a few of her close friends in Glasgow, but she was not there. Alerts had been set up at all UK airports, ports and railway stations in case she tried to leave the country. Although not under arrest, her visa had expired, and naturally, her parents were worried about her welfare.

Unlike Erin, there was absolutely no trace of her. The last time she had been seen was on Saturday afternoon, leaving a local charity shop where she had bought a pretty black cocktail dress and a pair of high-heeled sandals. Tracy paused on reading this - this seemed like a strange thing for a young woman travelling alone to be buying in Inverness, but maybe she was buying it to take back to Italy for somewhere she was going. Tracy made a note of the name and address of the shop along with the assistant's name, who it appeared had come forward in response to a poster Natalia's parents had put up in the local supermarket. She also made a note to ask her parents this, when she got around to speaking to them.

Looking at Natalia's blog, there were plenty of selfies and a few of her with other travellers she must have met along the way. No one instantly jumped out, and there didn't appear to be any particular person who appeared more than once or twice and never at more than one location. But that still didn't mean somebody hadn't been following her.

Her last post had been on Saturday, the 19th of July 2014, with a promise of updates regarding something 'new and exciting' she was attending that evening with a post to follow as usual the following evening, only this post never came. Natalia seemed to make most of her posts around ten pm.

Tracy *Googled* Saturday the 19th of July 2014 to see if there was any big festival or event on that evening in Inverness, but finding nothing, she logged out for now, baffled but planning to come back later when she'd had a chance to read through the other files. Right now, her stomach was growling, indicating it needed more than coffee this time.

As she stepped out of her office and into the hallway, she soon realised most of the day shift had gone home, including Betty, as it was just gone six o'clock. It was time she was heading home now too. She was still getting used to these new hours, but there was no switching off for Tracy. Once she was hooked on a case, she was like a dog with a bone - she ate, drank and slept on the case. Nothing else mattered. Sadly, her family had realised this too and suffered the consequences. Despite everything, she was a damn good cop, and she was convinced she would prove her worth again.

Tracy returned to her dark empty cottage, cursing herself again for forgetting to leave a light on. She really must invest in some smart plugs, then at least she could switch them on from work before she left. She had at least left the heating on, so the place was nice and cosy, unlike the night before. Heating some leftover lasagna Betty had given her, she poured herself a glass of Rosé and settled in front of the fire to read over some more of the case file.

The last phone call Natalia had made was on Thursday evening when she had called her grandmother in Italy as it had been her eighty-fifth birthday. They had spoken for forty-five minutes. Officers had spoken to her grandmother at the time of her disappearance, who confirmed Natalia had been her usual happy self, full of stories from all the fantastic places she had visited on her trip. She had sent her grandmother some photographs via *'WhatsApp* and had sung Happy Birthday to her. There were no calls to or from any numbers that her parents didn't recognise, but the last text message sent by Natalia to an unknown number was very interesting to her.

This last text was sent to an unknown number on Sunday afternoon at five forty-seven. It simply read, *'On my way. See you soon '*, finished with a smiley face emoji. The police had tried to trace the phone, but it was switched off and it was a pay-as-you-go or what's known in the business as a burner phone, so there was no way of tracing who it belonged to. The phone was located within a ten-mile radius of the hostel where Natalia was staying when this text was sent, meaning this person was close. Was that just a coincidence? Somehow, she didn't think so.

Officers at the time had suggested this may have been her trying to buy drugs from a local dealer - something Natalia's parents had vehemently denied. Sadly, this was not impossible, but that still didn't explain her disappearance. Thinking of the black Range Rover seen around the time Erin disappeared did make her wonder. This kind of car with blackened-out windows was often the car of choice for drug dealers. Not one to be judgmental, but she had seen it herself many times down in Glasgow. But the smiley face emoji bothered her.

DS McGregor had never bought drugs before, but she had certainly dealt with many over the years who had and she knew you didn't sign off a text to someone like that with a smiley-faced emoji. This struck her as more like the kind of text you sent someone you knew or wanted to get to know. There had been a one-word reply, *'Ok,'* which meant Tracy knew meant only one thing - this person either was the last person to see her, or they knew where she was headed that night. Either way - she had to find this person. But this might be like trying to find a needle in a haystack.

The dreams were back again that night, only this time, instead of the body of the dead boy, it was the bodies of the four missing girls she saw - pale and lifeless with their arms outstretched, reaching out to her covered in mud and leaves.

21

Tuesday 25th October

Klara

Back in the office bright and early again, DS McGregor carefully opened the third case file. Klara Eriksson, the youngest of the girls, was a twenty-one-year-old medical student on a gap year from Sweden. She travelled to the UK on the 24th of July 2015, where she stayed in London initially with friends in Knightsbridge before moving up to the Scottish Highlands in late November. Whilst there, she had taken a job as a ski instructor at Glen Eden Ski Resort near Braemar.

Having lived in Stockholm her whole life, Klara was only 25km from some of Sweden's major ski resorts. She had learned to ski at the age of four and had gone on to sit her level 1 and level 2 instructors' qualifications as soon as she turned seventeen. She had previously worked as an instructor at Flottsbro Alpin, the biggest ski resort in Stockholm, at weekends and holidays. But, she had been afforded the privilege of having skied at some of the best resorts all over the world with her family. DS McGregor figured her family must be pretty wealthy. Skiing was not a cheap hobby, and neither was staying in Knightsbridge – never mind as a student!

Reading on, she discovered Klara had arrived in the highlands at the end of November ahead of Scotland's official ski season, which runs from December to April, where she had been offered a position as a ski instructor for the season. While working there, she had been staying in the nearby Duddingston Castle hotel, which a quick check on *Google Maps* revealed it was situated around five miles from Glen Eden ski resort.

The hotel website showed that it was a stunning Scots baronial-style laird's mansion built in 1510, nestled in a 6500-acre estate. Surrounded by breathtaking mountains, rivers, glens and a golf course, it looked stunning but not the sort of place you'd imagine a student on a gap year would be staying. Tracy's eldest son, Callum, had taken a year out between university to backpack around Australia with his friends. They had lived in hostels and, when they were feeling a bit flush, had splashed out on an out-of-town B&B, with all four lads squashing into one room.

Once ski season was over, Klara travelled up to

Aviemore with some of the friends she had made at the ski resort. They stayed in one of the lodges and went hiking in the Cairngorms National Park together. By early June, they had gone their separate ways, and she had headed up to Inverness alone, where she had been last seen on Sunday, the 25th of June, 2016.

Her parents, Lars and Freja, had officially reported her missing on the 30th of June, as she usually spoke on the phone with them every Thursday night. They had panicked when they hadn't heard from her as usual, and couldn't reach her as her phone had been turned off. They had called the hotel where she was staying, who had checked her room and found it empty despite the fact she was not due to check out for another week.

The keys to her rental car were found lying on the desk, along with the key card for her room. All of her belongings were gone. A forensics search of her room had revealed nothing except Klara and housekeeping's prints. However, just like in Erin's disappearance, the room had been cleaned after Klara had disappeared. Klara had been caught on camera leaving the hotel on Sunday at 6:57 p.m. She wore jeans, white Converse and a pale blue blazer with a cross-body handbag. This information had been taken from the hotel's CCTV footage. Tracy would want to watch this video herself.

Investigating officers found no footage of her returning

to the hotel, so it was presumed she had never returned. So, where was her luggage then? There was no mention of her carrying luggage in the police report. Tracy had so many questions swirling around in her head. She hoped this footage might have some answers for her.

She loaded the CCTV footage from the hotel, the night Klara was last seen, onto her laptop and pressed play. Klara had been staying in the luxurious Ness View Hotel, a beautiful Grade B-listed building. Not yet familiar with the area, she paused the video and did a quick search online. According to the hotel website, it was originally a 19th-century house before it was turned into a five-star luxury hotel. Nestled in a secluded canopy of trees, you would never know it was in the middle of the town centre. Its central location meant it was ideally located for exploring the Highlands and the city centre. Tucked away on the banks of the River Ness, it was just a ten-minute drive from Loch Ness and a mile from Inverness Castle.

Turning back to the video footage, she moved it forward until she reached the footage of Klara leaving the hotel. Klara bounces out of the front doors at reception, turns right, walks past the car park and continues down the long gravel drive towards the large black front gates. She walks through the gates, and it looks as if she may have continued walking straight on the path alongside the river. Tracy noticed that, other than her small handbag, she had none of her luggage with her, and this footage confirms she left alone and was on foot. There was no one following her - or was there?

Tracy left the video running whilst she got up to grab another coffee. Just as she returned to her desk, she noticed a black Range Rover reverse out of a parking space underneath a tree and drive off in the direction Klara had been heading in. Adrenaline pumping now, she put down her coffee, rewound the footage, and watched it repeatedly.

Although she'd only watched for around twenty minutes or so, there had been no footage of the driver entering the vehicle, so she figured they must have been sitting there for a while. She rewound the footage until she eventually found the car driving into the car park. According to the time on the recording, this vehicle entered the car park at 16:33 and parked nose-first underneath a large tree. The driver was smart enough not to drive too close to the camera.

The sun visor was down despite it being overcast, and whoever was driving had parked underneath a tree between two other large vehicles, making it impossible for anyone to see who was inside. As she let the footage run on, no one emerged from that vehicle. They just sat there until fifteen minutes after Klara left. What on earth were they doing?

The car pulled out of the car park at 19:12. Zooming in, she should have been able to read the number plate, but there was just a completely blank reflection shining back at her where the number plate should be. This could mean only one thing - the person or people in that car did not want to be traced for whatever reason and had deliberately concealed the plates. This illegal move can be quite easily achieved by either fixing a self-adhesive polycarbonate cover over the plate or by spraying the plate with a polycarbonate layer. Up close, this cover is invisible to the naked eye but makes the plate unreadable to most, if not all, infrared cameras.

Of course, she would need to watch more footage as this person could simply be a guest at the hotel, but somehow, she very much doubted that. Why would you sit in your car when you could have sat inside? Watching this video had only made her even more convinced she was onto something, but with no number plate or potential suspect, going to the ACC would have to wait for now. Plus, she needed to tread carefully. She was new to the station, and with her track record, she didn't want anyone to think she was criticising fellow officers' handling of these cases. Buzzing from this find, she was keen to read on and see if she could find any more similarities between the cases.

Officers had interviewed the hotel staff and all of the friends Klara had travelled from Aviemore to the Cairngorms with. They had also trawled through hours and hours of CCTV footage from local businesses to see if there was any clue as to where she might have gone. There was a list of names and short statements from each one. Tracy made a note to cross-reference them with everyone who worked in the hostel in case there was perhaps anyone who had worked in both places - although she figured this would probably be too easy.

Officers checked the train and bus stations and even the local airport. All were drawing a blank. Mobile phone records again showed her phone had been switched off sometime after she had left the hotel that Sunday evening and had never been switched back on again, making the investigating officers suspicious that she had staged her disappearance. DS McGregor wasn't so sure. Given the evidence on the CCTV, she was even more convinced this was all too much of a coincidence. Three almost identical-looking girls, all simply vanishing into thin air. She didn't know how or why, but she felt these disappearances were definitely linked. And she was yet to look at the fourth case.

Betty popped her head around the door at 17:30 to say some of the team were heading out for an Indian if she wanted to join them? Tracy knew she probably should, especially as it was a good way for her to get to know everyone, but she wasn't ready to finish up yet. She was only just getting started. Pulling an overripe banana out of her bag, she politely declined and poured herself another coffee. This would have to satisfy her rumbling tummy for now as she read on into the evening.

Klara's parents, Lars and Freja, had flown over

immediately, along with their son Hugo. They had demanded more be done to look for their daughter and had searched the streets themselves, handing out flyers they had printed to anyone and everyone. They had even hired a private investigator who couldn't find any trace of her either.

Once Klara had been officially missing for six months, they finally went home, but her father rang the ACC once a month looking for an update on his daughter's case. Tracy sighed, she knew she would have to speak to him soon and update him on her discovery, but she also knew she would have to run this past the ACC first. And she needed hard evidence. She had a car and a hunch - but without a registration plate, could not prove it was the same person and wasn't more than just a coincidence. Either way, neither was a conversation she was looking forward to having.

Tracy logged into Facebook and trawled through Klara's posts. There were several posts from her time in Aviemore and Glen Eden. Again, all happy posts of her having fun, by the looks of it. Before this, her posts were full of her time in London with her friends - shopping in Harrods, riding the London Eye, visiting Buckingham Palace and the Tower of London and plenty of them partying in a beautiful penthouse apartment with phenomenal views overlooking central London, which Tracy presumed must have been where the girls had been staying.

Going back further were posts of her with her friends at

home in Sweden, with her parents and various other family members. There were posts of her when she was younger - horse riding, some of her competing in dressage competitions and winning some trophies. There were photographs of her skiing and posts of her in scrubs on her first hospital placement at medical school.

Her status listed her as being in a relationship with Sven Lindstrom, a fellow medical student. This immediately struck her as odd that neither of her parents had mentioned this when interviewed. And, where was he? Surely, he would have rushed over to Scotland the minute she went missing. There was no mention of him anywhere in the reports, and it certainly didn't look like investigating officers had spoken to him.

According to her Facebook account, they had been dating since meeting during her first year at university. Tracy wondered if he had continued with his course whilst Klara had decided to take this gap year alone. She also wondered why on earth you would take a gap year part-way through a course as intense as medicine. Most students usually do it before or after university.

This made her wonder if something had happened between them, or maybe with her parents or even on the course itself. Tracy thought it slightly odd that no one would mention him, especially since they had been together for three years. She was also beginning to think it strange that

Klara should decide to just take off on her own, especially when she still had another two years to go before finishing her medical degree. Her eldest son, Callum, had been forced to do this due to the Covid pandemic which had effectively changed everyone's plans. But given the option, he would have preferred the gap year before he started his course.

It was too late to speak to anyone now, but after a quick search on the university website, she found the contact details for the medical school. Tracy wrote the name and number on her notepad, planning to speak with them first thing in the morning. She also printed off a copy of the names of all the employees at the hotel, which she planned on cross-referencing with those at the hostel and with the DVLA in case any of them owned a black Range Rover. A quick glance at her watch revealed it was 20:10, definitely time to head home. The glazier was starting at her house today, and she was keen to see his progress.

Although it was dark, as soon as Tracy pulled into the driveway, she could immediately see the difference in the front of her home. It had been completely transformed from a dreary old, dilapidated cottage into a sleek modern version of itself. She stood back and admired it for a few minutes. Her gorgeous new front door had been installed, too, so she had to make her way around to the back of the house as she didn't have a key for the new door yet.

Using the torch on her iPhone, she squeezed past the

overgrown rose bushes at the side of the house and fumbled around until she found the bolt on the gate; sliding it across, she continued along the dark path until she could just make out the light coming from the kitchen extension. Thankfully the guys had left a light on in there for her.

She let herself it and shoved another ready meal into the microwave before wandering around the house to admire her lovely new windows from the inside. John, the glazier, had left her a note on the kitchen table along with her new front door keys. He hoped she was pleased with everything and promised to return the following day to finish the job. She removed one and popped it straight onto the ring with her car keys in case she forgot in the morning. The new back door would be in by then too, so she didn't want to be locked out.

Looking around, she was not disappointed. Although anthracite grey on the outside, she had opted for white on the inside. They looked amazing, and best of all, for the first time since moving in, no drafts were coming through. She was also amazed at how quiet the house was now. Time to think about that dog once all these renovations are over. She shouted to *Alexa* to play some Depeche Mode and sat down at the kitchen table with her microwave meal for one.

22

Wednesday 26th October

Katie had enjoyed a leisurely day yesterday. She had spent the morning wandering around Inverness Museum and Art Gallery, stopping for a bite to eat afterwards at one of the little cafes inside the old Victorian Market, which is a charming little shopping arcade built around the end of the 19th century. In the afternoon she had strolled out to the Botanic Gardens, which thanks to the bus tour she discovered were only thirty minutes away. She was enchanted by their secret garden, which was tucked away at the back through a ramshackle gate.

Today, she was up bright and early as she'd booked a day trip for herself that visited Cawdor Castle in the morning, followed by a tour of Glen Ord distillery in the afternoon. Although Katie wasn't a whisky drinker, her dad was, and the man in the tourist office told her no trip to the highlands would be complete without a trip to at least one of the many local distilleries.

Feeling a little tipsy after the three free samples, she picked up a bottle of 12-year-old single malt whisky as a gift for her dad, as her parents had promised to come and visit her in Inverness for Christmas.

While she was enjoying herself, her admirer was never too far away, watching her every move. Biding his time, getting to know her again. He didn't take the tour with her, but he followed along behind the bus, stopping at each place they visited. No one noticed that an extra person was tagging along with them, they were all too absorbed in their surroundings.

23

DS McGregor stopped by the hostel again on her way to the station. She wanted to ask for a list of employees around the time both Erin and Natalia had gone missing, and she also wanted to know if Klara had ever stayed there. The girl in reception was very accommodating. She had to check with the head office first, who confirmed they were happy for her to release this information. Tracy was disappointed to learn it would probably take a few days, though, as they'd have to go through two different computer systems. Still, they promised to email this directly to her as soon as it was available, which was better than nothing.

There was no record of Klara ever having stayed there. Given how wealthy her family appeared to be, this had been a bit of a long shot, but she felt it had been worth checking, especially given that two of the four girls had stayed here, even if it was just to rule it out as a possible connection.

Once she got into the office, she called Professor Anderson at the Karolina Medical Institute, where Klara and Sven were both students. She got through to her secretary, and left a message, asking her to call back as soon as she was free.

Meanwhile, she started looking into Klara's financial records. Just like Erin and Natalia, her parents had been fully supporting her. Nice one if you could afford it, she thought to herself. But then again, if she and Rob had the money, she knew they would have done the same for their son. Callum and his friends had worked in bars, restaurants and even for a short time as strawberry pickers to support themselves on their gap year. Just like the other two, there had been no large withdrawals before she went missing, and there had been no withdrawals after she was last seen on CCTV. She couldn't help but think she was missing something.

She considered asking for the three girls' full banking records, which she knew would take time and require their parents' authorisation. Still, she knew the ACC would demand a damn good reason for her asking for these, so thought she would put this on the back burner for now. Erin's parents knew she was looking into their daughter's disappearance, but she had yet to talk to Natalia and Klara's parents. She would have to tell them both at some point though, so she figured there was no better time than the present. Although she'd have to keep quiet about any links she'd found between other cases at this stage, as the last thing she needed was her new ACC breathing down her neck.

She decided to start with Mr and Mrs Eriksson. Mr

Eriksson rang the ACC religiously on the first Monday of every month for a progress report on his daughter's disappearance, so she thought he might be quite pleased we had contacted him for once, plus there was an up-to-date telephone number on the system for him. She dialled the number and waited. His PA answered the phone. Mr Eriksson was the CEO of Svenska Handelsbanken, one of the largest banks in Sweden. She was put on hold for a few minutes before being finally put through to him.

He had a strong Scandinavian accent but spoke perfect English. DS McGregor introduced herself and explained who she was and her role in his daughter's case. He was keen to listen to everything she had to say and, despite being a very busy man, seemed in no rush to get rid of her. It was evident in talking to him that he would do anything to discover what had happened to his daughter.

She was careful what she told him at this stage, though, as she didn't want to say anything until she had the evidence to fully back up her hunch. He told her he would assist in any way he could, offering to take his private jet and head straight to her. She quickly explained that wasn't necessary at this stage, but she did ask if she could speak over Zoom with him and his wife that evening. He immediately agreed, and they exchanged details and scheduled a call for 8 pm. She knew she shouldn't take work home with her, but she was determined not to let this go. This time she was 100%

focused on the case and nothing else.

While waiting on the hostel staff list, she ran a DVLA check on all the staff from Ness View Hotel. She instantly got a match - the manager Mr David Forsyth owned a black Range Rover from April 2014 to March 2017. This could cover the time when Natalia and Klara disappeared but not Erin.

Excited, she looked further into his DVLA history. He had a black Audi Q5 registered to him from 2017-2021 and a navy-blue BMW iX3 currently registered to him. Before this, he had a dark grey BMW X5 registered to him between 2010 to 2014. She printed off these details, which had the registration plates for each.

He had been on duty during the day of Klara's disappearance, but according to his statement and that of reception staff, he left the hotel at around 5 pm that day. She went back to the CCTV footage again and rewound it to 16:50. Sure enough, there was a tall, well-built man dressed in a navy suit seen leaving via the main reception at 17:07. He made his way over to a black Range Rover, which was parked in a space directly in front of the reception, climbed in and drove off. She could clearly see his registration plate as he drove down the driveway, proving there was nothing wrong with the camera.

Deflated, she closed her laptop, knowing she could probably cross him off as a suspect. It wasn't him. The other black Range Rover with the concealed plates was already sitting in the car park and continued to sit there for a further fifteen minutes after Klara left the hotel. She sat back in her chair and sighed.

Natalia

DS McGregor opened Natalia's case file again and took out the contact details for her parents, and gave them a call. Her father, Simon, answered the phone in fluent Italian but quickly switched to English as soon as she spoke. She apologised for calling out of the blue like this and, not wanting to alarm him, immediately said she didn't have news but wanted to update him and his wife as soon as possible that she was working on their daughter's case. Hearing this, he relaxed a little and expressed his gratitude that someone was finally looking back at his daughter's disappearance. He wanted to know all that she knew.

Again, she was cautious with her choice of words and told him her investigation was in the very early stages. She informed them she was going right back to the start and, as a former DCI in the CID, intended to look into all possibilities. Mainly what she needed from Mr and Mrs Robertson at the minute was some background on their daughter, her likes, dislikes, hobbies, personality, and state of mind when she took off on her road trip.

Simon was working from home, so he called his wife Sofia through into his study and put the call on loudspeaker so she could hear what Tracy had to say, allowing her to add any relevant comments.

They both said their daughter was a happy-go-lucky type of girl. She had excelled at school, and having an Italian mother and Scottish father was bilingual. This helped her get into Strathclyde University as an international student, where she studied mechanical engineering. She had graduated with a 1st class honours degree in 2013 but had decided to stay on and complete her Master's degree while she was there, as she was one of the few students in her class who had been invited to do so.

They were so proud of her, living away from home all these years, although her grandparents (Simon's parents) lived in nearby Renfrewshire, so they hadn't been too worried about her being so far away, as she had plenty of relatives living nearby all offering to keep an eye out for her. Her father had talked so fondly of his time growing up in the highlands (they had moved to Glasgow when he was sixteen), that she decided she wanted to travel and explore the area herself before heading home to Italy.

She had saved and paid for the trip, having worked in a local restaurant in the evenings and weekends while studying. It had been her treat to herself for all her hard work. She was excited about her trip, which she had meticulously planned and she set up a travel blog that he and his wife had religiously followed. Everywhere she went, she posted regular updates, and then one day, nothing.

Mrs Robertson, Sofia, got quite upset at this point and begged Tracy to find her and bring her home. Being a parent herself, Tracy felt for the pair of them. Much as she'd love to, this was a promise that she knew she couldn't make, but she did promise to do everything in her power to try and find out what had happened to their daughter.

She asked their permission to access her bank and mobile phone records, which they readily agreed to and were happy to put this in writing. Tracy said she would email them the relevant paperwork immediately to get started on this.

Tracy mentioned the items Natalia had purchased at the charity shop and asked if they knew of any event she may have been buying them for - perhaps a wedding or maybe a christening? Her parents couldn't think of anything immediately but agreed to think about it and let her know if they remembered anything afterwards. It had been so long ago.

Before she ended the call, she asked if they could remember if Natalia had told them anything about where she might have been headed on her last few days in Inverness. The phone was silent for a moment. Tracy wondered if she had lost connection when suddenly Mrs Robertson spoke and said she remembered her daughter mentioning something about a ghost tour or a visit to a haunted house. She wasn't quite sure which and couldn't remember if Natalia had given them any further details. Natalia was fascinated with ghosts and loved watching *YouTube* videos of people visiting spooky places.

Tracy felt the hair on the back of her neck stand up. This was not the first time she had heard this. She ended the call and thought back to the conversation she'd had only a few nights ago with Betty. Betty had mentioned several haunted places in Inverness, but only three were actual houses - Inverness Castle, Cawdor Castle and Loch Wood House unless you counted the theatre.

When she spoke to them later this evening, she made a note to try and casually ask Klara's parents if Klara had mentioned anything similar. Before she talked to them, though, she still had one more case file she wanted to read first - that of Jessica Fletcher, the fourth missing girl.

24

Jessica

Twenty-three-year-old au pair Jessica Fletcher from Canada was last seen on Saturday, the 28th of July, 2018. Jessica had travelled to the UK from her home in Toronto on the 1st of May to start a 24-month contract as an au pair with a local family, arranged via the Global Work and Travel agency. She was staying with the Stewart family in the separate granny flat of their five-bedroom detached family home.

Melanie and John Stewart had three boys, Josh, Oliver and Jacob, who were three, five and seven at the time. Mr Stewart was the CEO of a large pharmaceutical company and was often away on business, leaving his wife home alone with their three boys, who were a bit of a handful. Josh had cerebral palsy, so needed a lot of one-on-one care, making it difficult to care for the two older boys.

They had welcomed Jessica into their home to help take some of the pressure off Melanie when John was away, ensuring the other two boys didn't feel left out. Jessica's younger brother had cerebral palsy, so they decided she was the perfect match when the agency suggested her to them. It had taken a few months since they first met her for her visa to come through, but when it finally did, Jessica had packed up her things and headed straight over, eager to get started.

The boys and the family loved her. She had instantly slotted in as if she had known them for years. Oliver, who had been quite shy and reserved, was coming out of his shell, despite the short time she had been there and Jacob seemed to have bonded with her too.

They had been scheduled to go on a family holiday to Florida for three weeks, which had been booked before they hired Jessica. The plan was for Jessica to go with them, but as there had been a delay with her visa, she ended up staying behind. They had been devastated that she was missing out on the trip with them, but she had assured them there would be plenty for her to see and do whilst they were away. It was her first time in Scotland.

She had been an au pair in Australia and New Zealand for two years before coming to Scotland, so she was well used to being far away from home. They reluctantly said goodbye to her on the 15th of July and set off on their holiday. Jessica was already included on Mrs Stewart's car insurance as she used to take the boys to school and nursery, so they had given their permission for her to use Melanie's car whilst they were away. They were happy for her to do a bit of sightseeing herself. They even left her some extra money to cover groceries and fuel while they were away.

She had visited all the local places of interest, including Loch Ness, Urquhart Castle, the Black Isle, and Dunrobin Castle. They regularly FaceTimed each other, and the Stewarts said she had seemed genuinely pleased to hear of their adventures in Disney World and Universal Studios. She had appeared sad that she wasn't there enjoying it all with them.

The Stewart family last heard from her on Friday, the 27th of July, one week before they were due to head home. When they returned, Jessica and all of her belongings were gone. The house and car keys had been posted through their letter box. There was no note, and nothing had been taken; the house had been left immaculate. They contacted the agency which they had hired her from, but they hadn't heard anything from her and didn't seem to be able to get in contact with her either.

Finding this strange, the agency contacted her parents, who didn't even know she was in the UK. She had fallen out with them after quitting university and falling in with the wrong crowd. However, she had turned her life around and become an au pair, and Tracy would learn from Mrs Stewart's statement, had been desperate to reconcile with them.

Mrs Stewart had become really fond of Jessica, so

frustrated and worried, she contacted the police and reported her missing. Her disappearance was a mystery, but as all her belongings were gone, the police put it down to her simply leaving of her own accord. Tracy had to admit it did sound a bit like that on the surface, but at the same time, her gut was telling her that something wasn't quite right.

Through Interpol, Mrs Stewart had contacted Jessica's parents, Angus and Samantha, who had flown over from Canada to look for their daughter, handing out flyers in the town and securing them to lampposts as they searched the streets for any trace of her.

As a result of these flyers, a local hairdresser, Donna Lindsay, had come forward to say she had seen Jessica on the afternoon of the 28th of July. Jessica had come into her salon asking if she had any space to squeeze her in to have her hair done for an event she was attending that evening. She said Jessica had seemed excited about going somewhere but didn't elaborate, and as Donna didn't know her, she hadn't pushed for more information.

It had been a busy afternoon in the salon, and Jessica had just popped in unannounced to see if they could fit her in. Donna was heavily pregnant at the time. She was almost into her third trimester, so her feet were aching, having been on them all day. Still, when she initially tried to say she was fully booked, Jessica had looked so genuinely deflated that she reluctantly agreed.

She had straightened Jessica's curly hair and pinned it up, leaving a few loose strands. She looked very glam. Donna presumed she was maybe an evening guest at a wedding reception. There were several large wedding venues in and around Inverness. Investigating officers seemed to agree. Tracy, however, didn't think this seemed possible, because she couldn't have known many people in Inverness. Yet, no one had questioned this or followed it up.

Thinking back; Erin was possibly on her way to meet someone, whilst Natalia had been seen buying a cocktail dress and heels the day before she went missing. Now this. Could this somehow be linked? But she had looked at events in and around Inverness the day Natalia went missing and drawn a blank. She was pretty sure if she did the same for Jessica, she would also be met with nothing, but it was still worth checking. Five minutes later, a *Google* search came up with nothing apart from the Highland games and the national Whisky festival. Neither of these were the type of events you would either have to wear a cocktail dress to or have your hair done. This case was getting stranger and stranger, and she couldn't help but think she was missing something.

Like the other girls, Jessica's mobile phone was never found, and her bank account hadn't been touched either. Still, she would like to request the records for herself to see if there were any patterns or connections between the missing girls. Anywhere they might have visited in the days leading up to their disappearance.

A glance at her watch told her it was 5 pm, time to head home, as she wanted to have dinner before she spoke to the Eriksson's at 8 pm. Plus, she was eager to see if John had finished the rest of her windows yet.

She parked her car in front of the rather dilapidated garage and headed up to her new front door. Letting herself in, she headed through the hallway past the living room and straight out to the back of the house. The kitchen now had a beautiful set of bifold doors where the old sliding doors had been, giving a clear view of her somewhat overgrown garden.

The house seemed so much warmer. She turned the key in the lock and, lifting the handle, slid the three doors back until they had collapsed like a concertina against the far wall of the extension. She stepped through them onto the overgrown patio and stood back to admire the house from the outside. Although the light had faded and darkness was creeping in, the light from the moon was enough for her to see the back looked just as good as the front of her house. She felt a tear of pride at what she had achieved in such a short space of time.

The decorator was scheduled to start in the living room next week. After he had finished, she planned to stain and varnish the floor herself. She would have painted herself, but the ceilings were just too high downstairs, and there was some remedial plaster work to be done where some of the walls had crumbled away when she'd stripped the paper off them. Although she was handy, this was one task she'd rather leave to the professionals.

Feeling the nip in the air, she stepped back inside and pulled the doors over, carefully locking them behind her. She changed into comfortable sweatpants and popped another ready meal in the microwave. The free-standing oven looked rather scary, and it was so ancient that she hadn't tried it yet. Hopefully, her building warrant would come through soon for her building works, and she could look forward to choosing her new kitchen with a modern oven.

***

The Eriksson's called her right on time. Tracy had settled herself into the snug with the log burner on, setting her laptop up on the coffee table and angling it so they couldn't see she was wearing sweatpants.

They were a glamorous older couple, and it was immediately apparent how attached to their daughter they were. Mr Eriksson was still wearing a suit, whilst his wife was wearing a pretty pale pink pussy bow blouse with black trousers. She had blonde hair with Carmel highlights, cut in long wavy layers with a side fringe. Her eyes were the palest blue. Although she must be in her mid-fifties, she didn't look a day over thirty-five. Tracy wondered to herself if she used Botox. Her husband's hair was pure white in comparison. He was a jolly man with small gold-rimmed glasses.

Tracy introduced herself mainly for Mrs Eriksson's benefit and explained her role in their daughter's case. She talked about her extensive experience and how she was determined to find out what happened to their daughter, but to do this, she would need them to be brutally honest with her. They both nodded vigorously and said they were willing to do anything to discover what happened to their daughter.

She tried to put them at ease before asking about the boyfriend, talking about simple things. What kind of a child she had been; how their relationship was with her whilst she was growing up and her relationship with her older brother? They talked animatedly about their daughter, and it was pretty clear they had a relatively close relationship with her.

She then carefully steered the conversation towards the gap year and whose idea it had been. They seemed a little uneasy with this, and it was Mr Eriksson who spoke first, saying his daughter was struggling with the pressures of living away from home and studying for such an intense course, and he had been the one to suggest she take some time out. Some of her friends from school were living in London, so she had gone to stay with them initially before moving up to Scotland. Her tutors had been very supportive, and the university agreed she could take one year out of her course. Her parents had fully funded and supported her time out. Although she could see no reason for them to lie, the professor from the medical school in Sweden hadn't called her back yet, so she fully intended to confirm this with them when she spoke to them.

Seizing the opportunity to ask about the boyfriend, she first asked if anything, in particular, had happened to make their daughter feel this way? They both said no - almost a bit too quickly. So, Tracy asked if she might have disagreed with someone, maybe a tutor or perhaps a fight with her boyfriend? She noticed them both tense up at the mention of a boyfriend. Mr Eriksson spoke first, asking her why she would think that? Realising she had touched a raw nerve and not wanting to antagonise them, she backed down and said she was just curious, with his daughter being a pretty young woman.

To change the subject, Tracy then asked how much luggage Klara had taken with her? Her mum said she had taken two large suitcases, a matching carry-on, and a handbag. DS McGregor figured she wouldn't be flying economy then, as that was way more than your standard allowance. When she asked if they were anything distinctive about them - her mum said they were bright red Louis Vuitton suitcases.

Finally, Tracy asked if they knew if their daughter was interested in ghosts? They both looked at one another rather bewildered before saying 'yes' and asking how on earth she could have known that. She told them it was just a hunch she was working on, but she knew neither of them actually believed her. She just hoped they wouldn't go straight to her ACC; she wasn't quite ready to deal with him yet. So far, he had pretty much left her to her own devices.

She finished the call by promising to keep in touch regularly with them but asked if, in the meantime, they would mind sending over their daughter's banking and mobile phone records. She also asked if it was possible to speak with some of her friends that she had been staying with in London. They agreed to both.

She closed her laptop and scrolled through Netflix, not really watching anything, before finally heading up to bed. Exhausted, she tossed and turned most of the night, dreaming about each one of the girls again - lying dead, beside Robbie.

25

Thursday 27th October

On Thursday Katie caught the number 27 bus out to Culloden battlefield, where she spent the morning in the impressive visitor centre; marvelling at the numerous artefacts and displays along with the 360-degree battle immersion theatre, which transported her straight back to 1746, and the heart of the action.

After a hearty bowl of delicious homemade soup and an enormous scone and jam, she wrapped up warmly before venturing out onto the eerie moor. Just like every other day, he wasn't far behind her.

As she followed the gravel path around the battle lines, past the front-line flags and the many soldiers' graves, a sudden gust of wind caused her scarf to blow off and go sailing through the air. Before he knew what was happening Katie had turned on her heels and was coming charging towards him, chasing after her scarf. Caught off guard out in the open, he panicked at first as he realised there was nowhere for him to go. This was it! They were about to meet – face-to-face for the first time in years.

Adrenaline surging, he gallantly tried to catch it for her. The scarf eventually landed a few feet from where he was standing. They both reached for it at the same time, locking eyes as they did so, although his were shielded behind the dark glasses he was wearing. He paused for a moment, instantly transported back in time. To him, it felt like yesterday since he had gazed into those beautiful blue eyes, oh how he longed to take her in his arms. Lost in thought, it took him a few minutes before he realised she was speaking to him. She had no idea who he was. He reluctantly handed her scarf back to her and wandered off. Annoyed at himself, he would have to be more careful in future. He had revealed himself too early. Maybe she wasn't ready to acknowledge him yet.

Meanwhile, Katie stood rooted to the spot, blushing at her brush with the handsome, moody stranger who had wandered off muttering to himself.

26

DS McGregor had just sat down at her desk when her phone rang, Professor Anderson from the Karolina Medical Institute was returning her call. She apologised for not calling back the day before but had been out of the office all day interviewing for a new faculty deputy head. Tracy explained she was looking into the disappearance of Klara Eriksson and wondering if she could possibly shed some light on why Klara had taken a gap year. Knowing she was probably out of her jurisdiction, but chancing her arm anyway, she also asked if she could check on another student at that time, the boyfriend, Sven Lindstrom.

Professor Anderson went very quiet, so quiet Tracy had to ask her to speak up. The poor lady seemed genuinely petrified and asked if she told her something; could she keep it strictly between them? She knew she could get into serious trouble for talking to her about a former student, but felt Tracy had a right to know. Tracy assured her their conversation would stay between them.

Professor Anderson took a deep inhale and then began her story. Klara and Sven met in her first year at university.

He was in the year above her. He was on a scholarship programme and came from a modest working-class background, his mother a nurse and his father a factory worker, whilst Klara, in comparison, was from one of the wealthiest families in Sweden.

He was very charming and also very clever. The girls loved him, and by all accounts, Klara's parents loved him too. They quickly became inseparable, moving in together, but by midway through her second year, Klara had become very withdrawn. She had gone from being this bright and vibrant girl to a meek, passive individual who no longer took pride in her appearance.

Her friends and lecturers noticed she had stopped wearing make-up and started wearing frumpy, baggy clothes. She had stopped participating in any of the extracurricular activities at the university and seemed to do everything with Sven. Some of her tutors had tried to talk to her, but he was always there, lurking around in the background.

Things eventually came to a head in her third year when she collapsed on clinical placement in one of the local hospitals. When one of the doctors examined her, he was horrified to discover she was covered in bruises. Some old, and some very new ones, all carefully placed where no one would see them - abdomen, back, top of legs etc. It turns out Sven was bipolar and had been mentally and physically abusing her for months. She had collapsed that morning as he had struck her so hard in the stomach that he had caused her to haemorrhage, resulting in her needing an emergency hysterectomy. If she hadn't collapsed in the hospital, she would have died through blood loss.

Sven was immediately arrested and remanded in custody without bail, pending the court case. He was expelled from the university, and Klara was given as much time off as she needed to help her recover. Klara's parents were keen for none of this to come out as they are fiercely private people and wanted to protect their daughter as much as possible. They also felt guilty for having been taken in by him.

Tracy was horrified when she heard this and understood now why they wouldn't want to mention any of this, especially if they thought this information would mean no one would take their daughter's disappearance seriously. They probably thought if they'd told the police this at the time, they would have thought it sounded as if she had disappeared deliberately and committed suicide after all that had happened to her. To be fair – who could blame them?

Professor Anderson went on to say the case never went to trial as Sven was mysteriously found dead in his cell one morning by one of the guards. He hanged himself, but on what no one knows, as he was held in a windowless cell and was supposed to be watched twenty-four-seven. She then said in a voice that was barely more than a whisper that the Eriksson's are a very powerful family in Sweden. Tracy couldn't help but think she was trying to say she wondered if Mr Eriksson had something to do with his death.

Professor Anderson said that she had been to visit Klara in the hospital after her surgery. She was heavily sedated at the time, but she remembered she looked different somehow as if a huge weight had been lifted. It was almost as if the real Klara was slowly re-emerging. She spent several months in therapy at a private clinic before planning this gap year.

Klara had stopped by her office to sign some paperwork before she left for London, and they had chatted over a coffee, where she seemed optimistic about her future and was looking forward to returning to her studies the following autumn. Although her physical scars had healed, it was clear she was still working on the mental ones and needed a bit more time, hence the year out, but she was a fighter. He might have stolen her ability to become a mum naturally, but she was determined he would not destroy her life.

She had left her office with a spring in her step and was looking forward to seeing her friends again and escaping her suffocating parents for a little while as they now never let her out of their sight. As a parent herself, Tracy understood this.

Tracy thanked her very much for sharing this with her

and promised not to mention it when talking to her parents, and she genuinely meant it. If Mr Eriksson was as powerful as Professor Anderson suggested, she wanted to stay on his good side. She hung up the phone and sat silently for a few minutes staring at the handset, thinking about poor Klara and all that she had gone through. She wouldn't blame her for running off, but the person she had watched in that video had been walking with a spring in her step, her ponytail bouncing between her shoulder blades. Just like the girl Professor Anderson had described. She certainly didn't look to her like someone who was about to take her own life.

Tracy wondered why on earth Klara would have left her Facebook profile as being in a relationship with such a monster. Logging back on to take a closer look, she quickly realised Klara hadn't actually posted anything herself in a very long time. She had been tagged in every single post since her arrival in the UK by one of her friends.

She did a quick search on *Google* and found a tiny article about a Sven Lindstrom, aged twenty-four, who had hanged himself in prison whilst awaiting trial in 2015. There was no mention of what he was on trial for. She couldn't help but wonder if perhaps Mr Eriksson had had something to do with this after all.

She looked over at her whiteboard and, grabbing her marker pen, started to add up what she knew so far about each girl's disappearance - looking for a pattern, something she must be missing.

Erin Doherty; American citizen; aged 23; five foot three; blue eyes; dark brown curly hair; travelling initially with friends but on her own for the last week; last confirmed sighting Sunday the 5th of August 2012; wearing jeans/pink blouse/white Converse/pink bag -? going on a date or meeting someone; witness places Black Range Rover near the scene (no number plate details available); no access to a car; phone switched off; bank accounts untouched; possible visit to a haunted house before disappearance?; all her belongings were left behind.

Natalia Robertson; Italian citizen; aged 24; five foot four; blue eyes; dark brown curly hair; travelling alone; last confirmed sighting Saturday the 19th of July 2014; black Range Rover spotted on CCTV footage of her leaving the car rental depot only days before her disappearance (no plates); spotted in charity shop buying a fancy dress and heels; final text message sent and received to an unknown number indicating she was on her way to meet someone Sunday 20th. July; Mum mentioned a possible visit to a haunted house; no possessions left behind at the hostel; keys returned.

Klara Eriksson; Swedish national; aged 21; five foot three; blue eyes; dark brown curly hair; last confirmed sighting Sunday the 25th of June 2016; wearing jeans/blazer/ cross body navy bag/white Converse; black Range Rover caught on CCTV possibly following her from her hotel - number plates concealed; had access to a car, but this was left behind; no belongings left behind yet other than a small cross body bag - she was not carrying any of the rest of her belongings at last known sighting; rental car keys and room key left neatly in her room; interested in ghosts.

Jessica Fletcher; Canadian citizen; aged 23; five foot three and a half; blue eyes; brown curly hair; working as an au pair; family she was working for were on holiday at the time of her disappearance; had access to a car; last confirmed sighting Saturday the 28th of July 2018; had recently had her hair done as if she was headed out somewhere special; no mobile phone found; bank accounts untouched; all possessions gone.

Looking back at the board, she could see so many similarities between the cases, but she still didn't have anything concrete - other than their appearance at the moment that tied them all together. She knew she was onto something, though she could feel it. If only she had a registration plate for that black Range Rover. Time to look back through their social media accounts again. This time she was looking for evidence of them visiting the same places.

She logged into each girl's account and started making notes of all the local places each one had visited. By 1 pm, she had compiled this information into a table and cross-referenced each location everyone had visited. There were plenty of matches but nothing was standing out to her yet. Her head pounding, she rubbed her eyes and went to grab another coffee.

27

On her way home from her trip to Culloden, Katie finally bumped into Lily, who invited her in for a coffee, which turned into dinner and a few glasses of wine. Lily's apartment had a very similar layout to Katie's, except it was much larger and had a huge kitchen diner. It was very modern, with white walls and porcelain floor tiles throughout, not at all what Katie was expecting.

The white walls were adorned with beautiful artwork, including a painting of a ballerina mid-pirouette. She looked familiar, but Katie wasn't sure how. Turned out this was a watercolour of Lily as a young lady. Lily was a retired former prima ballerina. She had travelled the world with the Royal Ballet company and, consequently, had lived in many different countries. She was originally from the highlands and had always vowed to return to her roots one day.

She was seventy-five, but Katie wouldn't have put her a day over sixty. She still practiced yoga daily and invited Katie to join her sometime. She was divorced and had a son and a daughter, both married and three grandchildren who all lived in America. Katie didn't mean to pry, but Lily was such a fascinating lady who was so easy to talk to. It wasn't long before she told her the whole story about Matt and April and why she had ended up here. Lily listened intently but never once passed judgement on her. Before she knew it, three hours had passed, but what a lovely three hours it had been. It was so nice to finally have a friend.

Katie returned to her apartment, vowing to try the yoga class sometime. Some younger girls went along, too, so Lily had offered to introduce her to them. At the end of the month, some of the group took turns to meet up at one another's houses for drinks and a takeaway. This sounded just like what Katie needed. Hopefully, she could work it around the shifts for her new job.

Katie told Lily all about her plans for Saturday. Turns out Lily had known Mr and Mrs Campbell-McNair quite well. They had been a pillar of the community and often donated large amounts of time and money to support some of the local charities. She had been distraught when she heard they had died. Lily said the accident had always puzzled her, though. Emilia had come home from Paris that weekend as she was convinced she had a stalker. He or she had even broken into her apartment one night. She had come back unexpectedly one evening as she'd forgotten something on her way to a gallery show and found a window open, the curtain flapping in the wind. There was also a smell of expensive aftershave lingering in the air that she didn't recognise. The police in Paris hadn't been much help as there were no signs of forced entry, so she had come home to ask her dad for help as she had been absolutely terrified after that. He had been planning to hire a private investigator and a security team to keep a watchful eye on her.

Emilia had been a very experienced rider; this was her own horse whom she had raised from a foal. It didn't make any sense, even after all this time she said no one could ever figure out exactly what had happened that day. Lily had always wondered if her stalker had followed her home. But the police ruled out foul play, stating it was just a tragic accident.

She said Fraser had never been the same after this. He had called off his engagement and spent much of his time overseas or in London, leaving the running of Loch Wood House to the Brown family, who looked after the grounds. It was only in the last few years that Fraser had started to retake an interest in the house.

As she lay in bed that night Katie thought back to the horse she had seen in the corner of the photograph of the crash scene, perhaps Lily was right. She wished she had mentioned it now. Although, maybe Lily would have thought she was crazy. She drifted off to sleep, looking forward to her day tomorrow.

28

Friday 29th October

Last but not least, on Katie's list, was a trip to the world-famous Loch Ness. After all, she couldn't end her week without a chance to look for Nessie - the famous Loch Ness monster. As she didn't have access to a car, Katie settled on another day trip from the town centre that consisted of a return coach journey to Loch Ness, a cruise across the world-famous waters and entry to the historic ruins of the mighty Urquhart Castle.

In true Scottish style, it started raining as soon as the bus arrived to pick them up in Inverness. Katie was glad of the raincoat she had returned to grab before leaving that morning. There was no rain forecast, and it had been sunny when she first left the apartment. Still, she had read so many reviews online about the eerie mist accompanied by a cold, harsh wind that often blows over the loch, even in the middle of a hot summer's day, and thought it might make a good windbreaker.

The dark, peaty waters kept their secrets that day – there was no sign of Nessie, although she had laughed when a few kids on the tour took great delight at pretending to some elderly passengers that a piece of driftwood was the monster. It had a few people fooled, with people clambering over the seats to get a better view, until the captain let them borrow his binoculars. It became a bit of a queasy ride towards the end, though, and Katie was glad when they were back on solid ground. Thankfully the rain had stopped by the time the cruise ended, but the wind had picked up.

By the time they made their way down to Urquhart Castle, the wind was so severe it could cut you in two. She felt she might be blown away when walking between the gatehouse and Grant Tower in the Nether Bailey. Her hair was in knots by the time she got back on the bus – there was no way she was getting a comb through it, so she sat with it in a tangled mess the whole way back. Sad at there being no sight of Nessie today, there was no doubt she had had fun and had a natural glow about her with all this fresh air. Slowly the real Katie was starting to re-emerge.

Careful not to make the same mistake as yesterday, he slowly tailed her in the Range Rover today, hiding behind the privacy of the blackened glass. He watched from a distance at Urquhart Castle, using his binoculars to follow her movements. As he left her that evening, he was smiling to himself. Only one more day until he made his move.

They would be together soon.

29

A little after 11:30, Betty popped her head around the door to let Tracy know a large parcel from America had just arrived for her, finally - Erin's duffle bag! Excited, Tracy grabbed her phone and headed out to the front reception. On seeing the size of it, she asked the duty Sergeant, a lovely young lad called Stuart, if any of the interview rooms were free and if he wouldn't mind helping her. On finding out room four was free, he lifted one end of the large parcel, whilst she grabbed the other and they made their way along the corridor together.

With her parcel safely inside, she closed the door behind her, remembering to pull across the occupied sign on the outside of the door. It felt good to be back inside an interview room. She had thrived on this part of the job, and her attention to detail often left suspects squirming in their seats whilst she caught them out on their lies. Sadly, she wondered if she would ever be doing anything like that again. Maybe if she kept her head down here for a few months, all might be forgiven, but somehow, she doubted that. She might have to stick to this type of detective work for the rest of her career.

Back to the task in front of her, she pulled on a pair of blue examination gloves and tied her shoulder-length mousey brown hair up into a ponytail. Using the pair of scissors Betty had given her, she began cutting open the packing tape used to seal the large box. Inside the box, wrapped in mountains of green bubble wrap, was the red duffle bag.

Before opening the duffle bag, she placed a clear plastic sheet on the table and began carefully lifting the contents out one by one, laying them flat on the table. A force of habit for her when dealing with evidence. Although she knew this was a cold case, and any evidence from this bag would be long gone, she carried on in her own meticulous fashion regardless.

The clothes at the top of the bag were neatly folded, indicating they must be the ones her mum said she had washed, whilst the ones at the bottom were quite badly crushed as if they'd been stuffed in there for years. They mostly smelled musty, but if you held them close to your nose, even after all this time, there was still a faint hint of a fruity floral perfume coming from a pretty pink jumper; she wondered how many times Erin's mother had done this since her daughter disappeared—trying to take comfort from it in her grief. She placed the jumper down on the table and emptied the bag.

There was an iPad; a charger; a make-up and wash bag - all with products still inside; a hairbrush; a hairdryer, and a set of hair straighteners with a UK adapter plug still attached to them. There was also a well-used copy of Italy's *Lonely Planet* guidebook along with a U.K. one which was in a slightly better condition.

In the large zipped pocket at the front of the bag, she found it was stuffed full of tickets, leaflets, receipts and maps for all the places she presumed they had visited on their travels. She placed these in a pile to one side, planning to come back to them later to see if there was anything useful amongst them.

The bag was pretty full, but she laid everything out before her, making her own list of every item, carefully photographing each as she went along. She was trying to figure out if any of her clothes (other than what she was wearing on the day she disappeared) were missing and was hoping the powers of social media would help her with that task. Although this wouldn't determine what had happened to her, she felt by doing this; she could at least try to prove that Erin hadn't intentionally disappeared.

Laying them all out in neat bundles on the table, she could see there were two pairs of jeans - both skinny style, one blue, one black. She counted seven t-shirts - two white; two black; one navy; one coral, and a light pink one. There were nine vest tops - two white; two black; a black and cream stripy one, and one each in red, navy, yellow and grey. There were three pairs of shorts – denim, navy and khaki. Three cardigans - one each in navy, black and cream. Two jumpers - pink and grey woollen jumpers.

She counted three floral summer dresses in green, blue and red—two floral blouses - one in blue tones, the other in black and pink. She counted three bras - two black, one white, ten pairs of underpants and six pairs of trainer socks. There was a pair of Victoria's Secret short pyjamas, two pairs of black leggings and a black long quilted Berghaus jacket that had been rolled up and tucked into the hood for storage.

There was a pair of khaki combat trousers, an old grey Pennsylvania university hoodie and a rather well-worn pair of navy canvas Converse. Finally, wrapped inside a plastic bag at the bottom of the pack, she found a long black silk strapless dress and a pair of high-heeled jewelled sandals. This struck her as strange as everything else in the bag was so casual; even the summer dresses were floaty tea dresses, but this was full-on glam.

She checked the label and discovered it was from *Coast.* She was pretty positive they didn’t exist outside of the UK, meaning only one thing - Erin must have bought it while she was here. Tracy didn't remember seeing her wearing anything like this on any of her Facebook posts. She took a couple of extra photographs of it and the shoes, intending to email her friends to see if they recognised it. Looking closely at the sandals, she could see they had been worn and somewhere gravelly, as tiny pieces of red gravel were embedded in each of the leather soles. She photographed this too, not yet knowing how but she had a strong feeling, that these were somehow connected to her disappearance.

She went through the pockets of the jeans and the jacket, adding the few crumpled receipts she found to the large pile of papers that she had found within the front pocket of the bag.

Laid out together like this, she had to admit this did seem like this probably was everything Erin had brought with her; and thinking back to when her eldest son had backpacked around Australia, she was even more convinced this looked like a similar amount of stuff that he had taken with him. The girls, if they were a similar size, might even have shared clothes.

She suddenly had a thought - the iPad! There was no mention in the police report if anyone from the tech team had ever examined it. Feeling quite excited, using Erin's travel plug she plugged it in and left it on charge in the corner, hoping it might reveal where Erin had been headed that evening. And if her iCloud had been backed up, any photos taken on her phone in the last few days before she disappeared might also be on it.

Whilst she waited on it charging, she turned back to the pile of leaflets, tickets and receipts. She sorted them into bundles of type and country. This seemed to take ages, but she was only really interested in the ones from in and around Inverness, so she had to further sort the UK pile into little bundles from Scotland, England, Wales and Northern Ireland. Eventually, she was left with a more manageable bundle from Scotland.

Separating this further, she was left with an even smaller pile from the highlands which included a ticket stub from Inverness Castle, a hop-on-hop-off bus ticket, an Urquhart castle and Loch Ness day trip ticket and leaflet; Cawdor Castle ticket and information leaflet; Duff house ticket and map; a receipt for lunch for three people at the Glenfiddich distillery; a theatre ticket for a performance of Swan Lake at Eden Court theatre on Thursday the 26th of July 2012; a ticket for a day trip to John O'Groats and the far North with '*Timbuktu And Back Tours*' and finally, a ticket for a day trip to the Isle of Skye and Eileen Donna Castle with '*Robbie Robb's Small Group tours*'.

There were website links for each of these tours on the tickets. Looking each one up, Tracy could see they were still in operation today and transportation was included from Inverness town centre, which explained how Erin and her friends managed to see so much without hiring a car. Although this was the more expensive way to do it, it gave you the benefit of having a tour guide meaning they could find out a little about the history of the places they were visiting whilst they were there, and more importantly for foreigners, it meant you didn't have to negotiate driving on the opposite side of the road from what you were used to—a much safer way for all.

Tracy thought she wouldn't mind going on some of these trips herself, they sounded terrific, and the photographs of the scenery and attractions looked stunning. She couldn't quite believe she now lived near some of these beautiful places. Maybe when she'd cracked this case, she'd allow herself a bit of downtime to explore the local area.

She took one last look inside the bag to ensure she had everything, and there at the very bottom, poking out from underneath the bottom lining, was a scrunched-up piece of cream parchment paper. She lifted it out and tried to smooth it out. The writing was completely smudged, and there was no way to make it what it said on it, but it looked like it might be a water-damaged leaflet for somewhere.

She was about to dismiss it entirely until she turned it over, and there in the centre, she could see a faded picture of a house or castle. On closer inspection, she could just about make out the wording along the top, Loch Wood House. Although it might just be a leaflet Erin had picked up, she added it to her list of places Erin had visited, as Erin must have thought it important if she'd hung onto it.

She turned back to the iPad, which was only sitting at 1% charge, she tried turning it on, but as it had been off for so long, it wouldn't move past the screen with an image of a charging battery on it, she hoped it maybe just needed to charge for a bit longer. After all, it probably hadn't been used in over a decade. Disappointed, she carefully packed Erin's clothes back into her duffle bag and put the rest of her travel souvenirs back into the front zipped pocket.

She put the local tickets and leaflets into a clear evidence bag for now, along with the water-damaged one, and removed her gloves, discarding them into the bin in the corner. Erin's parents had trusted her with Erin's bag, so not wanting it to go missing, she decided to take it back up to her office with her for now, along with the iPad, which she duly plugged back in again when she got there. She tried switching it on again but had no luck. It looks like she might have to leave it charging over the weekend.

She suddenly realised it was after 3 pm, and she had been so carried away looking at Erin's things she had missed lunch again. Her stomach was growling like mad. She grabbed a tuna sandwich and blueberry muffin from the café next door and made herself another coffee before she sat down to figure out the timeline of Erin's movements in Inverness using the receipts, ticket stubs and Facebook posts.

She knew from speaking to Mr Johnson, Mollie, and

Olivia that the girls had arrived in Inverness on Tuesday, the 24th of July, where they had planned to stay for two weeks, taking them up to the 7th of August. Mollie and Olivia had headed back down to Edinburgh on Tuesday, the 31st of July, leaving Erin on her own for seven days. She printed off a July/August 2012 calendar and started recording Erin's whereabouts on it.

On Tuesday the 24th of July, she wrote - arrived in Inverness. Opening the evidence bag, she took out the pieces of paper and started arranging them in date order. She discovered that on Wednesday the 25th, they took the hop-on hop-off bus tour and visited Inverness Castle. On Thursday the 26th, they went to the Glenfiddich distillery in the afternoon (she wondered if the girls had taken a tour) and the ballet in the evening at Eden Court. On Friday the 27th, they went on a day trip to Skye. On Saturday the 28th, they went on a day trip to Loch Ness and Urquhart Castle. There were no tickets for anything on Sunday the 29th, but from looking at Facebook, they had been out partying on Saturday night, so presumably, they were at the hostel nursing hangovers. Monday the 30th was their last full day together, where they had taken another trip, visiting John O'Groats and Dunrobin Castle.

On Tuesday the 31st, Erin had accompanied her friends to the train station. Wednesday, the 1st of August, she visited Cawdor Castle on her own. Thursday the 2nd, she had visited Duff house, again on her own. There were no receipts or tickets for Friday the 3rd, Saturday the 4th or Sunday the 5th - the day she potentially disappeared. She turned back to Facebook. Her last post was from Duff house, which she could see now was actually on the Thursday.

Erin had commented on some of her friends' posts and had spoken to them on Friday night, so she added this to the timeline. Under Sunday the 5th, she added Heidi - 18:30 and the black Range Rover sighting. So, there was only Saturday, the 4th of August, when other than the phone call to her parents, there were no known movements or contact for her.

Tracy looked back at the iPad. Seeing no change in the lock screen, she decided to head home for the weekend. Disappointed, she had a feeling she would have to hand it over to the tech team on Monday anyway to have it unlocked.

30

Saturday 29th October

By the time Saturday night arrived, Katie was actually feeling quite good about herself. She had made a friend and had enjoyed the last two weeks exploring her new surroundings. The hairdresser had worked her magic and teased her tight curls into sophisticated waves, which she had left loose, framing her face and covering her shoulders. Her new golden highlights added warmth to her face, complimenting the rosy glow she had gained from being outdoors so much these past two weeks.

The girl in the nail bar had recommended candy pink to compliment her new hairstyle, which had helped her make the final decision on her outfit for the evening. She had chosen to wear the black dress. Although she knew black can sometimes be seen as being quite sombre, she was feeling slightly nervous about the whole thing, so she thought it would probably be easier to blend into the background if she was wearing black, plus the matching shoes for this outfit weren't quite so high so would be easier to walk in.

This evening, she had been a bit braver with her eye makeup, emphasising her pretty blue eyes. Diamond earrings and a faux diamond tennis bracelet finished the look off. As she stood in front of the mirror, Katie hardly recognised herself. She had spent so much time moping around after Matt she had almost forgotten how good it felt to be all dressed up. A quick check at her watch reminded her she would have to head downstairs in a few minutes if she were to make the bus on time. She had booked a taxi to take her to the pick-up point as she didn't fancy walking the 1.4 miles into town, especially not in these shoes.

As she was walking downstairs, she met Lily, who almost didn't recognise her as she looked so different. Lilly gave her a quick hug and asked her to pop in for a coffee the next day to tell her all about her evening - if she wasn't too hungover. Katie hugged her back and promised she would before racing off downstairs to her waiting taxi.

By the time the taxi pulled into the station Katie was feeling quite anxious again. What if she was overdressed? What if no one else turned up, or everyone she met was creepy? It was too late to back out now. She needn't have worried; another nine anxious-looking people were waiting outside the train station when she stepped out of the taxi.

She walked over to the group, and once she had checked, they were also waiting to go on the tour, she introduced herself. There were four girls and five guys, all close in age to herself.

The girls, Suzy, Ellie, Lizzy and Rebecca, knew each other already. They were all radiographers and worked in the X-ray department at Raigmore Hospital. Hearing she had come alone, the girls quickly welcomed her into their group. Katie immediately felt relieved. It was nice to meet some friendly faces, and knowing these people would become some of her new colleagues, helped her relax a little.

The guys, Mike, Chris, Gordon, Richard and Joe, had all gone to school together and seemed friendly too. Maybe this night would turn out to be fun after all.

At 19:00 prompt, a black executive travel minibus pulled into a space outside the station. Katie felt her stomach lurch – there was no going back now. This was it. The driver swiftly hopped out and slid back the side door to the minibus, revealing a very extravagant and luxurious interior.

This was no standard minibus; this was full-on luxury celebrity style. Katie had never seen anything like it. It had plush reclining leather seats, individual tables, mood lighting, a glass roof and a 40-inch TV screen playing music videos on the back wall. There was a Nespresso coffee machine and two fridges.

The boys held back, allowing the girls to board first. Katie, who somehow ended up first in line, opted for one of the single seats behind the door on the vehicle's passenger side. Before they pulled away, the driver clicked open a box behind his seat. It turned out to be a pop-up purpose-built bar containing a rack of champagne flutes and invited each one to help themselves to a welcome glass of prosecco complete with a strawberry on top. Katie noticed three more full bottles of prosecco chilling on ice, waiting for them to top up their glasses.

Katie couldn't help but notice how handsome the driver was, and judging by the comments from Suzy and Lizzy, the other girls thought so too. He was over six feet tall, of athletic build, with short dark hair and a closely cropped beard, and was wearing a very expensive looking dark grey suit with a white shirt, black tie, black leather gloves and despite the privacy glass and the fact it was dark outside a grey chauffeur's cap. Katie thought he wouldn't have looked out of place at a James Bond audition.

The girls were whispering and giggling away amongst themselves, joking if he was going, then this night wouldn't turn out to be too bad after all. Katie felt an immediate pang of sadness as she thought about how if they'd been here - her friends Heather and Michelle would have reacted in exactly the same way. April would have been right in there; she would probably have had his number by now. But this night was not about April. April was gone from her life. She wondered to herself if she might get the chance to chat with him later, although maybe this was just the bubbles going straight to her head.

The coach journey was fun, and it wasn't long before the conversation started flowing between them all. Of course, the prosecco probably helped with that.

Katie quickly found out Mike worked in finance, Chris was a paramedic, and Gordon was an off-shore engineer who was only home for the week before heading out to the rigs again. Richard was a forest ranger, and Joe worked for Historic Scotland as one of the custodians of nearby Urquhart Castle. Katie thought he had looked familiar when she first saw him, but couldn't quite think why. She wondered now if she might have bumped into him on the trip she had taken the day before. He seemed nice, shy but was starting to warm up a little.

The girls seemed really friendly too. Suzy was a great laugh. By the time they arrived at the venue, Katie was beginning to feel much more relaxed about the evening, but she realised she was also starting to feel quite tipsy. She made a mental note to herself to slow down on the drinking. She didn't want to make a fool of herself, especially as there was every possibility she would bump into the girls again at work and maybe even Chris if he was stationed nearby.

It was pitch dark outside when they arrived at the entrance to the estate. The two large ornate black metal gates to the private road swung open as if by magic as soon as the minibus approached, revealing a tar-macadam driveway lined with trees with black coach lanterns on either side lighting their way. They looked exactly like the ones Katie had seen in the Halloween video, only these were much bigger. A small gatehouse to the right of the gates was made of old white sandstone. Smoke was billowing out of the chimney. Katie wondered who lived there. It looked like a magical little place.

They travelled along the road in the pitch dark for around three-quarters of a mile before the road narrowed into a single track. Katie tried to look up at the night sky, but her vision was obscured by conifer trees as tall as the eye could see. She wondered if they had been there since the house was built.

The old-fashioned lanterns adorned either side of the road and continued to light their way. After what felt like another ten minutes, they slowed as they reached a fork in the road. The driver branched off to the left. Katie wondered what lay down the path to the right. There were no lanterns that way, only darkness.

The road surface had now given way to tightly packed red gravel, crunching under the wheels and weight of the vehicle. The group sensed they must be almost there, as they could feel the bus was beginning to slow down. Sure enough, they went around a tight bend and up a little hill, and then, as if by magic, the house suddenly appeared in all its glory. Katie felt herself gasp.

It was breathtaking, bigger than anywhere she had ever visited, and even more impressive than she had imagined. The online photographs didn't do it justice; she couldn't believe it was still privately owned. It was enormous. You would have to be seriously rich to own and maintain a property of this size.

The driver effortlessly drove around to the left of the fountain, pulling up just in front of the entrance, which was in the centre of this impressive building. The main building, made of Ashlee sandstone, was built on a square plan, three storeys high with a raised basement level. It had advanced corner towers, and breaking eaves with domed roofs and cupolas. Two large identical arc-shaped wings flanked either side of the main building. A ram's head staircase in the centre of the building led up to the house's principal floor and main entrance.

Four enormous pillars stood above the entrance marking the front facade of the building, each one taking their share of the weight of the pedimented centrepiece, which was finished with exuberant armorial carvings of statues of classical figures. Two extra-large black metal coach lanterns illuminated the steps up to the front door. The sheer scale of the staircase alone, with its beautiful carved archway overhead, was overwhelming. At the foot of the stairs on either side was a carved statue of a full-sized lion.

The driver swiftly opened the side door and started

helping everyone out. Katie eagerly accepted his hand as she didn't want to trip on the tiny step on the way out and make a fool of herself. She was suddenly feeling quite nervous again and lingered behind everyone.

As they climbed the impressive stone staircase, Katie couldn't help but feel someone was staring directly at her. She turned around, half expecting someone to be behind her, but no one was there, not even the driver. He had left as swiftly as he dropped them off, and if she squinted, she could just about make out the headlights of the minibus through the trees as it was heading back out the way they had come.

She paused on the stairs to admire the building for a few more minutes, letting the others go on in front of her. Shivering, she peered into the pitch-black forest, but it was impossible to tell if anyone was there. Something made her feel uneasy, though, sending a cold shiver up her spine. She pulled her fur bolero up, clasping it tightly around her neck and quickly sprinted up the rest of the stairs to join the others. As she reached them, she told herself she was being ridiculous - it was a dark and chilly October evening, and she was probably just nervous.

Doormen in morning suits stood on either side of the eight-foot glazed oak double doors, welcoming each of them into the house. A woman in the corner was playing the harp. As they entered, they were handed a name badge, which Katie carefully pinned to her dress.

The inside of the building did not disappoint. It opened up into an equally impressive hallway with a beautifully polished cream and black marble floor. Beautifully ornate columns lined either side of the large room with doorways (all of them closed) leading off in multiple different directions. Katie was anxious to explore. She wondered just how much of the home they would be allowed to see. It was so sad they were unable to take photographs.

Ornate gold leaf and navy chaise longs were tastefully placed between the columns underneath the floor above. But it was the grand double wooden staircase that took centre stage in this room. It had a blue and green tartan runner held in place by sparkling gold bars. Your eye was immediately drawn upwards, though, to the impressive gold and crystal chandelier hanging down from the ceiling, which had to be more than thirty feet high.

Katie glanced around, drinking in her surroundings, all whilst trying to imagine what it must have been like to grow up in a place that was so grand. It took her breath away. It was not shabby, and there was no smell of dampness. The walls were tastefully decorated with old paintings of beautiful ladies, all in period costumes, presumably some of the previous ladies of the house.

At the bottom of the staircase on either side was a waiter with a tray of yet more prosecco for everyone. Another butler was on hand to remove everyone's jackets.

He appeared from nowhere and floated away again just as quickly, almost unseen. Katie closed her eyes for a minute and let herself imagine what it might have been like to live in this fantastic house with someone attending to your every need.

She was interrupted in her thoughts again, though, as she felt another cold shiver but instantly blamed it on her outfit choice for the evening. The blue dress with the ruffles would have been a much wiser choice to tour a drafty old home. She could have kept the cover-up on if she'd worn this one. She found herself smiling now. She must be getting old, as this was something her mum would have said. She accepted another glass of prosecco and, as she took another mouthful, instantly felt the bubbles go straight to her head again. Hopefully, the food would be served shortly.

They were instructed to head upstairs to wait for the rest of the group before meeting their host for the evening. Katie continued to drink in her surroundings for a few more minutes, listening to the restful music and admiring the beautiful paintings before climbing the stairs behind everyone. Everywhere she looked seemed even more impressive than the last. At the first landing, before the stairs turned left or right, there was a gilded table with what Katie presumed were priceless antique urns. She would love to have taken photographs, but as they had been instructed not to, her phone stayed firmly in her bag.

Above this table was a sizeable life-size portrait of a young woman. She couldn't have been much more than twenty. The frame was a more modern style than the other paintings and from the style of her clothing, appeared to have been painted relatively recently. The woman was wearing a blue floral sundress and was sitting outside a café overlooking the Eiffel Tower. Although you couldn't see who she was looking at, she had a big beaming smile on her face, and it was evident from her skin tone she had a touch of the sun. She was beaming from ear to ear and looked absolutely radiant. The artist had signed the bottom right-hand corner of the painting. It wasn't a name, just signed– *The Sculptor*. Katie wasn't familiar with his work but noticed the attention to detail was exceptional. It was almost like she was looking at a photograph rather than a painting and although she didn't know the person, the artist seemed, in her opinion, to capture the essence of the person. He or she was a very talented artist.

As Katie looked more closely at the girl's features, she couldn't help but notice their similarities. They had the same dark curly hair and blue eyes and were of a similar build, and although it was impossible to tell exactly how tall she was as she was sitting down, she looked as though they could be close in height. If she didn't know any better, this could almost have been a portrait of herself; ridiculous, she smiled to herself. There goes that wild imagination of hers again.

She wondered if this could perhaps be the Laird's twin sister, Emilia. There had only been photographs of her on her horse in the news article, so she had no idea what she looked like.

Suddenly she felt that cold shiver again, like someone was watching her every move. Boring into her very being. Determined to shrug off the nerves this was creating, she turned to catch the others. Her daydreaming had made her lag behind again. From this landing, a sign pointed everyone towards the right staircase. Katie could see at the top of these stairs that the last of the guests were being ushered into an equally impressive room facing the stairs. From her position, she could just about make out it also had elegant furnishings in similar colours to the hallway.

On entering the large room, Katie could see three large windows on the right-hand side with views overlooking the entrance and out into the gardens beyond, all with beautiful thick silk brocade curtains held back by large rope tie-backs. Roller blinds had been drawn two-thirds of the way down the large windows. In the centre of the opposite side of the room was a large marble fireplace, which Katie was glad to see had been lit.

A gilded mirror hung above the fireplace; an old decorative carriage clock below it sat in the centre of the mantle. Compared to the stairwell, the room was dimly lit by two crystal chandeliers similar to the one on the stairs but on a much smaller scale. The white ceiling in the room was eloquently plastered in a neoclassical style, with deep ornate coving. The room had been wallpapered using a beautiful silk textured duck egg blue paper. Again, beautiful paintings adorned the walls, but they were all landscapes instead of people this time. Katie wondered if they were local places of beauty and made a mental note to ask the host if she got the chance before she left.

The dark oak and gold leaf furniture that she presumed would typically have been set out in this room had been moved to the far left-hand side nearest the door and was roped off to guests. It was probably expensive, or old or maybe both. Katie guessed they wouldn't want the guests to damage any of it.

She noticed several wooden chairs with navy cushion pads had been laid out in a semi-circle in front of the fireplace. Behind them and to the far right of the room were two large wooden tables containing silver trays of cold canapés, sandwiches, sausage rolls, haggis balls and pastries. Ornate silver cake stands held mini snowballs, chocolate tiffin cake, shortbread, gingerbread, and little individual glass jars containing strawberry or raspberry panna cotta deserts. In the middle of each table piled high were two silver trays containing Scottish tablet cut into generous square pieces.

Another table in the centre contained rows of freshly poured prosecco, complete again with strawberries on top.

Katie headed over to join the small queue at the food tables and helped herself to a napkin and a plate. She filled her plate with sandwiches, sausage rolls and salmon canapés, followed by a slice of gingerbread and a tiny strawberry panna cotta desert, desperately hoping this would help soak up the alcohol.

She decided to be brave and try the haggis balls, too, as she'd never had haggis before. It was surprisingly delicious. She vowed this would be her last as she helped herself to another glass of prosecco. Balancing her plate on her knee, she sat on the left nearest the fireplace beside Suzy, one of the girls she had met on the ride over. Several other people were arriving now. Soon the seats would be full, and she guessed the evening would begin. There was no sign of the host yet.

As she tucked into the delicious food, she had a lovely conversation with Suzy, who was very friendly and easy to talk to. She discovered Suzy had grown up on a farm in nearby Forres, a little village outside Elgin. She had moved away to Glasgow after school for university. On graduating as a radiographer, she worked in both Glasgow Royal and the Western General but had always planned to return to her home area at some point.

That time had come two years ago when her mum had sadly had a stroke, and she had come home to help her mum and dad move out of the farm and into a converted bungalow. Just as she'd been planning to return to Glasgow, a job had come up in the radiology department at Raigmore as the superintendent radiographer in charge of CT, so she had returned home permanently. The other girls were her colleagues and, as she suspected, were similar in age to Katie.

The room was becoming quite noisy now as everyone started conversing. Katie counted thirty seats when she first arrived, and all but two were filled. By the time they had finished eating, it was almost 9 pm.

Just at that, the clock on the mantelpiece struck nine, and the music from downstairs ceased. As if by magic, the host for the evening suddenly appeared. She was shocked to see it was none other than Fraser Campbell-McNair, the current Laird himself! Now that was a surprise – for everyone. Katie thought he looked even more handsome in person, but that might be the prosecco talking.

31

Fraser Campbell-McNair was an athletic six foot four, tanned with dark brown shortly cropped hair and a face of designer stubble - what Katie would describe as roguishly handsome, with the brightest blue eyes that seemed to sparkle despite the low lighting in the room. He was dressed in a green and blue tartan suit with a white shirt, navy tie and dark brown brogues. Katie wondered if this was possibly the family tartan. There was no doubt about it; he looked good, but boy, did he know it. Suzy rolled her eyes in agreement with Katie.

Fraser started by introducing himself and the staff in the room, which Katie thought seemed nice that he acknowledged them - maybe they had been wrong about him, and he wasn't so bad after all. As he looked around the room he appeared to hesitate slightly as his eyes rested on her. Katie blushed as she suddenly realised he was staring intently at her. She shuffled in her seat, feeling slightly embarrassed and a little uncomfortable. Moving swiftly on, Fraser thanked everyone for coming and welcomed them into his home. He hoped they had enjoyed the food, which had been prepared locally using local ingredients.

The salmon was caught fresh from the loch, and the strawberries and raspberries had also been grown on the land. It turned out they supply some of the local restaurants and cafés and are pretty famous for their Loch Wood jam which can be purchased in some of the nearby farm shops and delicatessens.

Katie made a mental note to look out for some the next time she was in town. The strawberry panna cotta she had tried was delicious. The tablet was also made from an ancient Campbell family recipe, handed down via the generations and is still made here on the estate today. Although they made it for their many events, it was only available to purchase at the Christmas and Halloween markets. Shame, she thought, as it was delicious.

Fraser moved on to talk about the history of the estate, confirming most of what Katie had learned online. The main part of the house had been designed and built in 1745 by the esteemed Scottish architect William Adam with stone from his own quarry. He sadly died before the project was completed in 1755. The task of finishing the project and adding the large wings on either side had been left to his son Robert Adam, also an esteemed architect who was famous for designing, amongst others, Kedleston Hall, which Katie fondly remembered visiting once as a child with her parents as it was part of the National Trust.

The carved figures over the door were of the Greek

gods Diana, Mars and Orpheus and were a precious reminder of the baroque neoclassical design that Adams was famous for. Although mostly unaltered structurally, there had been a few Georgian and Victorian additions by various family members over the years as they strove to put their own stamp on this magnificent home. These could primarily be seen towards the back and side of the building and within some of the rooms. It was steeped in history and contained many priceless paintings and artefacts. Queen Victoria and Prince Albert were even rumoured to have stayed the night after journeying further north following a stay at their beloved Balmoral estate.

The entire basement level had been turned into a private museum by his great-grandfather, housing a vast collection of sculptures, ancient relics, and artefacts built up from the family's travels all over the world. It boasted the largest collection of butterfly species from all over Asia.

Katie was fascinated; she would love to have seen this but guessed as this was a ghost tour, it would probably be out of bounds. She was secretly a little disappointed as a tour of the home sounded much more enjoyable. Perhaps she could suggest this if there was the opportunity to provide feedback afterwards.

Fraser explained that the family had built their fortune through the East India Trade Company, allowing them to travel and develop the estate into what it is today. Now the family primarily generated their income from the property and land they owned, both here and abroad. Fraser spent most of his time abroad now, but it was evident by how passionately he spoke of the place; that he still saw this as his home. Looking around, Katie could see why but imagined they must do very well for themselves. The place seemed immaculate, and unless other parts were in ruins (which she very much doubted), it didn't look like they would need to sell any of their precious artwork to survive anytime soon.

He spoke a little of his childhood, mainly spent here, although he and his sister had gone to boarding school in Europe. This was a family tradition which his parents had maintained. Their summers had all been spent on the estate - fishing, swimming, horse riding, hunting, building dens and tree swings. A million miles away from Katie's childhood.

Unsurprisingly he didn't mention the death of his parents or sister. Instead, he said he had inherited the family title and estate in late September 2003. Katie thought she detected a slight waiver in his voice as he said this and immediately felt drawn to him and his sadness. She couldn't imagine losing your whole family in such tragic circumstances and what this must do to you. At that moment, she wanted to reach out to him but quickly realised how inappropriate that would be. He was a stranger, and she wasn't in uniform now.

He cleared his throat and changed the subject, returning to the evening in hand. He suspected they had heard enough about him, and it was time to get on with the ghost tour. They were reminded again not to take any photographs.

As this was a singles evening, he revealed each name badge had a symbol printed underneath their name, which denoted the first partnership for the evening. After that, you were free to pick and choose your next partner. He explained they would be provided with a small torch lantern between them and were invited to follow along behind him in their pairs.

As they embarked, little bells would ring every ten minutes allowing the guests to switch to a different partner. Katie winced a bit; for a moment, she had forgotten about this part of the evening. She was glad she had met some of the guys on the bus; at least if she was paired with one of them, she thought she should be ok. They had all seemed nice enough to talk to; it was just Joe who was very quiet. However, as the evening was also a tour she figured this meant they wouldn't have much time to talk, and the darkness would help to mask any awkward silences.

Gordon nervously approached her as it seemed they both had penguins on their name badge, so it looked like she was partnered up with him first. She was secretly relieved and glad they had already met. Once everyone was paired up, they were issued with their lanterns and were ready to begin.

32

Fraser led the way, but not out through the main door as expected - he opened a secret door hidden in the wood panelling to the far right of the fireplace. Someone let out a gasp. Maybe this would turn out to be fun, after all. He led them up a dark spiral staircase, past several closed doors - Katie wondered if they were also secret like the one they had entered this staircase from - up to an attic room at the top of one of the turrets. The servants used these passageways to keep them hidden from the occupants and guests.

At the end of the staircase was another doorway much smaller than the rest. They entered a small room which had a vaulted ceiling. Katie guessed they must be in one of the corner turrets. The room was full of dust, and she could make out rows of eerie-looking large dolls with black eyes staring back at her from a series of shelves. She shuddered. One of the girls let out a scream when she saw them at first.

Fraser explained this room was an old storage room used to house the family's suitcases at one point. There were rumours it was haunted by the ghost of a young servant girl who had sneaked up here to sleep one day whilst on duty.

She had become locked in somehow, and her perished body was found a year later curled up inside a large pram with a cover pulled around her. The family and other servants presumed she had just returned to her family in the neighbouring village. Right then, an old doll's pram started rocking in the far-right-hand corner of the room. A few people jumped. Someone let out another scream. Katie couldn't tell if it was the same person as before, but even she had to admit that if that had been staged, it had freaked her out too.

They briefly looked around the rest of the room, examining the pram, which didn't look like it had been rigged to perform. Katie felt the hairs on the back of her neck stand up. She had to stop herself from clutching Gordon's arm. Even with the dim light from the lanterns, she thought Gordon looked pretty freaked out too.

There was no other entrance into the room, only a window, but given they were four floors up, there was no way anyone else could have sneaked in and out of the room unnoticed. Perhaps they had genuinely encountered a ghost. Still, she remained open-minded. She had had at least three glasses of prosecco by now, possibly more, as the servers seemed to sense an empty glass and had gracefully swept in a few times and filled their glasses whilst they were busy talking.

Gordon seemed nice and, like Suzy, was easy to talk to.

It wasn't long before conversation started flowing between them. He had just turned thirty. One of his mates from the rigs had signed him up for this evening as a bit of a laugh. Not wanting to come alone, he had roped his mates from home into joining him.

This evening wasn't his only birthday celebration, though. The boys had been to Prague for five days in the summer. Katie had been to Prague herself, so they were able to chat about some of their escapades, although she was sure the lads' trip would have been a more booze-fueled weekend than the sightseeing trip she had experienced with Matt. Although she felt no spark between them, he was the perfect gentleman.

Once everyone had had their chance to look around, Fraser led them back down the stone staircase to the doorway leading them, this time out onto the second floor. They exited the passageway through another hidden entrance into a smaller but more lavish room than the one they had started in. It was still big enough to take the whole group with room to spare, though, and it was full of furniture.

Although still pitch dark, the lanterns enabled them to have a good look around the room, with just enough light to afford them the pleasure of admiring the beautiful coffered ceiling and ornate Greek geometric style cornicing. More chandeliers were hanging down from the ceiling, although these were on a much smaller scale than before.

This room had a stone fireplace with a festoon of foliage carved across the centre and figures carved into either side. The wallpaper was a rich blue colour with a fleur-de-lis pattern on it. It had been set up as a dining room with a large oak table and elaborately carved chairs dominating the centre of the room. Katie immediately recognised the style as that of Thomas Chippendale, which Fraser later confirmed.

Ornate eighteenth-century tapestries adorned the walls. A large silver candelabra sat in the centre of the table. Cabinets, also carved by Thomas Chippendale, lined one side of the room, each full of expensive-looking matching dishes, silverware and crystal glasses. Katie wondered if this was the room she remembered seeing on the website, which had been set up to host a rather large dinner party, but it was hard to tell in the dark.

Suddenly a tiny bell rang from somewhere deep in the corner of the room—time to switch partners already. The last ten minutes had felt like no time at all. Chris stepped in, this time by her side. She couldn’t help but notice, he was quite handsome. This evening was turning out to be ok after all.

This room hadn't always been used as a dining room. At one point, it had been used as a drawing room by one of the young ladies of the house, Elouise. She had retired to this room every day after breakfast to write a letter to her future husband, who was away on a six-month tour of the Orient with his father. Sadly, their ship had sunk on the way home, and everyone on board had perished. She had refused to accept he was not coming back and continued to write letters to him for six years following his death, before finally accepting he wasn't coming home. She had poisoned herself in this very room. It was said she could often be heard either by her quill frantically scratching the paper or by her screams as she died in agony from eating deadly nightshade she had picked from the garden.

Everyone was silent while they waited with bated breath for the scare in this room, but it never came. They were met only with silence, although Katie thought if she listened hard enough, she could almost make out a faint scratching noise. But that might just be her imagination. She asked Chris if he had heard anything, but he said he was sorry, but he hadn't.

They moved out of this room and down into the massive dark hallway. There were no windows here, so Katie figured they must be in the middle of the house now. The light from the lanterns cast shadows on the floor. Katie almost screamed when she saw the shadow of a giant creature on its hind legs standing before them. It turned out just to be that of a black bear, preserved through taxidermy and positioned in such a way as to scare them in the dark.

Further, along this long hallway, she noticed two

complete suits of armour positioned on either side of one of the rooms, almost as though they were standing guard against whatever or whoever was inside. Katie shuddered again, wondering if anyone was inside one or both of them, waiting for an opportune moment to jump out and scare one of them. She hoped it wouldn't be her as she passed by as she was so gullible she knew she would likely fall for it and make a fool of herself. When everyone passed by with no incident, she exhaled, knowing she was letting herself get carried away. They continued along the long hallway before entering the room at the far end.

This room was equally as stunning. Although dark, it had the striking classic gilt interior you would expect from William Adam, creating a romantic yet elegant atmosphere. This room was known as the North drawing room.

It had high ceilings, white walls and frieze-style crown moulding etched in gold paint. The fireplace surround was finished to match. Even the panels of the doors had gold edging on the inside. Another Thomas Chippendale table stood in the centre of the room underneath another elegant gold chandelier. The walls were adorned with priceless artwork by Naismith, and Katie thought she also spotted a Picasso, all in gold frames, which hung from the ceiling on gold chains. Beautiful floor-length blue silk curtains with rope tie-backs framed the two large Venetian-style windows. Katie was drawn to look out of the windows, trying to orientate herself, but it was impossible as she couldn't see anything at all as it was pitch black outside.

She figured they must be at the back of the property, although it was hard to tell. She thought she could almost make out the walled gardens if she peered hard enough. Around the room's walls were dark wood chairs with blue cushions in matching fabric to the curtains. A large oriental-style rug in various shades of blue dominated the centre of the floor.

As they talked, she discovered Chris shared her passion for architecture and stately homes. He had studied history at university before joining the ambulance service and was currently stationed at Inverness following a three-year secondment on the helicopter based in Glasgow. Being from Scotland, Chris preferred castles and offered to show her around some of his favourites sometime if she was interested. She wasn't sure if he was asking her on a date or not but thought she might just take him up on his offer. He was really attractive, and the conversation was easy with him. They agreed to swap numbers at the end of the evening.

This room had another sad tale of death and romance. In 1855 one of the ladies of the house died on the eve of her wedding. She had been poisoned by her sister, who was secretly in love with her fiancé, although these feelings were not reciprocated, and he later died of a broken heart. A memorial to them was located in the walled garden next to the spot where he had proposed to her. Her ghost was said to be heard pacing this room at night as she plotted her revenge on her sister. Just at that, a clock in the hallway struck ten o'clock. The sudden noise made everyone jump.

The sound of another bell could also be heard in the background. Chris thanked her for her company and gently kissed her hand before gallantly moving on. Her next partner was someone she had never met, an older gentleman named Rodger. He was a retired Royal naval officer, twice divorced with three grown-up children, who now owned and ran a successful salvage company. Although he was older, he took good care of himself and looked like he still regularly worked out.

However, although he was pleasant enough to talk to, Katie was secretly quite pleased he did most of the talking as she had absolutely nothing in common with him. He also seemed to rather like the sound of his own voice. She found herself rolling her eyes at him a few times and was thankful for the darkness so he couldn’t catch her doing so. She had a feeling this was going to be a long ten minutes.

It wasn't long before they were moving again, this time up a central stairwell. This staircase was not as grand as the one in the main entranceway but, nevertheless, was still pretty impressive. A little moonlight came in from the large sash windows, making it easier to take in their surroundings this time.

Looking down, she could make out doors into various rooms below her on the first and basement floors; looking upwards towards the upper floor, another magnificent coach lantern hung down through the middle of the stairwell on a gold chain. Panelled walls on either side of the staircase were finished in the same cream and gold design she had admired in the North drawing room. These walls were also covered in family portraits and images of men on horseback surrounded by hounds. Fraser explained who everyone was whilst they climbed the staircase.

They followed Fraser up onto the third floor and into a room on the left-hand side. This was a much smaller room than the ones they had been in previously. As they entered, Katie could see it was a bedroom. It was decorated again in the same simple elegant Adam's style with cream walls and a Vitruvian scroll design crown moulding, the repeated scroll pattern was also painted in gold. The rims on the door panelling were finished in gold to match. Above the door frame was a gold-edged pediment similar in style to that over the front entrance, minus the carvings. This room also had an impressive plaster ceiling with festoons of foliage and patterns of the Greek acanthus plant circling the impressive oval centre piece, which held another gold and crystal lamp.

The centrepiece of this room was the large four-poster bed complete with red brocade curtains, swags and matching bedclothes. In the far corner, was a dressing table with a matching red upholstered chair and two full-length gilded mirrors. Katie noticed the bedclothes looked rumpled and lumpy like someone was lying on them.

Fraser was busy telling the group this room was supposedly haunted by his great-grandmother, who had died of TB in this very room. Servants and guests tell stories of hearing coughing and spluttering noises coming from this room, even in broad daylight. Some even refused to clean this room alone to this day. Katie looked back over at the bed and felt herself shiver. She wondered if this lady was perhaps lying there now, watching them all, wondering what on earth they were doing in her bedroom. Someone coughed at that moment, frightening her, until she realised it was only the person standing beside her.

The tour continued through long dark passageways and unlit servants' corridors with several more stories of tragic events over the years in the many beautiful rooms. Katie met many different people throughout the evening, some interesting and a few who were incredibly difficult to converse with. Still, she had enjoyed herself and had loved exploring the tiny part of the house they had been permitted to visit, even if it had been pitch dark. She would have loved a daytime tour.

The evening finished up back where they began, in the main foyer. By now, it was almost midnight. Katie couldn't believe it was so late already. The time seemed to have flown by. They were treated to a final glass of prosecco and some more of the famous Loch Wood House tablet whilst they mulled about in the foyer together, waiting for their transportation home.

Everyone seemed quite drunk, Katie included. Katie swapped numbers with Chris and agreed to meet up with him one day through the week. He was on day shift until Thursday but offered to pick her up on one of his days off to explore some of the local attractions together. Katie told him she would like that, and she meant it.

While talking to Chris, though, Katie couldn't shake that intense feeling that someone was watching her again. She shivered and shrugged it off. But she should have trusted her instincts. There was indeed someone watching her. He had been watching her the entire evening, and he was not happy at the attention she was attracting. This was not part of his plan. He hoped this would not be a complication. It would not stop him, though. She belonged to him, and he had waited a long time for her to return to him. No one was going to stand in his way. He would make sure of it.

33

Katie decided to go to the bathroom before she left. It was located on the ground floor, near the entrance to the family museum Fraser had spoken about. She would have loved a quick peek inside but thought it best not to. Although she appeared to be alone, anyone could come down at any moment and she didn't want to get caught snooping around.

When she came out of the bathroom, she bumped straight into Fraser. She startled him at first as he wasn't expecting to find anyone down here, and least of all her. Most of the guests had left already, the rest were making their way down to the waiting taxis and minibuses. He thought she was gone.

She reminded him so much of Emilia it was painful to talk to her. He was struggling with being so close to her. But he tried to put his feelings aside and asked her if she had enjoyed herself. She told him she had very much and thanked him for the hospitality. Seizing her chance, she asked if she could have a private tour of the house sometime? He hesitated, Emilia had suggested this to their parents many years ago, before politely saying he would discuss it with

Scott, who was the event organiser (and unofficially his right-hand man on the estate). Fraser explained he didn't usually get involved in these events, but he had decided to fill in for Scott tonight - give him the evening off.

Sensing he was anxious to get away from her, they exchanged a few more pleasantries before Katie excused herself as she didn't want to miss her ride home. Fraser assured her they wouldn't leave without her. Scott would make sure of it. He had the planning of these events down to a fine art. Suddenly remembering she wanted to ask him about some of the paintings, she turned back to speak to him, but he was gone - almost like he had vanished into thin air.

She made her way back along the way she had come and was startled to discover she was the only one left when she stepped back into the foyer. Everyone else was gone, including the staff who had been there earlier. Panicking, she hurried over to the door, anxious not to be left behind.

As she was walking down the steps, she could see a single black limousine. That uneasy feeling of being watched was back again. She pulled her fur bolero up around her neck and hurried down to the waiting vehicle, hoping it awaited her.

She opened the door and relieved to see a placard with her name on it resting on the parcel shelf, climbed into the back seat. Privacy glass separated her from the driver. As it was closed, she presumed they didn't want to talk. That was fine with her. She was tired. It had been a long evening. A freshly brewed jug of coffee sat on the small table before her, alongside a china cup and saucer.

The coffee jug slotted neatly into a hole, she guessed, to prevent it from being knocked over whilst the vehicle was moving. Feeling a little tipsy from all the prosecco she had drunk, she poured herself a cup, helping herself to two small cartons of milk from the little bowl which was neatly slotted into another hole, next to the coffee pot.

She slid her shoes off and rubbed the balls of her feet before allowing her bare toes to sink into the plush black carpet, enjoying the warmth of the vehicle. It felt good to take her shoes off, her feet were hurting from all the walking she had done tonight, and it had been a long time since she'd spent that long wearing a pair of heels. As she sipped her coffee, she put her head back on the leather headrest and, before long, closed her eyes. A moment later, and she was out for the count, the remnants of her coffee spilt on the floor. Only she wasn't sleeping.

34

He had to move quickly. He wasn't sure how much coffee she had drunk; therefore, he wasn't sure how long she would be out for. It could be minutes, could be hours. There was no way of telling.

On leaving the estate, he sped off towards her apartment, careful not to break the speed limit and attract unnecessary attention. Although he knew the local constabulary very well, he didn't want to risk anyone seeing him with her.

In no time, he arrived at the front door to her apartment block, careful to ensure he pulled up underneath the cover of the canopy above the front door, thus obscuring the rear of the vehicle from the CCTV camera he had clocked during his earlier visits. He hung around just long enough to make it look like someone got out, even getting out himself and opening the back door to make it look like he was helping someone out. Only no one did get out. The dark cap hid his features perfectly. He even stood for a minute as if he was seeing someone safely back into the building, chuckling to himself at how gallus he was being.

Once he got back in and drove off, he headed out of the driveway before doubling back on himself and heading to the rear of the property, parking next to the woods out of view of any resident's windows or cameras. He exchanged his suit for dark jeans and a jumper with a dark woolly hat pulled low over his ears. Lifting her handbag, shoes and jacket, he sneaked into the building through the rear entrance he had left unlatched. Thankfully no one had noticed and locked it.

He had disabled the security camera there earlier in the week and hoped no one had discovered and reported it. It had been relatively easy to get into her building. No one questioned the polite delivery driver, complete with a cap pulled down over his face, who arrived at the same time as a young couple with a baby were leaving. He had even helped lift the pram down the steps for them.

He sneaked up to her apartment unseen and let himself in using her keys, careful not to touch anything. With no time to look around, he placed her shoes at the front door as if she had just kicked them off. He put her handbag on the counter in the kitchen and hung her jacket over the back of one of the leather chairs at the breakfast bar.

Wearing gloves, he closed the bedroom curtains but pulled back the duvet and ruffled the sheets to make it look like someone had slept there. He returned to the kitchen and made it look like someone had hastily made toast, leaving the dirty dishes on the countertop. Then he lifted her trainers and some running gear out of the wardrobe before carefully letting himself back into the quiet hallway, taking her keys with him. He contemplated taking her mobile phone but decided against it in case anyone tried to trace it. He wasn't entirely sure what, if anything, she had agreed with the guy he had seen getting close to her earlier, but he knew she had given him her number. He decided it was probably safer to leave her phone in her apartment. That way if he did contact her, by ignoring him, he would hopefully get the message.

Carefully he made his way down to the notice board, now looking for the flyer, but it was nowhere to be seen. Damn, it was gone. He hoped it wasn't still back up in her apartment. He hadn't seen it lying around in there, though. This made him uneasy, and he hoped no one would come snooping and spoil his plans for her. Still, he had no time to go back up to her apartment to look for it, she could wake up anytime, and although it was late, there was always the chance that someone might see him. Plus, if anyone did come looking, he had been smart enough to make it look like she had returned home. Technically she did, so even if the police came looking for him, he wouldn't exactly be lying.

If he had only put a light on when he entered her kitchen, he would have noticed she had it neatly pinned to the fridge for all to see. He had knocked it onto the floor when he closed the refrigerator.

He made his way carefully and silently back out the way he had come in and crept back to the car, taking care not to be seen. A quick look inside confirmed his prize was still out for the count. Mindful not to be caught with an unconscious lady in the back of his car if the police were to pull him over, he lifted her out of the back seat and popped her gently into the boot.

The car had a large enough boot he could lie her completely flat. He laid his jacket over her to keep her warm, then swiftly changed back into his chauffeur outfit and headed back towards Loch Wood House. Number plate recognition technology meant the gates swung open for him as soon as he approached them. For the second time this evening, Katie made her way along the long driveway, only this time, unbeknown to her, she would be taking that unlit road to the right after all.

This road led straight behind the main house, past the walled gardens, continuing along behind the orangery and the stable block before finally ending at an old abandoned double-storey Victorian outbuilding. Built in 1840, this had been the servant quarters at one point, but had long since been abandoned. It was on the periphery of the estate, backing onto vast woodland.

No one came out here anymore. The entrance was hidden behind an overgrown hedge. The road, which had turned to a dirt track, was covered in brambles, and he hoped he would be able to back the limousine out of there without causing any damage to it when he was done. He usually brought the Range Rover when he came down here as it was much more suited to this rugged terrain—still no point in worrying about that now.

He carefully opened the boot, changing back into his dark clothing from earlier. Thankfully, she was still sound asleep. He watched her for a moment, silently breathing in and out - so peacefully, before carefully lifting her out and carrying her into the house and up the two flights of stairs to the attic, as if she weighed nothing at all. He gently laid her on the clean mattress he had prepared on the floor before placing a gag over her mouth. He bound her feet together with masking tape and handcuffed her hands to an old column-style radiator, all while talking sweetly to her. She had changed her hair, he noticed, and he liked it. The handcuffs had a bit of play in them as he had welded a short chain between them to make them a little longer.

The heating had been disconnected as the building had been long abandoned, so he placed a blanket over her as he didn't want her to freeze to death. That wasn't part of the plan. Once he was sure her bonds were secure, he left and locked the door behind him, taking the keys. Although he doubted anyone would check, he was anxious to return the car before anyone realised it was missing.

35

Saturday 29th October

Not one for a lie-in, Tracy was up early again. It was a beautiful crisp day outside, so she was keen to make the most of it and finish what she had started in the front garden, especially now that her new windows and doors were in. Plus working out in the garden helped take her mind off her failures. The front garden was a lot more manageable than the back, she would eventually need a landscaper to tackle that, but the front should be relatively simple to keep - once she tackled how overgrown it was.

The cottage was a typical Victorian-style property with a front door in the middle and a window on either side. A path led straight down to the gate from the front door, and a second connecting path led underneath the window in front of the snug to the garage and driveway. There was a stretch of grass on either side of the path, which she had cut and edged the other night and flower beds underneath the windows.

She dug over the flower beds, removing all the dead and overgrown plants and weeds ready for planting in the spring. When she'd finished that, she trimmed the front hedge that framed her property from the footpath. Standing back to admire her handiwork, she decided to remove the dilapidated front gate as it was letting the front of the house down now.

After lunch, she visited the local garden centre and picked up two small bay trees and two black plant pots, which she thought would be perfect to sit on either side of her lovely new front door. By the time she finished that night, she was exhausted but pleased with all she had achieved. It certainly was a massive improvement from when she bought the property. The lady who owned the house previously had been a bit of a hoarder, so when she first viewed the property, you couldn't even open the front door. Tracy was the complete opposite.

That evening, she treated herself to another long soak in the bath. She was lying there enjoying the heat, which seemed to soothe her aching muscles and couldn't help but think about the case. The dress and sandals were still bothering her.

Although no stranger to dressing glam for a night out, Erin had been backpacking for a year living primarily in jeans and a t-shirt. Why would she need such a glam outfit in Inverness of all places when she was there alone? Then there was Natalia, who was also travelling alone but had been seen buying something similar before she disappeared.

And finally, there was Jessica, who had gone to the hairdressers to have her hair done in a rather sophisticated style for a night out in a town where she knew hardly anyone. Was there a link here?

Klara was the one she knew the least about, but she was nonetheless convinced all of their disappearances were linked. And she was convinced the owner of the black Range Rover had something to do with it too. If only she could find a way to trace them.

She suddenly wondered if any more CCTV footage was stored at the time from Ness Walk hotel and made a note to check this first thing tomorrow. She wasn't scheduled to work Sunday, but having nothing other than gardening and DIY to fill her time with, she was happy to throw herself into the case.

Sunday 30th October

Logging in from home on her laptop, she could see there were indeed more files. There were several days' worth of CCTV on either side of Klara's disappearance. Although she had the log burner on, it was still a bit chilly, so she grabbed the throw off her bed and curled up on the sofa with her laptop on her knees.

She decided to start with the Friday before Klara went missing first. Surveillance is soul-destroying but can be highly satisfying when you find what you are looking for. She went through the whole day, fast-forwarding through some parts of it. Klara left that day at precisely 10:02 am, headed over to her blue rental car and drove out of the car park turning right as she exited the hotel. She didn't return until 4:55 pm. She emerged again twenty minutes later, dressed in running gear and headed off along the river path. Just as she had done the night she disappeared. She returned to the hotel at 18:15. There didn't appear to be anyone following her, and so far, no signs of the mysterious black Range Rover. The only black Range Rover parked in the car park was the one belonging to the hotel manager, and she had already ruled him out as a suspect.

Deflated, she turned her attention to the Saturday recording, the day before Klara went missing. As expected, there were many comings and goings at a large hotel over the weekend. Klara went for another run at 10:07 am, returning at 11:30 am. As she watched, Klara left the hotel again on foot at 12:30 and returned at 16:30 carrying lots of shopping bags. She carried on watching, and at 19:00, Klara emerged again.

This time she looked very glamorous in a stunning royal blue bodycon style pencil dress with capped sleeves and a deep v-neck back. Her hair was down and styled in relaxed waves, and she was wearing silver high-heeled sandals and carrying a small silver clutch bag. She stepped into a waiting taxi and sped off. Where on earth was she going? Tracy took note of the taxi registration plate, although she knew with the length of time that had passed, she would be unlikely to find out this information now. With the pandemic, it was even possible the firm was no longer in business.

Klara returned to the hotel that evening in a black limousine at 12:42 am, and just like the black Range Rover, the license plates appeared to be deliberately obscured. Privacy glass again concealed the driver. Damn it! - she closed her laptop. Frustrated she threw it down on the sofa beside her - just when she thought she might have something. Rubbing her eyes, she padded into the kitchen to make something to eat. While waiting for the kettle to boil, she opened the cupboard and took a couple of paracetamol. Her body still ached from all the manual work from the day before, but now her head was pounding as she had been looking at the computer screen for so long.

She decided to go for a walk to clear her head. Pulling on her wellies and parka jacket, she headed out of the house, turned left, and headed down toward the village. It was a crisp day but pleasant enough if you were in the sun. Before reaching the little village, she wandered along the footpath past other cottages and farms. The village had a couple of small shops and a café. She popped into the café and picked up a coffee before returning home.

As she was walking, she started thinking about Klara's luggage. The original report said her hotel room had been cleared, meaning she or someone else must have done this. The rental car had been empty, so nothing had been left in there, and she presumed the hotel would have noticed such distinctive luggage if it had been left behind in storage uncollected.

However, just to be sure, she gave the hotel a quick call to check - as she suspected nothing matching the description of Klara's bags was still there. She asked the concierge what the process was for anyone who wanted to store their luggage with them. The concierge told her anyone leaving luggage after check out was given a ticket, which they had to produce when they returned to reclaim it. Their luggage was kept in a locked storage room near reception. Only the concierge on duty and the manager held the key. She asked if they happened to keep a record of stored luggage. He put her on hold whilst he checked their records, only to confirm they had no record of any luggage ever being stored from that particular room over the dates in question. Thanking him, she rung off. She knew now she would have to go back to the CCTV footage, to see if there were any clues about its whereabouts.

Headache gone, she settled back in to watch the Sunday footage. Klara emerged at 12:30 in her running gear again and, after setting her pacing watch, returned at 13:25. There was no sign of her again until she left the hotel on foot at 18:57. Tracy let this tape run, fast-forwarding through sections where no one came or went. Sure enough, there was no sign of Klara returning to the hotel that evening either on foot or by car.

She watched Monday’s and Tuesday’s footage, there was no sign of Klara. Same with Wednesday's footage. Just as she was about to give up for the night and go to bed, she suddenly noticed the black Range Rover pull into the parking lot, parking in the same spot as before. It was Thursday at 7:30 am. It sat there for an hour and a half when the driver's door suddenly opened.

A tall, well-built man emerged wearing smart dark clothing, black golf gloves, and a golf cap pulled down low over his face. She tried zooming in, but making out any of his features was impossible. He was Caucasian with designer stubble. That was all she could definitively make out. Using the entrance into the hotel as a gauge of height, she would place him somewhere between 5ft 11 inches and 6ft 4 inches tall, possibly around 15-16 stone.

It was impossible to tell age, but if she were to guess based on stature, she would have placed him somewhere between mid-thirties and fifty years old. Whoever this is, he was smart enough to know he was being watched. He never once looked in the direction of the camera. He walked calmly over to the reception and made his way inside. She took a few screenshots of him. At the moment, he was the only suspect she had.

He then re-emerged at 11 am, carefully ensuring he left alongside several other guests who were also checking out. She paused the video as there, just to the right of the camera, she could see he was carrying two bright red suitcases with a sizeable matching hold-all slung over his body. Tracy couldn't believe what she was seeing.

She rewound the recording and watched it again just to be sure, zooming in on the luggage she had *Googled.* There was no mistaking it - this had to be Klara's missing luggage, but where was Klara, and why hadn't she collected it herself? It was impossible to see if anyone was in the passenger seat of the Range Rover, though, so she guessed she could have been waiting for him in the car.

But there were so many things that didn't add up. The deliberately concealed number plates, parking in the car park for hours on the Sunday before Klara emerged, then driving off only minutes after she left. And if Klara had known him, why had she walked past his car on the Sunday evening? Why hadn't he just picked her up from the hotel?

Whoever he was - he had her luggage, and since she was the only one registered as a guest in that room, he had to have had her room key. She had to have either gone willingly with this person or something sinister had happened to her, but either way, she was now even more convinced this person knew where she was or what had happened to her.

Turning back to the video, she pressed play and watched as he popped the luggage into the boot of his car, got in and drove off. He was heading left as he exited the car park. Excited at what she had found, she was also wary about sharing this information. She still had no actual proof that anything sinister had happened to any of these girls. Her findings were all still circumstantial. It was possible that these cases weren't connected at all, and if Klara's father was as powerful as the professor had suggested, perhaps someone could have targeted his daughter to get to him.

Still, if this was the same person and she had discovered he was targeting young girls, she knew she would have to decide soon when to speak to the ACC about her findings. She was close, but not quite there yet. Careful not to let history repeat itself, she decided to sleep on it. By morning, she had decided to wait a little longer.

36

As the dawn light trickled in underneath the tiny gap at the bottom of the old war regulation black-out roller blinds, it slowly made its way along the floor until it pooled onto Katie's face. The light and heat from it gradually began to stir her from her sleep. Groaning, she could feel the classic symptoms of a hangover, that familiar blinding headache and overwhelming thirst as though her tongue was stuck to the roof of her mouth.

Cursing herself now for drinking too much the night before and not entirely trusting herself to move yet (for fear of being sick), she lay there for a few more minutes in a desperate bid to try and steady the accompanying dizziness.

Once she was satisfied she could move without vomiting, she tried to roll over to pull the duvet back up over her head and go back to sleep, but her arms appeared to be stuck, panicking she tried to move her legs next and quickly discovered they wouldn't move either. Initially, she thought she had just wrapped herself up in the duvet, but then she realised something was over her mouth. Panic began to set in. What the hell was happening to her, she thought. And, where was she?

Forgetting the dizziness and nausea for a second, her eyes sprung wide open, and she immediately felt her heart begin to beat faster and faster until it felt as though it might burst right out of her chest. She tried desperately to focus on her surroundings, but everything was just a blur. The whole room was spinning. In a desperate bid to try and work out where she was, she lifted her head, only to be fought back by yet another wave of nausea. With a gag over her mouth, she knew she couldn't risk being sick as being a nurse; she was well aware she ran the risk of aspirating and dying. Defeated, she lay her head back down and closed her eyes, waiting for the nausea to pass. Tears formed and spilt down her cheeks, splashing onto the mattress. At the same time, she tried to slow her breathing as she knew panicking wasn't going to help her any.

She lay there for what felt like an eternity before gingerly opening her eyes again. When confident she would not be sick, she slowly lifted her head, trying to take in her immediate surroundings. Although her vision was still blurred, she could make out enough to let her realise she was not in her own bed, but deep down, she had already known this.

She appeared to be lying on a mattress, facing a wall she didn't recognise, with her hands secured by handcuffs to an old column-style radiator. The cream paint was flaking off the radiator, and behind it was a thick dirty skirting board that looked as though it hadn't seen a duster or a paintbrush for many years. The old-fashioned patterned wallpaper above it was peeling away from the wall. The room smelt musty and damp. This was not her home. She had no idea where she was. Tears filled her eyes again as she thought about her family, wondering if she would ever see them again. This made her start to sob, which increased her breathing again and, with it, her heart rate. Realising this wouldn't help her, she lay back down on her side, closing her eyes and curling her legs up toward her as best she could, while trying to steady her breathing again. She tried desperately to remember what on earth had happened to her.

The house tour, although hazy, was slowly returning to her. She remembered she had been on a ghost tour of a stately home. But it had been opulent and warm, not dusty and damp like this. The style of this room was all wrong, too, the ceiling was low, and from her limited view, there was only one small window. Although she thought, she had probably only visited a small part of the house, so maybe it wasn't all the same. But how had she ended up here, wherever here was? There had been others there, too; slowly, her memory was starting to return. She remembered talking to some girls and an attractive guy, exchanging numbers with him. Wouldn't they have realised she was missing? Surely, they would have realised she wasn't with them on the journey home? Then she remembered going to the bathroom and missing saying goodbye to some people. She had been the only guest left when she returned, but then she remembered getting into the back of a black limousine - so she must have left – mustn't she?

Something must have happened to her on the way home, had someone been waiting in her apartment or in the bushes outside? Exhausted, she tried to get some rest; she knew she had to be able to think straight if she was going to get out of here.

She must have drifted off. When she woke up, the light had moved around to the room's opposite corner. Her stomach growled; she was starving. Having no way to tell the time, she wasn't sure how long it had been since she had last eaten or drank anything. Her throat was parched, the gag not helping any. Opening her eyes, her vision seemed slightly clearer now, and she could tell she was still wearing her dress from the night before, and she could feel her underwear was still intact, which was a relief. Her shoes were gone, though, as was her jacket. She wasn't sure if they were somewhere else in the room.

A dark brown woolly blanket was covering the lower half of her body, so she wasn't sure what was holding her legs together. It didn't feel like handcuffs, so maybe she could get this off. Her arms were aching from being stretched out in front of her, the handcuffs digging into her wrists. She knew she would have to try and sit up if she were to get a better view of her surroundings, and she desperately needed to get this tape off her mouth.

Wriggling closer to the radiator loosened her arms a bit; bending her knees, she pulled herself in towards the radiator, gradually bringing her face close enough to pull the tape holding the gag in place off her mouth. She took a deep inhale of air and then promptly burst into tears. Her wrists were sore, and she felt like she had no circulation in her legs.

Going into survival mode, she lay on her back and pulled her knees up, bringing her feet up to her bottom; she then shimmied up the radiator until she was in an awkward sitting position. With her back against the wall, she shimmied her hands back down the radiator trying in vain to reach the bindings on her feet, but it was useless; whatever was binding them was far too tight.

The air smelt damp and musty as if the room hadn't been used for a long time, yet the mattress she was lying on seemed new, as did the blanket, which meant this was planned. A single bulb hung from a cord in the middle of the room. There was a doorway facing her and another to her right-hand side, which she thought might be a cupboard. There was no sign of her shoes, handbag or jacket. The only other piece of furniture in the room was a single white wooden chair, which had been placed near her as if someone had been using it to sit there watching her. She shuddered at the thought of this. The only sound was the rain which was battering off the window and the roof above, and if she strained hard enough, she thought she could hear the wind rustling through leaves outside. She watched and waited until it was dark.

She must have dosed off again as she was woken immediately by the sound of footsteps outside the door. Suddenly a key turned in the lock, and she was blinded by a torch shining straight into her face. She could make out a large shape filling the door frame in the shadows. This was a very large man. He never spoke; he just checked her bindings were still secure and thrust an open bottle of water into her hands. Frightened he would take it from her, she gulped it down, finishing it all. He then handed her a ham sandwich which she quickly devoured. Wrapping another blanket over her shoulders, he turned and left without uttering a word, locking the door behind him.

Katie breathed a sigh of relief before bursting into tears again. He hadn't renewed her gag, so this must mean she was being held miles from anyone who could hear her cries. What on earth did he want from her, though? He can't be all bad if he fed her and wrapped her up, she thought to herself. Maybe she could convince him to let her go if she could just talk to him. Her eyes felt heavy again, and before she knew it, she was fast asleep from the sedative he had crushed up and laced within the water.

37

He was enjoying this. He hadn't planned initially on kidnapping her, but this was turning out to be more fun than he thought it would be - letting her believe she might escape, giving her false hope before the end. Just like she had done to him, leading him on all those years.

Soon she would join the others, where she belonged.

38

Monday 31st October

Back in the office, Tracy printed off the screenshots she had taken of her mystery man. She pinned his picture underneath Klara's column on her whiteboard and reviewed the evidence she had collected already.

She knew from speaking to Heidi that a black Range Rover had been seen in the vicinity around the time Erin had disappeared, and now she knew for certain Klara's luggage had been removed from the hotel by a man who owned or had access to a black Range Rover. A black Range Rover had also been seen on CCTV outside the car hire company, possibly following Natalia, although she had no solid proof this was even connected. Jessica was the only one without a link to a black Range Rover.

She pulled up a local map on *Google* and printed it off. Pinning it to the whiteboard, she then marked the location where each girl had been last seen using little red-coloured magnets. She placed one at the youth hostel; one at Ness

View Hotel; one at the hairdressers and she put a final one at the Stewart residence, where Jessica had been staying. Standing back, she could see these girls had been staying roughly within a mile of each other. The car hire depot where Natalia had been seen handing her keys back was also within this mile radius.

Returning to her DVLA list from 2012, she decided to run another check to see if any of the same people still owned the same, or a similar car in 2014 and 2016. When she had this list, she further narrowed her search to those within a 10-mile radius of the Youth hostel where both Erin and Natalia had been staying and Ness View Hotel, where Klara had been staying, and then cross-referenced them, placing blue magnets at each of their addresses.

This time she was left with just four people. Billy McVey, the retired pub landlord living with his wife around the corner from the hostel. Marie Katz, the forty-eight-year-old business lady living in town with her partner Mac Rennie at the time of all four girls' disappearances. Johnny Baird, the fifty-four-year-old self-employed builder and Dr Andrew Wilson, the seventy-nine-year-old retired GP.

Grabbing her keys and handbag, she headed out armed with this list; now that she had an image of a suspect, she thought it was time to visit some of these people, even if it was just to eliminate them.

As he lived nearest, she decided to start with Mr

McVey. Although he didn't sound on paper as though he fitted the profile, she didn't want to rule him out just yet. She knew as well as anyone not to leave any stone unturned when it came to a police investigation. Someone else who did fit her profile could have had access to his vehicle. Luckily, the couple still stayed in the same house. They lived in a 1980s-style detached home with a green garage door, which looked like it could do with a coat of paint. The metal gates to the property were painted the same colour of green as the garage door.

As she parked on the road outside their home, she noticed they still owned the same car. Taking her phone out, she tried snapping a photograph of it. The registration plate was clearly visible. However, that didn't necessarily mean anything, as polycarbonate coverings are designed to be removed. She made her way up to the front door and rang the bell. A stylish lady dressed in black trousers and a blue flowery blouse answered the door. After Tracy showed her warrant card and introduced herself, Mrs McVey, or Wilma, as she insisted Tracy call her, invited her inside.

Their house was lovely and warm, and a fresh smell of coffee came from the kitchen. Wilma ushered her into the sitting room and asked if she could make her a tea or coffee. As she was doing so, she explained that her husband, Billy, was out buying a newspaper but would be home shortly. Tracy accepted a coffee and made herself comfortable in a cosy armchair beside the fire while waiting for her coffee.

Trying to keep things as casual as possible so as not to raise any suspicion, she told Wilma she was looking into some cold cases, including Erin's disappearance. She showed her the picture she had brought with her of Erin. Wilma said she remembered it well. Erin had been the same age as their eldest daughter when she went missing. Her disappearance had really rattled them. She said the whole thing had made her husband quite paranoid for a while afterwards, always asking their daughters where they were going and how they were getting home when they went out. He insisted on driving them everywhere. Wilma said it had driven the girls up the wall.

She remembered the police had come round the doors afterwards asking if they had seen Erin or noticed anything or anyone suspicious hanging around. She and her husband had been working in the pub that evening, so, as usual, they hadn't gotten home until well after midnight. Nothing had struck them as being out of the ordinary. The street was as quiet as it usually was. Neither of them could recall seeing anyone hanging around. Wilma said their youngest daughter Kristen, had been home that evening, but their eldest daughter Melissa had been out with her boyfriend (now her husband). She thought the girls would have also spoken to the police, but couldn't say for certain as it had been such a long time ago.

Tracy noticed the living room was full of family photographs. Seeing Tracy looking at them, Wilma lifted a family photograph from the sideboard and pointed out her daughters to Tracy, along with various other family members. Just as Wilma finished showing her the pictures, Billy appeared newspaper in hand. He was a small, round gentleman, no taller than 5 ft 6 inches, definitely not the man she had captured outside the hotel on the CCTV. Neither were either of their sons-in-law. One was Asian, and the other was wheelchair-bound from a motorbike accident he had been in when he was just twenty-two.

Tracy casually enquired about their car, asking if they remembered whether they had driven to work that Sunday evening. Wilma stated they always drove to work, so yes, they would have done, and when asked where they parked, she said it would have been parked behind the pub all evening. She wondered if anyone could have had access to their keys, but Billy confirmed he always kept them in his trouser pocket. Thankfully neither of them asked why she was asking about their car. Satisfied they had nothing to do with this, she thanked them for their time and left.

Back at the car, she decided not to get back in but to visit Dr Wilson next. That way, if the McVey's were looking out of their window, they would see her go to a few more doors and not make them wonder why she had just come to their house. A brand-new silver Mercedes A-class SUV was parked in his driveway, so hopefully, that was a sign he was home.

She rang the doorbell and waited. After a few minutes, a tall thin gentleman with thin white hair and a neat beard answered the door. Although he was seventy-nine, he stood perfectly straight. It was apparent he took good care of himself, but he, too, definitely wasn't the man she had seen on the CCTV. He was smartly dressed in a blue shirt which was open at the neck, with navy trousers, and she noticed he had dark grey moccasin slippers on his feet. He also invited her in for a coffee which she politely declined.

Again, she gave him the same story she had given to the McVey's. He vaguely remembered Erin's disappearance but couldn't say he had seen her on that Sunday or at any other time. His wife had been very ill with breast cancer and had been undergoing a combination of chemotherapy and radiotherapy. He had been looking after her himself as they hadn't been able to have a family, so it was just the two of them. They had two nieces and a nephew who all lived down south, so as his wife had passed away, he was all on his own now, but he finished by telling her he had a great bunch of friends. He was off to play golf with three of them that afternoon.

Careful not to raise suspicion, she casually asked if he owned a black Range Rover in 2012. He thought for a moment before stating that he probably did, it had been several cars ago for him, but when he worked it out in his head, he confirmed he had. She asked if he could possibly have been parked on the road that evening. He said he didn't think so, as he always put his car in the garage at night. Noticing he had a double garage, she had no reason to doubt him. She thanked him for his time, as he clearly had nothing to do with this either.

While in the area, she decided to try Johnny Baird. He lived with his wife Sarah and their four kids in a large sandstone detached house on Crown Avenue, around the corner from the Youth Hostel. Johnny had a police caution on record at age nineteen for being drunk and disorderly in the town centre after a local rugby match, but that hardly made him a criminal.

There was a dark grey seven-seater VW Touran parked in the driveway. Johnny's wife, Sarah, answered the door. She was a small, mousy woman with long red hair tied up in a ponytail and pale green eyes. Wearing gym gear, she was obviously just returning from or heading out to the gym. As they chatted, Sarah revealed she was just back from spin class, having dropped the younger kids off at school. She immediately invited Tracy inside, apologising for the mess on the way through to the kitchen, as having four boys, her house was always somewhat chaotic. Tracy sympathised with her; her own hallway had often looked like a bomb had hit with the number of sports bags and shoes her boys had left lying around whilst growing up. Sarah said her husband was at work just now, but she was happy to help in any way she could.

Just like the other neighbours, Sarah didn't recall anything helpful either. She had been home all day Sunday as they were packing to go on holiday the following day. They only had two boys then and had been off to Florida to stay in her sister's villa for two weeks. The twins had been a bit of a surprise addition to the family six years ago.

Sarah remembered the night well, as her husband had popped out early in the evening to price up a job for when they returned. She had been mad at him as their flight to Florida via London had been leaving Inverness at seven am, and as they had to be there three hours early to check in, she had insisted they all try to go to bed early that evening. With him out, she had been left to get the kids ready for bed on her own whilst trying to finish off some last-minute packing. But he was always working. He was constantly on his phone even while they were away on holiday.

He ran his own construction business. On hearing he had been out that evening, around the time Erin had disappeared, Tracy was rather keen to meet him now. She didn't want to sound too eager, so she casually asked when he might be home if she needed to speak to him too. Sarah said he was usually home around six most evenings.

Just before she left she asked how Sarah liked the VW.

Sarah replied she preferred the Range Rover but this one was more practical now there were so many of them. Tracy casually asked when they had got rid of the Range Rover, Sarah confirmed it would have been sometime in 2016. On hearing this Tracy left for now, but vowed to herself to return that evening as perhaps Johnny might just be the person she was looking for, as this might explain why there was no black Range Rover linked to Jessica's disappearance.

Last on her short list was Marie Katz. She and her partner Mac had recently built their own home on the outskirts of Roseisle, a pretty little village in the parish of Duffus near Elgin. It was a fifty-minute drive away, so she headed to the supermarket to pick up a pack of sandwiches and a bottle of water.

The drive to Roseisle was delightful; within no time, she was driving through the beautiful countryside. It was so refreshing after living in the city all these years. She loved breathing in all this fresh air. The satnav on her vehicle eventually took her down a single-track road. As she neared her destination, she had to squeeze into a passing point to let a tractor pass before finally pulling up in front of their home.

The house was a large one-and-a-half-storey L-shaped barn-style home, finished with larch cladding and a smooth white render, with black aluminium windows. The L-shaped end of the home featured an overhang creating a covered deck area with three sofas surrounding a fire pit. Trees lined the plot, and there was a detached triple garage to the right-hand side with modern black doors. A raspberry-coloured Range Rover Evoque was parked in front of one of them. The garden at the front was still a bit of a quagmire. Tracy was beginning to wish she'd brought her wellies with her. Still, she stepped out of the car into the mud and squelched towards the enormous black front door, hoping the car parked out front meant someone was home.

A bell chimed deep within the house. A fresh-faced woman dressed in black yoga pants and a light pink sweat top covered in paint answered the door. Almost out of nowhere, a silver tabby appeared between her legs, curious to see who was at the door. This was Marie; she seemed much younger than her forty-eight years. She quickly invited Tracy in. Tracy removed her shoes which were covered in mud, and left them outside at the front door. The floor was a beautiful grey polished concrete. It looked cold, yet it felt warm underneath her socks. She figured they must have underfloor heating.

Marie took her along the hallway and led her into the vast open-plan kitchen/living space, which took up the entire L-shape overlooking the decked area she had noticed as she approached the property. It had a double-height ceiling with a glass balcony above. The whole room was painted white. The kitchen, situated in the corner to the right as you walked in, was a very pale grey wood with copper handles and sparkly grey quartz countertops. A large darker grey island with a butcher block worktop sat opposite the long bank of kitchen units. Copper lights hung down from the ceiling above the island. Tracy pulled out one of the bar stools and sat down whilst Marie filled the kettle.

After complimenting her home, she explained why she was there, showing Marie the photographs, this time of both Erin and Klara and asking if she knew either of them. Marie took a moment to look at each one. She said she vaguely remembered seeing posters for each girl around the town and in the local newspaper but denied interacting with either of them.

As Marie hadn't stayed near either girl, DS McGregor took a slightly different approach and, deciding to be honest, mentioned that she was there because witnesses had only recently placed a black Range Rover in the area around the time each girl had gone missing. She explained that, as a result, she was going around speaking to everyone who had owned a car like this around this time. She was following up on this lead on the off chance the person driving this vehicle had seen anything suspicious. Marie looked at the photographs again and said she couldn't remember ever seeing either girl, but it was so long ago.

Tracy thanked her for her time and, as she was on her way out, asked if Marie had ever stayed at Ness View Hotel. She said no, but her partner Mac, a steel fabricator, had built the new gates for the hotel. This suddenly became interesting to her. Tracy asked when this would have been, but Marie couldn't quite remember. She thought maybe sometime in 2015 or 2016, but she would have to check with him to be sure.

As she climbed back into the car, Tracy wondered if it was possible he might have been working at the hotel at the same time Klara had been staying there. He certainly would have had access to his partner's car. She decided to check the dates for this work with the hotel manager and look a bit closer into Mac.

She glanced at the clock in the car, 16:30. By the time she got back towards Inverness she would hit rush hour (although it was hardly the M8 rush hour traffic she was used to). Still, this would bring her back into town around the same time Johnny Baird would get home from work. As she had nothing or no one to go home to, she drove past Nairn and headed back into Inverness.

She called Ness View Hotel from the car and asked to speak to the manager. The girl in reception politely told her it was Mr Forsyth's day off and asked if she could help instead. Tracy thanked her but said she would call back the following day.

As she pulled up in front of the Baird residence, Johnny was unloading some of his tools from his white work van into the garage. He was a small squat man, around five foot seven, with hazel eyes and dark hair, greying at the sides. Tracy couldn't help but wonder if he possibly dyed his hair. His skin was tanned from working outside. Looking at him, he reminded her of a young Alex Salmond (the former First minister of Scotland).

He was wearing muddy orange construction boots, black jeans and a grey t-shirt that looked rather tight over his protruding gut (presumably from a fondness of beer) with a high-vis vest. As she introduced herself, he wiped his hands on his vest before firmly shaking her hand.

She already knew he wasn't the man she was looking for, but out of courtesy, she showed him Erin's photograph and asked if he may have seen her that evening or perhaps parked his car on the corner of the road near the hostel. He said he didn't remember seeing Erin before and would have no reason to park his car anywhere other than on their driveway. DS McGregor believed him. Not one to waste time, she thanked him and left.

Feeling slightly deflated, she popped into the large Morrisons supermarket on the way home to stock up, deciding to try and make herself a stir fry for dinner. She was still waiting on word back from Allan about the build costs for her new kitchen, so the antique oven was still out of bounds, but she had decided last night that maybe the hob didn't look quite so scary. Plus, she was getting fed up with microwave meals.

Thankfully, when she got home, the decorator had been, and her living room was starting to take shape. He would hopefully be finished by Wednesday. Then she'd have to wait a few days to let it dry out before staining the floor. Seeing Heidi's modern home inspired her to go with an off-white colour on the walls with a dark charcoal for the feature fireplace wall. She closed the door zipping back up the plastic door she had put up when she was sanding the floor to try and minimise the dust.

She poured herself a large glass of wine and sat in front of the fire in the snug while pondering the next stage of her investigation. Today hadn’t been a complete waste of time, she had ruled out three suspects and perhaps her suspicions about Mac would turn out to be correct.

39

Tuesday 1st November

Tracy started the day by contacting the manager of Ness View Hotel. David Forsyth had agreed to meet her at 11 am. When she arrived, he met her at reception and took her along to his office, where he had laid out coffee and pastries. She duly accepted. The Danish pastry she had chosen was delicious.

Conscious that everyone tended to know everyone in a small town, she pretended she was looking into security at the hotel asking specifically about key card entry to the rooms and whether or not it was possible to look as far back as the time Klara had been a guest with them. She sat through a half-hour explanation from David regarding hotel security and how it had been upgraded since then, so sadly this was no longer possible. Once he was finished, she mentioned the beautiful bespoke designed gates on the way into the hotel grounds. David told her proudly they had been made locally by Mac Rennie, who owns Rennie Mac Fabrications based in nearby Forres. She asked if they were new, and David told her Mac and his company had installed them in August 2016.

Time now to look closer into Mr Rennie. Back at the station, she ran his name through the police database - nothing. She ran him through the DVLA and saw he had several vehicles currently registered to him - a black Ford Ranger pick-up truck, a grey Ford Transit van and a red Ducati Diavel V4 motorbike. His license was clean, and the photograph was not much help as they are confined to your face so it doesn't give anything away about height and build.

She logged onto his website, hoping to find out what he looked like, but there were no photographs of him, just details of his services, testimonies from previous jobs, and photographs of his recent projects.

Deflated, she then tried searching the internet using just his name and Inverness. Several hits appeared. Some were Facebook links, which she ignored as she had no idea who she was looking for, and these could be anyone anywhere. As she scrolled down the list, she stopped, finding a newspaper article from the *Forres Gazette* in 2021. This story was about Mac Rennie, a local businessman who had jumped into the water at Findhorn Beach to rescue a young lad who had got into difficulty while paddle boarding with his friends.

He had been walking along the beach at the time, walking his dog, when he heard the boy and his friends shouting for help. Instinctively he had jumped into the water fully clothed and pulled the young lad to safety. There was a photograph of Mac with the young lad he had rescued, Ben McDougall, alongside the Lord Provost.

Although it was difficult to determine an exact height with nothing to gauge him by, she could see he was a tall, well-built man with dark receding hair and a short goatee beard. She pulled out her photograph of the black Range Rover driver for comparison. He had his face and head covered with the cap, so she couldn't see what his hair - if he had any - looked like. Without a face-on shot, it was impossible to tell if this was the same person or not.

Plus, this photograph was a more recent image than the one she had taken from the CCTV footage. They looked like they could be a similar build, though. She could place him at Ness View Hotel around the same time Klara had been staying there, and he had access to a black Range Rover, so she certainly wasn't ready to rule him out yet. However, she was well aware this wasn't enough to go on.

Stuck, she decided to call it a day. She took herself for a long walk along the beach at Nairn, stopping in for a fish supper on her way home. The fresh sea air had felt so refreshing, and it was nice to feel the wind on her hair. She slept like a log for the first time since arriving in Inverness.

40

He slowly opened the door and looked inside. She was sound asleep on the mattress, just as he hoped she would be. She was so peaceful, lying flat on her back. Her once wavy hair was starting to curl again and lay fanned out around her like a halo. He sat and watched her for a while, slowly breathing in and out. She looked so innocent lying there, but she would be just like the others – he was sure of it, pretending not to know him. Meeting her at Culloden that day had convinced him of this.

He studied her perfect features. Just exquisite. She would be his final masterpiece, but he wasn't in any rush. He had missed his deadline for this Halloween. He would have to wait until next year before he unveiled his final piece. Having waited this long for her to come back, he was sure he could wait a little longer.

Before he left, he placed another sandwich and bottle of water next to her, each one laced with just enough lorazepam to keep her sedated for a few more hours.

41

Wednesday 2nd November

Katie

Katie woke suddenly, just as she had done the previous day and the day before that. And just like the days before, she burst into tears as she realised her nightmare was still real. She was trapped, taken by some madman who had her chained to a radiator inside some dark and dingy room. Her limbs ached from being forced into the same cramped position for hours on end. Her throat was raw from crying and shouting. And she was wet, having soiled herself several times.

She turned around and noticed a plate beside her with a sandwich alongside a small bottle of water. The chain on the handcuffs had just enough play to enable her to reach them if she sat up. In doing so, she felt something sharp digging into her left breast. Wincing in pain, she looked down, trying to see what on earth could have done that to her. Shaking the blanket off, she realised it was her name badge from that stupid singles night, and it still had the pin attached to it. The pin had jagged her.

Edging herself as close as possible to the radiator, she slowly shimmied herself up into a seated position. Reaching across with her right arm, she managed to unclip the name badge. The pin was robust and quite sharp, a bit like a kilt pin. For the first time since she had been locked up in there, she suddenly felt a glimmer of hope and wondered if she could use it to get out of there.

She carefully hid it underneath the mattress for now, and knowing she had to keep her strength up, ate the sandwich and drank the water. It wasn't long before she drifted back to sleep, thanks to the sedative.

DS McGregor

Tracy was excited as she left for work that morning. She had decided overnight that she would try to speak to her new ACC today. Show him her findings so far and discuss where to go next. Maybe ask for some help tracking down the mystery Range Rover. When she entered the station, though, she could tell something big was happening. Only Jenny, a full-time civilian operative, was at the front desk.

All of the duty officers had been called into an emergency briefing.

Last night, the ACC received a call from an old friend about the daughter of a former colleague who was now living out in Florida. He and his wife hadn't heard from their twenty-nine-year-old daughter for over a week. She had been due to start a new job next week as a nurse at Raigmore Hospital but hadn't shown up to collect her ID badge or attend the induction programme, which was mandatory for all new employees.

Two officers had gone to her apartment that morning to check on her, and it appeared she may have gone running and not returned. He had officers searching all the local parks and known running routes, but there was no sign of her so far. This was the kind of job Tracy thrived on, but this was no longer her role in the police force anymore.

Saddened, she quietly retreated to her office and booted up her PC while waiting for the kettle to boil. Betty burst in just as she took the first mouthful of her coffee. She was vaguely excited but also had a rather grim expression which was unlike her. All she could say was – 'it's happened again!'

Puzzled, Tracy asked her what she meant. Betty was carrying a small brown envelope which she put down on Tracy's desk. Inside was a photograph - as she removed it from the envelope and turned it over to look at it, she almost dropped her mug. There staring back at her, was an image of yet another girl identical in looks to those of the other four missing girls. Except this was a photograph of twenty-nine-year-old Katie O'Connor, who was currently missing.

Tracy put down her coffee, pulled the pictures of Erin, Natalia, Klara and Jessica from her whiteboard and made her way along the corridor to the ACC's office. That time to speak up was now. Someone else's life was in danger. She knocked on the door and stepped inside on hearing permission to enter.

ACC Henderson was a tall, well-built, attractive man in his mid-fifties. He had a full head of grey hair, which he wore in a stylish pompadour style, which is short at the sides and rolled longer on top, swept back and up off his forehead. He had piercing blue eyes and was close-shaven. She had heard he was a fair man and had risen slowly through the ranks earning lots of respect from his colleagues as he went. Like her, he had spent much of his early career in the CID in Aberdeen and Edinburgh.

Tracy didn't beat about the bush; she just calmly sat and explained everything she had found out so far about each of the missing girls, before finally laying the photographs of each one in front of him alongside the recent picture of Katie. She told him everything about the links between their appearance, the fact they were all lone female travellers, and they had all disappeared at the weekend - roughly two years apart; the links with the black Range Rover and finally, although she wasn't quite sure how this fitted in yet, the haunted house link. And how she now believed that Katie's disappearance was somehow linked to this. At first, she thought she had overstepped the mark as the ACC just sat there staring at the photographs, and then he finally spoke.

His response was not what she imagined it would be - he stood up, grabbed his jacket and asked her if she'd like to go on a field trip with him. Delighted to be back out there doing what she considered real detective work, she jumped at the opportunity and almost skipped back to her office to grab her coat and bag. He was by the front door waiting for her. They drove directly to Katie's apartment. As he drove, he discussed all the details they had so far about Katie's disappearance, which was not much, to be honest.

Katie was the daughter of a retired police officer who was now living with his wife out in Florida. She was an only child and had moved to Inverness three weeks ago after splitting up with her fiancé. She was due to start a new job as a nurse practitioner at the accident and emergency department at Raigmore Hospital. She was a keen runner, and her mum and dad last spoke to her the previous Monday evening, as they did every Monday. When they couldn't contact her on Monday night, her dad had rung the hospital the following morning as she was due to start her induction this week, but they told him she hadn't shown up.

Worried he had called one of his old colleagues in Nottingham, who had then contacted the ACC directly. As a courtesy, he had offered to send some officers around to her apartment to check on her. The officers had to ask the building caretaker to let them in, as there was no answer at her door. On entering, they found her bed unmade and no sign of her.

They had checked her cupboards and, on finding no trainers, had concluded that maybe she had gone for a run and was possibly lying injured somewhere. Hence the reason for searching all the local trails and running routes, which so far had come up with nothing. He had officers canvassing the doors and the local neighbourhood looking for any information from anyone who might have seen or been in contact with her.

When they arrived, the apartment was already cordoned off with police tape, and an officer was stationed outside. He graciously tipped his head towards the ACC, obviously surprised to see him out of the office, and he also looked rather suspiciously at her. She guessed he was probably wondering what she was doing there, especially if he had heard the rumours about why she had been transferred here. Although they weren't sure if this was a crime scene yet, they both entered the apartment wearing gloves and a white paper suit. This way, if any evidence were present, it would hopefully have been preserved.

Tracy went straight into CID mode, moving methodically from room to room, snapping images of each room on her phone. As they entered the small hallway, she observed a pair of high-heeled shoes, one lying on its side underneath the radiator. Lifting one and turning it over, she saw someone had recently worn them to walk over gravel as tiny pieces of red stone were embedded into the leather soles. Just like the gravel, she had noticed on Erin's shoes.

She continued along the hallway, turning left into the kitchen. A little black faux fur bolero jacket was hung on the back of one of the bar stools. Picking it up and sniffing it, she could smell ladies' perfume mixed in with a sweet shampoo smell, indicating it had to have been worn relatively recently. But where would someone be going in a new town wearing something as glamorous as this? This was the very same question she had asked herself about the other girls.

A small delicate handbag sat on the countertop. Gently she opened it and slid out the contents. There was a Mac lip gloss in 'partial to pink'; a black leather card holder containing a credit card, bank card and driver's license; an unopened packet of hankies and a mobile phone, which had run out of charge.

On the countertop next to the fridge was a plate with a knife sitting on top. There were crumbs on the plate as if someone had recently made a slice of toast. The toaster was stone cold. No cups were lying around. Tracy found this strange, most people made tea and toast together. She went over and checked the bin - an uneaten slice of toast lay in the bin, neatly cut into four pieces. Opening the cupboards now, she was looking for the laundry basket. It was nowhere to be found.

She continued through the apartment, moving next into the bedroom. The curtains were haphazardly closed, and the duvet pulled back as if the bed had been slept in, but the person had left it airing, intending to come back and make it later. She opened the wardrobes; everything was nice and neat.

All of the clothes were hung in order of type and colour. Starting from the left-hand side were blouses and tops first, followed by skirts, dresses, trousers and jackets. All the hangers pointed in the same direction. On the shelf above were rows of handbags, again colour-coordinated, wrapped inside their dust bags. The bottom had shoe racks containing rows of neat shoes and boots. This was someone who liked everything in order. Either that or they were slightly on the autistic spectrum, she thought.

Tracy thought she could do with someone like this to help her organise her own home. She still had stacks of unopened boxes in her two spare bedrooms and was currently living out of a suitcase as she hadn't gotten around to buying wardrobes yet.

She found a purse in the bedside drawer. Emptying the contents onto the bed, there were some loyalty cards, two twenty-pound notes and a fist full of receipts from TK MAXX, Next and Asda. They were predominantly for home items, along with a few receipts for food.

Inside the zipped coin pocket, she found a receipt for £120 at The Loft, Inverness, from Saturday, the 29th of October 2022. New to the area, she had no idea what this kind of shop or business was, but if her suspicions were correct, she thought it might be a hairdresser or a beauty salon. She photographed it and put it back inside the purse, which she placed back inside the drawer, underneath the socks where she had found it.

She moved through into the en-suite, and there in the far corner of the room was what she had been looking for in the kitchen - the laundry basket. She tipped the contents onto the tiled floor and started sifting through them using a pen. There were the usual pants; socks; a black bra; a pair of pyjamas; towels; a couple of tops, and a pair of jeans but no dress.

She wandered into the other rooms, finding nothing but suitcases and a few boxes on the floor of the wardrobe of the second bedroom and just a very neat and tidy living room. She closed the doors on both of these rooms.

Wandering back into the kitchen to where the ACC was, she announced this scene felt staged to her. First, there were the fancy shoes, jacket and bag but no dress. She had searched everywhere. There had to be a dress as you don't wear jeans with a jacket like that. Granted, it was possible a dress could be at the dry cleaners, but there were no dry-cleaning receipts anywhere in her purse. And where on earth had she been going? She was new to the area and hadn't started work yet, so presumably hadn't made any friends here so far. There was no evidence that any friends from home had been visiting, which meant she was headed out alone, just like the other girls had been. This didn't make sense to her.

And the place was too neat. Everywhere in the apartment was immaculate; nothing was out of place. Yet there was the unmade bed, the bedroom curtains which had been hastily closed and the dirty dishes left out on the countertop. Then there was the uneaten toast they had found in the bin. She just didn't buy it that the person who lived here would go to the extreme of colour-coordinating her wardrobe, then go out and leave her curtains loosely drawn, bed unmade and dirty dishes lying around. That didn't add up.

The ACC turned to her and said he thought he might know where Katie was headed. One of the officers had come back from door-to-door enquiries. The lady next door, Mrs Davenport, had told them she met Katie on Saturday evening and she told her she was heading out to Loch Wood House on a ghost tour. They both looked at one another - time for them to go on another field trip.

Just as they were about to leave, Tracy caught sight of a piece of paper on the floor, poking out from underneath the fridge. Lifting it up for closer inspection, Tracy saw it was an invitation to an event at Loch Wood House. It was an unusual design, printed on parchment paper. The paper felt familiar to her somehow, but she couldn't quite think why. They bagged it for fingerprints.

They removed their gloves and white paper suits, discarding them in the bin on their way out. As they left the building, Tracy noticed there was CCTV, but the ACC was already on it. He had clocked it on the way in and had already spoken with the building owner, who, while she had been busy looking around the apartment, had put him in touch with the local security company. Officers were already on their way over to collect the recordings from the previous week.

As she was climbing into the ACC's car, she suddenly remembered why the paper looked so familiar - she had come across something similar while going through Erin's belongings. The writing had been smudged as the paper had become wet at some point, so she could not work out what it was, but now she was more convinced than ever that these cases were linked.

As they headed out to Loch Wood House together,

Tracy felt excited. This was her favourite part of the job, a role she had so desperately missed these past few months. It was obvious ACC Henderson missed this part of policing now too. Being stuck in an office all day was not the career he had envisaged when he first joined the police force. However, like Tracy, he had found himself eager to climb the ladder. She found out he was divorced with three teenage daughters.

It was a thirty-minute drive to Loch Wood House through more stunning scenery. The countryside was beautiful up here. There was no denying that. Even on the bleakest of days, it still lifted her mood. It wasn't long before they reached the gates leading them onto the private road. ACC Henderson got out and rang the buzzer. After a few minutes, it was answered. On hearing who was at the gate, they were buzzed through immediately, and the gates slowly swung open.

They drove past the small cottage at the gate and followed the tarmac road until they reached the fork in the road. Turning left, they headed towards the house on the red gravel track. Tracy was utterly mesmerised as soon as the house came into view, marvelling at the fact that this was someone's home. The ACC parked the car at the bottom of the grand staircase. They got out and walked up the stairs. Just as they were about to ring the doorbell, the door opened, and an imposing man appeared. He introduced himself as the Laird, Fraser Campbell-McNair. Tracy felt her heart racing – she didn't want to jump to any conclusions, but he was certainly the right height and build as the man she had witnessed taking Klara's luggage from the hotel.

After they all introduced themselves, Fraser led them through the impressive hallway into a smaller room at the back of the house. The room's walls were lined with books, some possibly older than the house itself. The fire had been lit, so the room was nice and warm. They sat on the two comfy leather wing-backed chairs next to the fire, whilst Fraser sat on the single chair facing them. An older lady, whom he introduced as the housekeeper Mrs Waddle, appeared at that moment, pushing a tea trolley filled with a freshly made pot of tea and some homemade scones. Tracy would have preferred coffee, but not wanting to seem rude, she accepted a cup of tea.

Once she had gone, they got down to business. They explained they were investigating the possible disappearance of a young lady who they believed may have attended an event held recently at his house. Fraser expressed his condolences to the young lady's family and immediately asked how he could help. They asked him what events had been held over the past five days. He lifted his iPhone and checked the business diary. Friday was the Mitchell/Hall wedding, and Saturday was the monthly haunted house singles evening. Tracy and ACC Henderson glanced at one another. She couldn't quite believe her luck. So that's what the *'tour with a difference'* was.

They asked him to explain a bit more about this event. He happily indulged them. The house was expensive to run; his parents had already started renting it out for weddings and film crews. It had been used in several period dramas, and magazine shoots over the years. When he had taken over the running of the house after his parents died, his friend Scott had suggested other ways he could raise money to help with the rising costs. Scott had devised the idea of running murder mystery weekends and a ghost tour that was also a singles evening.

Fraser hadn't been keen initially, but they had proven to be very popular, and each was usually full. Both were advertised in local hotels and B&Bs and on their website, meaning these evenings could be made up of a mixture of locals and tourists. However, they found the guests were usually more interested in seeing around the house than they were in a singles evening.

They asked for a copy of the guest list for both events and asked if he had attended either event himself. He said he had been at the ghost tour and admitted hosting the evening, giving his right-hand man the night off, but stated he had not been at the wedding. Tracy pulled out the photograph of Katie and handed it to him. She couldn't be sure, but she thought she noticed a flicker of recognition when he looked at it. He quickly handed her the photograph back, without another glance stating she possibly looked familiar but he couldn't be certain. Although she couldn't prove it, Tracy was convinced he was hiding something. He couldn't get rid of that photograph quickly enough.

They thanked him and having left him their card for him to email the guest list to, got up to leave. Fraser got up to show them out. As they walked back the way they came, Tracy noticed Mrs Waddle was busy polishing the brass rods in the main stairwell. Turning to acknowledge her, she looked up at the impressive chandelier. And that's when she saw it – the painting at the top of the stairs! She hesitated, feeling her heart race, this girl looked exactly like her missing girls. She tried to contain her excitement, but Fraser saw her notice it too.

As they reached the door, Tracy turned to Fraser and asked if they could also have the guest lists from previous events in August 2012, July 2014, June 2016 and July 2018.

Perplexed, he asked her why, as he thought they were investigating the disappearance of this young woman. Tracy said she couldn't tell him any more, as it was all part of their ongoing investigation. Visibly frustrated, he agreed but said this information might take longer to access. However, he would have his assistant email this information over to them whenever it was available.

As they drove back out through the estate, Tracy

couldn't help but feel she had rattled him. If he had hosted that event, he was bound to have seen Katie. Why had he hosted that evening in particular? And that painting in the stairwell – it could easily have been of any of the missing girls. She knew he was lying – but why? ACC Henderson thought so too.

And he was the right height and build for her mystery man in the CCTV footage at Ness View Hotel. Although she had kept that information to herself for now, knowing there would be no second chances for her this time, she was not about to make the same mistake twice.

42

Back at the station, officers were already painstakingly sifting through CCTV footage from outside Katie's apartment building. Tracy offered to take over and give them a bit of a break. Relieved, they welcomed the opportunity to step away from the screens for a bit.

By the time she took over, the officers had reached footage from the Saturday afternoon. Katie had been seen going for a run at 09:30. She was out for an hour and a half. She was then seen leaving again on foot at 12:25, returning at 16:50. It was apparent she had been to the hairdresser as her previously curly hair, which she had been seen wearing in a ponytail, had been teased into elegant waves. It looked like it had been highlighted too. So, Tracy was correct; The Loft must be a local hairdresser’s salon. She confirmed this, though by checking on *Google.*

A white taxi pulled up outside the apartments' entrance at 18:36. It sat for a few minutes before Katie emerged at 18:44 wearing a beautiful black knee-length dress teamed with a black fur bolero jacket, carrying a black sparkly evening bag. She was wearing high-heeled shoes that looked exactly like the ones that had been lying on the floor in the hallway of her apartment.

As she stepped into the waiting taxi, Tracy could see her dress looked very elegant. The sleeve of her jacket had slipped down at one side, revealing the dress was sleeveless. It had a high neckline with a fitted bodice and full skirt, complete with a tulle underskirt, which was just visible as she sat down. Zooming in, she could see the whole dress looked as though it was made of satin, but the skirt had a lace overlay with tiny black flowers embroidered on it.

She looked very different to her photograph, which she guessed may explain why Fraser was unsure when she had shown him the photo earlier. The picture they had of her was with her curly hair, and she was wearing a running vest and had no make-up on. She also looked slightly heavier in the photograph, although she was still tiny. But then again, he hadn't even given it a chance, he'd handed it back without a second look.

Going back to the surveillance video she wound the footage on. They knew from speaking to Fraser that the event ended around midnight, and the guests were escorted back to their hotel or residence afterwards. Tracy skipped through to 0:10 and watched slowly on from there. The ACC popped his head in, keen to determine if she had made any progress. She paused the footage and filled him in with the timeline she was working with. He asked her if she minded if he sat in with her whilst she watched on.

Glad of the company, she didn't mind one bit, and he had brought fresh coffee. They watched a young couple arrive back in a taxi at 0:32, having obviously been for a drink as they were staggering around, giggling and laughing, fumbling around for keys as the taxi cab drove off. Sometime after that, a young man walked up towards the front door wearing hospital scrubs at 0:45.

Then at 01:16, a black limousine pulled up at the front door. It was parked further forward than the taxi, affecting their visibility as the canopy over the door blocked their view. The driver's door opened, and a dark figure wearing a black wide-brimmed hat and tails got out and opened the back passenger door. The driver appeared to be talking to someone for a few minutes as he lingered outside before gently closing the car door, getting back in, and driving off. It was impossible to tell who or if anyone got out of this limousine. There was no CCTV inside the building. They rewound the footage and watched it again and again.

Feeling slightly deflated, she paused the screen. She still felt in her gut, just like the apartment, this was staged. Someone had gone to extreme lengths to ensure it looked like Katie had made it home that night. Watching on, Katie did not re-emerge via the front door either on Sunday, Monday or Tuesday. They both agreed on one thing now – it was time to let forensics process Katie's apartment. He made the call whilst she finished her coffee.

Returning to her office, she started thinking about the black Range Rover again. She had previously discounted all those registered outside a five-mile radius of the youth hostel, where Erin had been staying. This also eliminated those registered to outlying farms and stately homes, such as Loch Wood House.

She returned to her previously printed DVLA list, and sure enough, in 2012, there was a black Range Rover with a 5-litre V8 petrol engine registered to a Fraser Campbell-McNair, registration plate FR10 CMN. Cross-checking their records from 2014, 2016 and 2018, she found he was still the registered owner of a similar vehicle. She ran one final check and could see he currently had a 2021 model Range Rover sport D300 HSE diesel in Santorini black metallic paint registered to him.

This wasn't the only car he had registered to him. He also had a black 2021 model Audi R8 V10 Performance Spyder Quattro, and a 2019 BMW i8 petrol plug-in hybrid in protonic blue. Boy, did this guy love his cars! Tracy's ex-husband loved cars, so she knew how expensive each vehicle was. He was hardly struggling if he could manage to afford all of these cars and run that huge estate. Yet talking to him earlier, he made it sound as if he was almost destitute when he started hosting these events.

Tracy wanted to go back over and arrest him

immediately, but careful not to let history repeat itself; she decided to continue digging. She started by looking into Fraser's background. He was born on the 30th of November 1978, making him forty-four on his next birthday. Educated abroad, he had spent most of his childhood with his parents at the family home in Inverness. He had a twin sister Emilia who was sadly killed in a tragic accident alongside his parents in 2003, leaving him the sole heir of the family title and estate.

Logging into the police report from the accident, she could see from witness statements his sister had been home for a long weekend and had gone horse riding on the estate, as she often did, whilst her parents were out for the afternoon. As they returned from lunch at a friend's house, their daughter had come charging out of the gates at full speed, causing her poor dad, who had been driving, to swerve to try and avoid hitting her and her horse. But the horse had somehow panicked and changed direction at the last minute, causing them to plough into their daughter and straight into the path of an oncoming articulated lorry.

Mr and Mrs Campbell-McNair had been killed outright, whilst their daughter had clung on for three days on a ventilator with horrific internal and external injuries. Her brother Fraser, who had been on holiday at that time, had rushed back from where he was staying, where he had sat at her bedside holding her hand the entire time. He was absolutely heartbroken. The articulated lorry driver, who had survived the crash, had been breathalysed, as had blood alcohol levels been checked for Mr Campbell-McNair - both came back negative. No one was found to have been speeding.

From the photographs of the scene, it was impossible to tell what type of car they had been driving. The entire front of the vehicle had crumpled into the front of the lorry. The horse had been completely cut in half. Emilia had been partially thrown off her horse onto the side of the road; only her lower right leg had become trapped between the lorry and her parent's car, presumably caught in the stirrup.

She had suffered a fractured skull, causing a subarachnoid haemorrhage; a tension pneumothorax which had been treated on scene by the EMRS team after being correctly identified by paramedics; a fractured pelvis/left femur and a complicated crush fracture of the right tibia and fibula.

Her injuries were so severe she had been airlifted to Aberdeen Royal Infirmary. A CT scan revealed, in addition to the above, she also had a ruptured spleen, liver and bowel lacerations, along with various other fractures. She had undergone an emergency splenectomy, bowel resection, and right lower limb amputation, followed by pelvic fixation and burr hole decompression to relieve the pressure on her brain caused by the haemorrhage. Sadly, it was too much for her body to cope with, and the doctors had recommended switching off her life support after it was demonstrated through several sets of neurological testing, that she had no brain function.

A postmortem of Mr and Mrs Campbell-McNair revealed they had died of severe chest trauma. Mr Campbell-McNair had suffered from cardiac tamponade, whilst his wife had suffered a traumatic aortic dissection (ruptured aorta). Both had been pronounced dead at the scene. The only injury sustained by the lorry driver was a back injury, caused by the impact of the crash. The coroner's verdict had been that of a tragic accident. Tracy felt incredibly sad reading this. Almost an entire family was wiped out in one tragic event.

43

Thursday 4th November

Katie

The early morning sun on her face was causing Katie to stir again. Using her tongue, she could feel her parched lips were cracked and her limbs aching from the position she had been forced into for days on end now. She could feel she was getting weaker, which meant she would have to try and make a break for it soon before she lost what little strength she had left.

He was keeping her drugged, so she decided she wouldn't touch any more of the food or water he brought her that night. She lay back down on the mattress and closed her eyes as she tried to come up with a plan. Attacking him whilst she was still chained up was no good. Even if she somehow managed to stab him in the jugular artery, he could fall on her and squash her. Plus, she would still be chained up, and she'd die from dehydration and starvation as she doubted anyone other than her captor knew where she was. She would have to come up with another plan - and fast.

DS McGregor

Forensics were finished processing Katie's apartment. They had found no DNA or fingerprint trace of anyone other than Katie in her apartment, which was disheartening. This guy was good. A sweep of the building had, however, found a faulty lock on the back door of the apartment building, which led into the laundry room, together with a deactivated surveillance camera which had been tampered with at some point. This, too, was clean of prints, but it did at least prove it was possible for someone to access the building and possibly Katie's apartment undetected.

By mid-morning, the guest lists had arrived from Loch Wood House for all the guests who attended both the wedding and the ghost tour, and those for all previous events on the dates she had asked for - scanning the lists from the most recent events first Tracy quickly found Katie's name on the guest list from the ghost tour which took place on Saturday the 29th of October.

It wasn't long before she found the names of the other four girls - Erin Doherty, Natalia Robertson, Klara Eriksson, and Jessica Fletcher. Each one of them had attended the ghost tour. Placing the other lists aside, she started cross-checking them, looking for a pattern. In case the same person had attended the same event as all five girls, but she found none.

They decided to focus on Katie for now. Twenty-eight guests were listed as attending the event held on the Saturday evening. Meaning they had twenty-seven interviews to carry out, together with staff and background checks for everyone else who was there. This investigation was going to need all hands on deck. She was sure the ACC wouldn't mind if she lent a hand; after all, Katie's disappearance did appear to be linked to her cold cases, so she wasn't technically overstepping the boundaries of her job description. And, she was still a DS.

She was teamed up with PC Lesley Purdie, who had joined the police force ten years ago. PC Purdie was a local girl, so she knew some of the girls on the list. They decided to start interviewing the girls first, as Tracy thought this might help them open up a bit if they were interviewed by someone who knew them. As Suzy, Ellie, Lizzy and Rebecca all worked in the X-ray department, they started at the hospital. Thankfully, they were all on shift today, and the deputy radiology service manager was kind enough to lend them her office to give them some privacy to speak with each of the girls.

They spoke to each one in turn, starting with Ellie. Ellie could identify Katie, although it took her a few minutes as she noted that her hair was very different that evening. Instead of the tight curls in the photograph Tracy showed her Katie's hair was much longer as it had been straightened into long sophisticated waves and highlighted with soft honey tones.

Tracy asked what Ellie remembered about the evening. She described the house, the lavish spread of food and drink laid on for them, then talked a little about the tour itself. As you were paired off with someone at that point, she didn't pay much attention to what everyone else was doing. Plus, it had been dark. They only had a tiny little battery-operated lantern between each couple.

They had just been curious to see inside the house and had gone along with it being a singles evening as a bit of fun. Tracy asked about what she was wearing. Ellie explained they were all asked to dress smartly like they were attending a cocktail evening, so she, too, had been wearing a long black dress from Mango with sparkly straps. She had paired her outfit with silver wedge sandals and a silver clutch bag.

On the way over, she had spoken to Katie in the minibus, but as she had been sitting at the back beside Rebecca, she mainly had just exchanged small talk with Katie. Although she did remember the driver had been rather handsome in a moody kind of way, and she ashamedly admitted giving him a bit of a hard time once the alcohol started flowing.

Tracy and Lesley spoke to Lizzy and Rebecca, who confirmed everything Ellie had told them about the evening. They, too, had been all glammed up. Both of them had thought the Laird was very handsome, but agreed he seemed full of himself.

Suzy was the most helpful as she interacted with Katie a lot that evening, sitting beside her while they ate. Suzy talked freely about their time together from meeting Katie outside the train station; to her noticing, that Katie became quite friendly with one of the guys she met on the tour. She thought his name was Chris, as she recognised him from work. He was a paramedic. She was pretty positive she saw them exchanging numbers towards the end of the evening.

When they asked her if Katie had travelled back with them after the event, Suzy sheepishly admitted the very end of the evening was somewhat hazy, probably due to the amount of alcohol they had all had to drink. She didn't think Katie had been with them but couldn't be certain. Ellie, Lizzy and Rebecca had all said exactly the same thing. None could remember much about leaving the event or travelling home afterwards. All were ashamed to admit they had woken up in their beds the following day, none of them having any recollection of how they had gotten there.

Tracy asked if she remembered anyone else hanging

around Katie. Suzy hesitated momentarily before saying there was one strange thing that happened – right at the very beginning of the night, which might have been absolutely nothing. Excited, Tracy asked her to carry on. She told them when they discovered their host for the evening was the Laird he seemed rather full of himself initially, until he caught sight of Katie, almost as if seeing her there caught him off guard or something. He had stopped talking mid-sentence and just stared at her, only for a few minutes, but she had noticed Katie blush and look away. When she asked Katie what that was all about, she said she had no idea as she'd never met him before.

Using the list of names, the girls were able to identify from it which guys had been picked up in the minibus with them. Tracy and Lesley felt their next logical move was to speak to these guys, especially Chris. Although Tracy was still convinced Fraser had something to do with this.

As they left the hospital, they stopped by the ambulance station to see if Chris was on shift. Luckily, he was, and he was just returning from a job when they pulled into the parking lot. After asking his colleagues if they minded stepping out for a bit, he cleared some time with ambulance control and sat down in the mess room to talk with them. When they showed him Katie's photograph, he instantly recognised her. Tracy noticed he seemed visibly shaken when they told him she was missing.

He told them he had liked Katie a lot. They had exchanged numbers at the end of the evening, and he had planned to take her out tomorrow as he was on a few days' leave after finally finishing a run of day shifts at 7 pm that night. He admitted he had texted her the following day but was disappointed as she hadn't replied.

When they asked him how he got home, he too was embarrassed to admit that his memory of the return journey was also very hazy. He remembered being in the minibus but couldn't say exactly who had been in it with him. His hangover the following day had been pretty horrific, but he had simply put it down to the fact he didn't drink much and wasn't used to drinking prosecco.

Tracy and Lesley moved on to Gordon, as he lived closest to the ambulance station. He was loading his car with suitcases when they pulled up in front of his house. They had caught him just before he was due to leave for the airport, as he was off to the rigs for the next three weeks. He too recognised Katie and remembered spending a bit of the evening chatting to her, but like Chris had been so drunk, he couldn't remember the journey home either.

They moved on to Mike next, a financial advisor who worked from a small office he rented in the town centre. He also recognised Katie but said he hadn't spoken much to her as he had been too busy chatting to Lizzy that evening. They had hit it off and had been out on several dates since

Saturday. Just like the others, he could remember Katie being on the minibus at the start of the evening, but after that, it was all a bit of a blur to him, including their journey home.

Next on their list was Joe. Getting no answer at his apartment, they called him on his mobile. It turned out he was at work at Urquhart Castle. Looking at their watches, it was 15:30. The castle closed at 17:00. Keen not to waste any time, the girls jumped in the car and headed up the A82. They were there in just over thirty minutes, with Tracy still enjoying the breathtaking scenery en route. Lesley, who had grown up nearby, pointed out many places of interest as they drove there. Once this case was over, Tracy decided she would definitely need to take some time off to explore the area.

As usual, it was a very windy day at Urquhart Castle. The wind almost cut them in two as they made their way down to the visitor centre. When they got there, Joe was waiting for them. He told them the same thing that Gordon and Chris had, although he remembered Katie seemed quite jumpy while on the tour. She told him at one point; she felt someone was watching her. He didn't remember anyone in particular, acting strangely around her. However, he noticed one of the guys on the tour - a loud-mouthed, arrogant older gentleman whose name he didn't recall his name, had been quite leery towards some of the young ladies. He figured that was maybe all that was bothering her.

Last but not least from this group was Richard, who worked for the forestry commission, and luck would have it, he was in nearby Urquhart Woods today. A quick call to him confirmed he was still on site, so they agreed to meet him in the small car park before he finished. He was another tall man but thin with receding dark hair. Unless he had lost a lot of weight in the preceding years, he wasn't the man from the CCTV footage either. He also recognised Katie, but just like the others, he couldn't confirm whether she had been on the minibus on the way home or not.

Tracy and Lesley jumped wearily back into the car. They had now spoken to nine people, and although they had CCTV footage of someone possibly arriving back at her apartment block that evening, no one they had spoken to so far was actually able to confirm that Katie had left the house at the end of the evening. There were still another sixteen people on the guest list that evening, and judging by what she had heard so far, Tracy doubted they would be able to confirm this either. Still, they had to try - no stone unturned and all. Then, they had to move on to the staff.

As they drove back into Inverness, Tracy and Lesley couldn't help but think that it all seemed a bit too convenient that everyone they had spoken to so far had been so drunk they couldn't remember anything about getting home – was it possible they could all have been drugged? But by whom and why? It didn't make sense - unless someone had already planned to try and snatch Katie.

44

Although she had no concept of time, she knew that evening was approaching as the sun had gone down already, and twilight was creeping in. It was always dark when he came to check on her. She wondered if perhaps he had a day job or if this was the only time he could slip away unnoticed. Straining to listen out for him, she lay on her side, facing the wall, her right ear pinned to the ground. Eventually, she heard a car approach the building. Somewhere below her, to her left, a door opened, and it wasn't long before she heard the stairs creak under his weight.

When he reached the top of the stairs, she heard his heavy footsteps approaching her room. Her heart was pounding in her chest. The door was locked with a key which she could hear him turn in the lock. This time, the key must already be in the door as she couldn't hear him insert it. Maybe he was becoming careless. The door creaked on its hinges as it slowly swung open. She turned her head to look at him, but as usual, he held the torch high as he shone it towards her. Even as her eyes adjusted, the position of the light always made it impossible for her to make out any of his features.

She could see he was a tall, broad man. He wore dark clothing and had a balaclava hiding his face. For the first time, she wasn't sure if she imagined it or not, but she felt as if he was possibly somewhat familiar to her. He never spoke to her; he just checked her bindings and removed the old plate and water bottle, replacing them with new ones. For the first time, he leaned over her and lovingly stroked her hair. Placing a stray strand behind her ear. Shivering at his touch, she shied away towards the radiator. He smirked, pulled the blanket around her, and retreated the way he had come in.

As soon as he was gone, she reached underneath the mattress and felt for her pin; it was still there. His actions made her more determined than ever that tonight was the night she would try to break out of here. Ear to the ground again, she had switched position, although painful to do so, listening intently for his footsteps on the stairs. When she finally realised he was gone, she let out a massive sigh of relief, collapsed back on the mattress, and burst into tears again.

After she had stopped crying, she decided she had to try and get a grip of herself. She figured she had at least twenty-four hours before he was back again. She got into a more comfortable position, lying down, almost cuddling the radiator, and started to think. Her feet were bound together with masking tape. She had tried to pick at the tape using her fingers, but it was impossible as she couldn't get into a position where she could see what she was doing. The tape was also very sticky.

Thinking back to the pin, she wondered if she could use it like a saw on the tape. It wasn't sharp, but it was thick and strong and reminded her of a kilt pin. Lying on her back, she lifted her legs up first, then raised her arms. Bending her knees, she brought her feet in towards her hands. Her arms were stretched as far up as possible. Careful not to drop the pin, she held it firmly in her left hand and purposely tried a sawing action, but the tape wouldn't budge. If anything, it seemed to be making it tighter, and she could feel it was starting to cut into her ankles. Defeated, she lowered her legs.

Determined not to let this beat her, she thought about what else she could try. And then she suddenly remembered her dad had taught her how to pick handcuffs as a little girl. It was kind of like his party trick. You couldn't do it with the modern police handcuffs, but looking down at these, she could see these were really old.

Feeling the first bit of hope in the last few days, she shimmied herself up into a seated position. Taking the pin between her hands, she opened it wide and bent it until it was wide enough to use like a pick. She moved the pin into her right hand and started work on the lock. Her first few attempts failed, but she was determined to continue; it was her only hope.

Her arms were aching, and her wrists were bleeding, but just as she was about to give up, she suddenly heard that familiar click. She had done it - her left arm was free! She fed the cuff through the bar in the radiator, and her arms were free. Leaving the cuff dangling on her right arm like a bracelet, she wrung her hands, so grateful to be free.

She turned her attention next to her feet. Using the sharp end of the pin, she made several holes in the tape and scored away at it until she was eventually free. Gingerly she tried to stand, but immediately fell back down again onto the mattress. She was weaker than she thought, and it might also be the drugs he had given her. Taking a minute to steady herself, she looked around the pitch-black room, trying to take in her surroundings. There was only one window opposite her, a cupboard and a single door. She tried to stand again, this time having a bit more success. The room still spun, but it was gradually levelling out. She made her way over to the window and lifted the blind. The window was barred, and when she tried to open it, it wouldn't budge. She was also at least one floor up, so climbing out of here wouldn't have been an option, even if the bars hadn't been in the way.

She tried the door next, which was locked just as she had suspected. Her feet were sore walking on the wooden floor as the room appeared to be full of debris. She sat back down on the mattress and hit on the idea of tearing the blanket into strips to protect her feet. It wasn't long before she had completely covered each foot, using the tulle from her underskirt to create a bit of padding. It wasn't exactly comfortable underfoot, but at least it made it bearable, and she had a feeling that if she made it out of there, she was probably in the middle of nowhere, so she might have to make her way over uneven terrain to get help.

With her feet covered, she made her way back over to the locked door. Using her pin again, she tried the lock; it wouldn't budge, but she could tell the key was, as she suspected, on the other side of the door. She wondered if she could knock it out and somehow manage to get it. Looking around, she wondered what she could use. There was no point in knocking it out if she couldn't reach it afterwards. Using the rest of the blanket, she carefully folded it into a section the same width as the door and gently fed it out underneath as far as she could.

She then took her pin again, bent it back into a pin shape and began trying to push the key out. Eventually, it dislodged and landed half on the blanket and half on the floor. She gingerly started pulling the blanket towards her. The key moved a little at first, then stopped as it hit a dip in the floor. She paused before very gently pulling the opposite corner of the blanket. Slowly the key started moving towards her again. With her heart in her mouth, she watched the key come closer and closer towards her. As it was almost about to pass under the door, it hit another dip in the floor and fell off the blanket completely. Katie burst into tears.

Looking around the room, she was now desperate to reach this key. She glanced over at the sandwich he had left her. It was on a paper plate. Throwing the sandwich off, she grabbed the plate and took it over to the door. It was just wide enough to fit under the gap in the door. She carefully positioned the plate outside the door and used it to try and flick the key towards her. After a few tries, gradually, the key started moving. Patiently she waited until it eventually moved close enough that she could touch it with her finger. One more flick, and she was able to draw it in toward her. Grabbing it, she pulled it through, inserted it into the lock and turned the key. She flung open the door and stumbled out into the darkness.

Once her eyes adjusted to the dark, she could see she was at the end of a small landing. There were four other doors, all locked as she tried each of them as she passed along the corridor. Although she still had her pin, she was well aware this wouldn't offer much protection should that brute of a man re-appear. She gingerly climbed down the first flight of stairs, stopping briefly on the landing to make sure she was still alone.

This floor was identical to the one above. She tried all

the doors and found two of the rooms were unlocked. They were all empty and, just like the room she had been kept in, had bars on the windows. She returned to the second landing and descended the final set of stairs.

The front door was facing her. She ran over to it and tried the handle, but it was also locked. He must have taken the key. The windows to the side of the door were also barred from the outside. She would have to find another way out of here.

Using the moonlight coming in through the tiny square windows in the door, she could make out there was a long corridor leading behind the stairs. She had no option but to follow it and see where it led. The light from the door didn't stretch to the end, so she had to feel her way along the walls hoping the floorboards were intact and she wouldn't fall through them. Feeling her way along the walls, she passed several locked doors before finally coming to a room at the end. On finding this door unlocked, she turned the worn round handle and pushed.

The door opened inwards revealing a large room, much larger than the others she had been in. Although it was difficult to tell in the dark, it had what looked like easels set out along the back wall, and it had a large table in the middle, dominating the room. A little moonlight was poking its way through the windows, which also had bars over them. Making her way over to the table, she saw the table was smeared with something white. In the dark, she was unsure what this could be. Touching it, it seemed brick-hard, almost like dried plaster.

Wandering over to the first of the easels, she could make out several pieces of paper were pinned to it. There were layers and layers of them piled on top of one another. As she got closer, she could make out sketches of what looked like a woman. She made her way around all four before realising a final one stood in the centre of the room, next to the table. Compared to the others, it only had a few sketches pinned on it. It was so dark she couldn't quite make any of them out.

Feeling her way around the table, she wondered if there might be tools somewhere. She was desperately hoping there was something in here she could use to pry the bars off the window, or maybe even break down the door. As she was feeling her way around the room, she found a cord hanging from the ceiling. Pulling it, she discovered it was a light switch.

The whole room was suddenly bathed in a flood of yellow light. Initially, she had to close her eyes as she felt the bright light burning into her retinas. Slowly she was able to open them again. As she did so, she was startled by her surroundings. The table did indeed have dried plaster on it. Tubs of new plaster sat unopened underneath. In the centre of the table was a smashed sculpture of a woman's head, the eyes gouged out.

Opening the drawers in the table, she found an array of tools - tiny chisels, rakes, hammers, shapers and sponges. She lifted a hammer and chisel, placing them on the table while looking around to see what else she could find.

Every space on the walls around the whole room was covered in photographs and sketches of a woman. As she got closer, she saw they were of the same person. Some of the images looked posed, whilst others looked as if they had been taken when she had been completely unaware anyone was watching her. There were hundreds of them, spanning back years. The more she looked at them, the more familiar this girl became. Suddenly she realised where she had seen her before. She was the girl from the painting at the top of the stairs inside Loch Wood House! This was Emilia - the Laird's twin sister who had tragically died. She noticed some of the sketches were in a very similar style to the large one that hung inside the house on the stairwell.

Wandering over to the easels, she could see now each one held various sketches of other girls who looked eerily similar to Emilia. Looking through the drawings, she was shocked to find images of them in nearby places, all seemingly unaware they were being watched. Finally, she came to an image of each one hanging from a tree, each one obviously dead. She let out a cry, tears streaming down her face. Underneath these sketches were photographs of their lifeless bodies being moulded into statues. Their bodies were intact underneath the plaster. As she reached images of the final stages, she gasped as she suddenly recognised them - they were the creepy statues she remembered seeing on the website for the haunted forest Halloween tour.

Horrified, she made her way around all four easels. Sure enough, they were all images of the same thing. Finally, she found images of herself pinned to the very last easel - there were loads of sketches and photographs of her pinned to the top of the board. There was one of her coming out of her apartment block, several of her running, some of her at the singles evening and one of her lying sleeping on the mattress in the room above. There was even one of her in the café at the train station the day she arrived in Inverness. She shuddered and, realising her fate, promptly vomited into a nearby bucket. This man, whoever he was, was sick, and she would be the next statue if she didn't get out of here now.

Wiping her mouth on the back of her hand, she returned to the table and, grabbing the small chisel and hammer, calmly made her way back along the dark corridor towards the front door. She was going to break out of here if it was the last thing she did. She positioned the chisel, took aim and started around the lock on the solid front door.

45

Friday 4th November

Tracy was at the station bright and early again this morning. After yesterday's revelations, she hadn't slept much. She kept thinking about poor Katie, wondering if she was still alive. She felt within her heart, that the other girls were probably dead, but she hoped there might still be a chance for Katie.

The senior investigating officer (SIO) in charge of Katie's disappearance was DCI Neil Harper. He was already at his desk. She grabbed a few coffees and headed into the briefing room to join him. Her photographs and the information she had gathered on the cold cases had been included on the whiteboard that had been set up for Katie's disappearance. Looking up from his paperwork, he invited her to sit down so they could discuss the case.

Tracy learned whilst she and Lesley had been interviewing the people who attended the singles evening, he and his team had been busy looking into the employees from Loch Wood House. Initial background checks had found nothing suspicious. No one had any criminal records. They mainly employed foreign nationals to help with the catering side of the business. However, this had reduced significantly post-Brexit, and they now relied on students to fill these positions.

Given that they were chasing names from over a decade ago, it might take some time to track everyone down. So far, the only consistent employees were those who worked on the estate. These included the housekeeper, chef, gardeners and events manager. Family-wise, there was just the Laird.

The housekeeper Mrs Waddle, whom Tracy had already met, seemed an unlikely candidate. At sixty-two, she had taken over from the previous housekeeper only six years ago, so she wasn't around at the time of all the girl's disappearances. Background checks into her family showed she had no children and her husband was in a nursing home, after suffering a major stroke.

Most of the time, Fraser did his own cooking, unless he was hosting a dinner party when he would call on his chef. The chef, Charles, was in his late sixties and had been employed by Fraser's late mother and father. He often prepared the food for the events they hosted, and thus couldn't quite be ruled out of the investigation yet. However, Tracy had already discounted him as she knew she was looking for a younger man.

Which brought them on to the Laird. He was overseas a lot, and checking records, it looked like Fraser had been out of the country for all but Katie's disappearance. Tracy felt quite deflated hearing this, but given that she knew he travelled by private jet, she wasn't quite ready to rule him out just yet.

Moving on, there were some regular gardeners who worked on the estate, taking care of the ornate gardens used for weddings and providing general maintenance of the grounds whom he was currently looking into, and, finally, there was Scott Brown, who was the Laird's childhood friend and event planner.

Tracy's ears pricked up on hearing this. Fraser had briefly mentioned him yesterday, but she had been too busy watching Fraser's actions, she hadn't paid much attention. DCI Harper knew Scott, as they had gone to school together. He told her Scott's father had been the groundskeeper, his mum the housekeeper (before Mrs Waddle). They had lived in the cottage at the front gate before sadly passing away, within months of one another.

Scott was the same age as the Laird and, as an only child, had grown up on the estate with Fraser and Emilia. He remembered he was a bit of a loner, preferring to hang around the estate. As they looked into his background, they discovered he had followed Emilia to art school, where he had graduated with a BA honours in fine art, specialising in sculpture and watercolour.

DCI Harper remembered he had been quite cut up after Emilia's death, and seemed to remember hearing through the grapevine, that some time afterwards Fraser had taken him on as events manager. He had been in charge of planning and developing the business side of running the house, leaving Fraser to concentrate more on managing the property portfolio his parents had built up here and abroad. He assumed Fraser had given him this position as he felt quite sorry for him, having been so close to his sister.

They quickly discovered Scott ran the Loch Wood House website and often hosted many of the events he organised. In return, he stayed in his parents' old cottage and had a complete run of the estate. Tracy couldn't help but wonder if this included the use of the cars. Then she suddenly remembered Fraser Campbell-McNair had a black Range Rover registered to him. What if….?

Digging further into his background, Tracy could see Scott also had a share in a luxury car hire company, the same company in fact, that often provided transport for the events they ran at the house. The limousine! Klara had arrived back in a limousine and so had Katie – allegedly! Tracy quickly found the name of the company and looked them up online. Scanning their website, she found a list of vehicles registered to them along with their current drivers. She soon located the vehicle and the name she was after.

Excited, she turned to DCI Harper and asked if he had any photographs of Scott. A few moments later, he searched online and pulled up images of him alongside Fraser at various events. Tracy pulled out her phone and, scrolling through her photographs, found the image of the man caught on CCTV at Ness View Hotel retrieving Klara's luggage - there staring back at her was that very man! She was now 100% convinced of it. To double-check, she pulled up the footage of the limousine outside Katie's apartment - although he had shielded his face, from his stature she was positive they were looking at the same person. Sharing her findings - DCI Harper agreed.

They grabbed their jackets and tore out of the office. She drove while DCI Harper spent most of his time on the phone organising a warrant and a team to meet them at the house. It was only 07:30, but they knew time was running out. Hopefully, they would catch him before it was too late.

46

Katie could see dawn was beginning to break through as the light coming through the windows was changing to sunlight. She knew she didn't have much time left. Her hands were raw from chipping away at the lock with the tiny little chisel, but she was almost there. And she still had the handcuffs dangling from her right wrist. She could practically smell her freedom. One more swing of the hammer and the wood surrounding the lock disintegrated. Grabbing the handle, she used her last ounce of strength to free it from its grip. Stepping out into the fresh air, she collapsed onto the ground.

Quickly she picked herself up. Although she had no idea what direction to head in, she just knew she had to go now before he came back and realised she was free. She gingerly made her way down the stone steps and was about to head down the dirt track road when she looked down and saw the tyre tracks. Her heart sank as she realised this road could lead to civilisation and help, but it could also lead her straight to him. Turning back towards the building, she hastily made her way around it and headed towards the woods mindful of her step.

As she was making her way into the tree line, she thought she could hear the rumble of a diesel engine in the distance, fearful it might be her captor she froze, wondering if she should find somewhere to hide. Suddenly she thought she could see headlights through a tiny gap in the dense forest. They were still a fair way off, but they looked like they were headed straight for her. Terrified, she knew she wasn't far enough away from the building he had held her captive in. Looking down at her bleeding hands she knew she wasn't ready to give up. At that moment her adrenaline kicked in and she took off running deeper and deeper into the forest, no longer caring about her feet. She hadn't come this far to be caught now.

47

Scott was busy getting ready for the day ahead. Halloween was past, and there were no more events scheduled this weekend. With Fraser safely headed back to New York, he was free to do as he pleased on the estate again. It was time for him to get to work on his final masterpiece - his grand finale for Emilia!

He had taken the truck today as it was easier to transfer the bodies afterwards, and it was also easy enough to take down the lane to the old abandoned servants' quarters. The gardeners never came down here, and with his parents both dead, there was no one else left now who knew this building existed. It wasn't on any of the maps.

This had been a place where just he and Emilia went. They had called it their secret hideaway as teenagers, having found it together one Saturday afternoon while riding around the estate. It had been completely overgrown. They had removed the ivy from the front door and, with Scott's dad's help, repaired the generator, which supplied them with some light and heating. The water had been long turned off, but there was a well outside with a bucket attached to a pulley system, adding to the fun. He had experimented here with his sculptures, whilst Emilia had created some of her early masterpieces. They had spent many an afternoon there together. He had never wanted to leave.

It had seemed fitting to bring her back here, so they could be together forever. He hated the killing part and was sad it had come to that, but it was necessary as he was sure she would reject him again. She had shown no signs of recognising him when they met face-to-face last week at Culloden. It had to end this way. Hopefully, she would still be sleeping then he wouldn't have to look at her while he ended her life. He had put extra sedatives inside her water last night, just to make sure.

But, maybe he didn't have to kill her – what if there was another way? Maybe he could swoop in and rescue her, just like he had as a teenager when she fell off the rope swing into the frozen loch. He hadn't hesitated, like her stupid brother, jumping straight in and pulling her to safety. She had clung to him afterwards and told him he was her hero that day. It was then that he knew he loved her. He sped up, anxious to get to her, hoping his new plan would work.

As he drove through the hidden gates, he immediately saw the door had been burst open. The rage from earlier was back. He jumped out of the truck and ran over to the door examining the damage, panicking as it looked as though it had been burst open from the inside. Tearing up the stairs two at a time, he reached the door to the room where he had imprisoned Katie. It, too, was lying wide open, the key still on the inside of the door.

He quickly looked around the room, but he already knew she was gone. The water and the sandwich he had left the night before lay untouched. Enraged, he kicked them over and tore back down the stairs. He ran along the corridor to his studio – finding the door was wide open, and the light was on. He knew now he had to find her. Grabbing a length of rope from the back of the truck, he crashed out into the forest, smashing through the undergrowth. She couldn't have gotten far in this terrain as he knew she didn't have any shoes.

48

DCI Harper and DS McGregor were almost there, remembering to slow down on the final bend. She needed to make it there in one piece - they both did. Smoke was billowing out of the cottage's chimney at the gatehouse. Trying to play it cool, they buzzed the intercom to the house. No one answered. And no one moved inside the cottage.

Sensing they didn't have much time, Tracy was already looking at ways they could scale the fence. There were spikes at the top. Opening the boot and finding nothing useful, she removed her jacket. Rolling it up, she climbed up onto the bonnet of the police car and placed her jacket over two of the spikes. She was glad she was wearing trousers today. They both climbed over and jumped onto the grass on the other side.

They tried the cottage first, which turned out to be empty. Scott had been there recently by the looks of it, though, as the coals in the fire were still smouldering away. The kettle was warm, too, as if it had recently been boiled, and there were warm dishes on the draining board. Satisfied they had searched the entire place and found no one home, they decided to head towards the house. Backup would be here soon; hopefully, the dog handling unit wouldn't be too far behind them.

***

Katie was running mindlessly through the forest now, the trees becoming thicker and thicker. She had no idea where she was, and her feet hurt from stepping on the sharp twigs and rocks. Her makeshift shoes helped a bit inside, but they weren't much use outside; still, they were better than nothing. She had heard his truck pull up at the building where she had been imprisoned. And listened to his rage on discovering she was gone. She was sure she could hear him behind her, crashing through the forest.

Scott's father had been a hunter and had taught him how to track an animal. He put these skills to good use now. He knew she was weak and rightly guessed she couldn't be too far away. Soon he was hot on her trail.

***

DS McGregor and DCI Harper had made it to the house. Ringing the doorbell, they stood and waited, peering in through the window. Eventually, Mrs Waddle answered. She informed them that Fraser had left for New York that morning, and Scott had taken him to the airport. When they asked where Scott might be now, she seemed puzzled as she presumed he had let them in through the front gate.

They told her a little white lie and said the gates had been open, hoping she wouldn't check the CCTV or she would see their car blocking one of the gates, her jacket wedged over two spikes. They thanked her and made their way back along the drive as if they were leaving, but they had no intention of doing so. Permission to be there or not, they were looking for Katie as they knew her life depended on them. Just as they reached the fork in the drive, backup had arrived along with their warrant. One of the officers had climbed over the same way they had and opened the gates from the inside.

They jumped into the leading police van and tore through the estate, desperately scouring the terrain looking for any sign of Scott or Katie. Eventually, they came across the black Range Rover parked in the garage next to the stable block. Sure enough, an almost invisible clear polycarbonate strip had been attached to the front and back license plate. Leaving the forensics team with the vehicle, DS McGregor and DCI Harper continued searching the estate on foot alongside the ACC, who had joined them with officers Purdie, Logan and Price. The dog handling unit was on its way, as was the helicopter with the heat cameras.

They split up, fanning the area in a line looking for

outbuildings. It wasn't long before they stumbled upon the stable block, the ice house and finally, the old servants' quarters. The pick-up truck was still lying abandoned with the driver's door wide open, keys still in the ignition. They killed the engine and removed the keys. Officers Purdie and Price checked out the building whilst the others continued searching the area. They noticed the woods were very thick out here.

Suddenly they heard a scream coming from about half a mile away, inside the thickest part of the woods. They all sprinted off in the direction of the scream. Tracy got there first, closely followed by the ACC and DCI Harper. In front of them was Scott sitting on top of a terrified Katie. They noticed the rope around her neck.

Instinctively they all ran at him, batons at the ready. He was startled at first, not knowing where they had come from. Katie rolled to the side, gasping for breath whilst they wrestled him to the ground, and then she passed out. Eventually, they managed to restrain him, and Tracy did the honours of slapping the handcuffs on him and reading him his rights. Although not before he punched her in the face, breaking her nose.

Meanwhile, PC Purdie called an ambulance. Katie still had a pulse, but it was feeble. As they led Scott to the waiting police car, the paramedics carefully lifted Katie into the back of an ambulance. Her bleeding feet had been cleaned and dressed as best they could, as were her neck lacerations. She was wearing an oxygen mask, her breathing little more than a wheeze, unable to talk, but she was alive - just! A moment longer, and she too would have been gone.

49

Monday 7th November

Tracy gave the door a light tap and pushed it open. Katie turned to look at her and managed a very raspy '*hi*'. She was no longer on oxygen, and the wounds in her feet had been carefully cleaned and dressed. Her wrists were bandaged. The red ligature mark around her neck was just visible beneath her hospital gown. Tracy noticed it had begun to fade a little. It had been three days since they had rescued her.

A large bouquet stood on the windowsill. From the card, Tracy could see they were from Fraser Campbell-McNair. It seemed she had misjudged him. He had simply been upset by Katie's close resemblance to his beloved sister.

Chris lay asleep on a chair in the far corner; apparently, he hadn't left her side since she had been brought in. Her parents had arrived from Florida, but they had returned to her apartment to freshen up.

Tracy pulled a chair up beside her and sat down. Katie

raised the back of the bed using the hand controls so she was facing her. Her voice was still very weak, barely more than a whisper. But she was a fighter, and doctors were happy with her progress. Tracy knew she would have many questions and planned on answering them as best she could.

She started by explaining Scott was in love with Emilia. He had been for years. Sadly, from what they could piece together, it appeared these feelings were only ever reciprocated in his head. Fraser didn't remember them ever being any more than just friends. They had been as thick as thieves growing up, their love of art creating a bond between them. Scott had even followed Emilia to Paris initially when she moved there after art school but had been forced to return home when he ran out of money.

Seems Scott may have mistaken their closeness for love. But, he was not just in love with her; he was obsessed with her. The tech team had found hundreds of unsent emails to her on his laptop.

By the time Emilia moved to Paris, Fraser was spending less and less time at home, as he had met his fiancée, Isabella, but he still shared a close bond with his sister. She had admitted to him one evening, not long before she died that she thought she might have a stalker. Fraser had laughed it off, as Emilia always had a vivid imagination, but his parents had taken her seriously. He admitted that was why she had come home that particular weekend.

The day Emilia died, she had been out for an afternoon ride and it seems she had bumped into Scott. He had packed a hamper and suggested they enjoyed a picnic down by the loch—something they often did together as kids.

After sharing a bottle of wine, they took a boat out on the loch and ended up back at his studio as he wanted to show her what he had been working on while she had been away. The walls were covered in photographs and sketches of her, most of them taken without her knowledge. Some of them were taken in Paris after he had supposedly returned home.

The next part was a little hazy and had been pieced together by his ramblings in his emails, but Tracy and the team guessed seeing the walls covered in images of herself would have freaked Emilia out, and she must have realised at some point then that Scott was her stalker. He had even made a sculpture of her which they think he might have unveiled to her. At some point, he had tried to kiss her. Terrified, she had pushed him off and stormed out. She had jumped on her horse and taken off into the estate. Enraged, he had taken after her, pleading with her to return to him. He had chased her through the forest and right out into the path of her parent's car, ironically causing her death that day.

Despite her rejection, Scott had never stopped loving Emilia. Suffering from delusional schizophrenia, he continued writing to her after her death. When Erin stumbled upon the ghost tour completely by accident, he quickly became obsessed with her. She looked so much like Emilia, he convinced himself she had returned to him. He tried to get close to her, but we think he scared her with his strange behaviour towards her. By the time she confronted him about it, he had already lured her out into the forest, where he strangled her.

Natalia, he found by accident too, but for fear of rejection again, he lured her out into the forest and strangled her as well. After that, he started actively looking for girls who reminded him of Emilia - Klara and Jessica, respectively, and then yourself, believing she was taunting him now, by coming back to him and pretending not to know him. God knows when he would have stopped.

He turned the girls into moody faceless statues as some sort of penance for Emilia as she had rejected him all those years ago, placing them at various parts in the woods as it reminded him of their childhood where they would play hide and seek for hours. In case anyone asked, the Halloween enchanted forest tour gave him a cover story about what they were and why they were there. Their features were almost hidden entirely by their hair, so even if Fraser got too close, he would never guess they looked so much like his dead twin sister.

As Scott controlled the website, he had been able to engineer the questions for both the ghost tour and the murder mystery events, trying desperately to find his next Emilia. He began stalking the streets looking for her. As soon as found his next victim, he would try to lure her to an event where he could get close to her. Tracy explained he'd had to improvise with her as Fraser had given him the evening off.

They couldn't prove it, but they suspected everyone was drugged at the event, as no one could remember leaving. It would have been quite easy to have slipped something into either the food or drink that evening.

Forensics had been all over the place. The statues had been carefully removed and examined using CT. Sadly, each one was found to contain human remains. Using the sketches he had drawn, they were able to work out which statue contained the remains of each missing girl. Once their remains were separated from the plaster and sent for DNA, they would be returned to their respective families and laid to rest peacefully. Tears rolled down Katie's cheek. She had been so close to joining them. If it hadn't been for Tracy's tenacity she probably would have done.

The picture of Emilia that hung in the hallway at Loch Wood House had been painted by Scott. He had slipped it in with her belongings when they were shipped back from Paris after her death. Fraser presumed Emilia must have commissioned someone to paint it for her, so had hung it pride of place in the stairwell. The original photograph, on which it was based, was found in his studio along with several others. Emilia was sitting at a café overlooking the Eiffel Tower gazing into the eyes of a young man, clearly head over heels in love. Scott had also painted a very different version of that photograph with himself sitting in this young man's place. They had found it amongst the paintings in his workshop.

Katie thanked Tracy so much for rescuing her. Sensing her job was done, Tracy gently squeezed Katie's hand and got up to leave.

As she was leaving, Tracy noticed some visitors had appeared at the door - it was Suzy, Ellie, Lizzy and Rebecca with a big box of chocolates and a stack of magazines. Tracy looked over at Chris, who was still sleeping in the corner. She smiled to herself as she left the ward; somehow, she thought Katie would be strong enough to get over this.

Acknowledgements

I want to thank all my amazing proofreaders and my family and friends for keeping my secret these past few months – I couldn't have done this without you all!

Thank you also to my long-suffering husband who has tirelessly put up with my brainstorming as I worked through various scenarios for my characters.

And finally, I'd like to extend a special thank you to everyone who has bought and read my book. Your support is greatly appreciated.

About the Author

Alison lives near Glasgow, Scotland with her husband. By day she is the superintendent radiographer in charge of a busy MRI unit, by night she turns into a real-life Jessica Fletcher - iPad at the ready.

When she doesn't have her nose in a book you will find her out running; planning her next house project or foreign holiday or obsessively (her husband's words not hers) cleaning the house. All whilst listening to *Depeche Mode* or *James* on repeat.

This is her debut novel and is the first in a thrilling new Scottish crime series that introduces you to Police Scotland's very own tenacious female Detective Sergeant, Tracy McGregor.

DS McGregor will be back

Printed in Great Britain
by Amazon